"Is he dead?"

Andrew said, his voice choked with emotion as he gripped her shoulders. "Did I kill him? Oh, God, please don't tell me that Robert died."

"No, no," Kara said quickly. "Robert is holding his own. I saw you standing all alone and..."

Kara's words trailed off as she lost her train of thought. She was suddenly aware of the incredible heat that was rushing through her from Andrew's hands where they were still gripping her upper arms. Her breasts were heavy, achy, yearning for a soothing touch that only Andrew could provide.

Dear heaven, what was this man doing to her? She should step back, force him to remove his hands, but she was pinned in place by the mesmerizing depths of his dark brown eyes.

MacAllister eyes.

Dear Reader,

I can't begin to tell you how much I enjoyed writing this book. It was such fun to get together with the MacAllister clan again and see how everyone is doing, how big the kids have grown and who had added new babies to the family. I hope you, too, will feel as though you're visiting old friends.

I was delighted when my editor at Silhouette proposed bringing the MacAllisters back into all of our lives. They were very special to me when I first wrote their series years ago, and I was definitely looking forward to attending their big family reunion.

But as you will see as the story unfolds, the reunion does not go as planned. Out of the shadows of the past emerges another MacAllister, a secret son, who creates tremendous turmoil within the family.

But Andrew Malone also captures the heart of one of the MacAllisters, as well as losing his heart to her. In addition, there is a precious little baby, who is struggling to overcome a rough beginning in life and who is waiting for loving parents to take him home.

I want to take this opportunity to thank all of you for your continued loyalty and support over the years, and for the wonderful letters you've written to tell me that you enjoy my books. I appreciate all of you.

With warmest regards,

Joan Elliott Pickart

JOAN ELLIOTT PICKART

THE BABY BET:
His Secret Son

Silhouette Books

Published by Silhouette Books
America's Publisher of Contemporary Romance

SILHOUETTE BOOKS

THE BABY BET: HIS SECRET SON

Copyright © 2000 by Joan Elliott Pickart

ISBN 0-373-48409-7

All rights reserved. Except for use in any review, the reproduction
or utilization of this work in whole or in part in any form by any
electronic, mechanical or other means, now known or hereafter
invented, including xerography, photocopying and recording, or in
any information storage or retrieval system, is forbidden without
the written permission of the editorial office, Silhouette Books,
300 East 42nd Street, New York, NY 10017 U.S.A.

All characters in this book have no existence outside the imagination of
the author and have no relation whatsoever to anyone bearing the same
name or names. They are not even distantly inspired by any individual
known or unknown to the author, and all incidents are pure invention.

This edition published by arrangement with Harlequin Books S.A.

® and TM are trademarks of Harlequin Books S.A., used under
license. Trademarks indicated with ® are registered in the United States
Patent and Trademark Office, the Canadian Trade Marks Office and in
other countries.

Visit Silhouette at www.eHarlequin.com

Printed in U.S.A.

In memory of
HARRY CORNELIUS, JR.
One of the good guys

THE MACALLISTERS

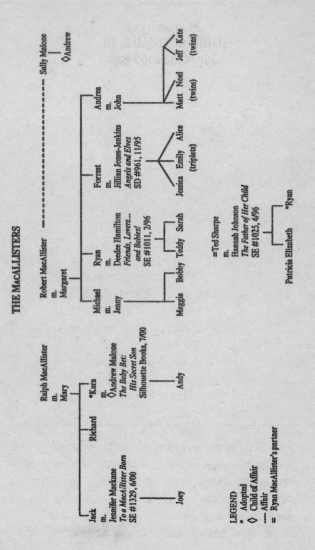

LEGEND
◊ = Adopted
◊ = Child of Affair
---- = Affair
= = Ryan MacAllister's partner

Chapter 1

It was New Year's Eve and people across the country were more than ready to celebrate the special event.

In Ventura, California, it was as though Mother Nature had decided to take part in the festivities by producing an unseasonably warm and crystal-clear night, allowing the party goers to show off their finery without the distraction of bulky coats. Excitement crackled through the air.

The sky was a lush cushion of black velvet for millions of stars, which glittered like diamonds across the heavens, leaving room for only a sliver of silvery moon. Fireflies danced through the darkness edging the city like a multitude of whimsical fairies carrying magical glowing wands.

Traffic was heavy, but smiling drivers exhibited

uncharacteristic patience as bumper-to-bumper vehicles crept forward on the main streets of Ventura.

But Andrew Malone was *not* smiling as he pressed the brake pedal of his sports vehicle yet again. The light six cars ahead of him had turned red.

He drummed his fingers on the steering wheel, a deep frown knitting his dark brows. The knot of tension in his gut coiled tighter, and a stress-induced headache throbbed painfully in his temples.

He glanced at the car next to him and saw a man in a tuxedo behind the wheel. The woman in the passenger seat threw back her head, apparently laughing, revealing a dazzling smile as dangling earrings swung next to her pretty face.

Party time, Andrew thought, switching his attention back to the now-moving traffic. Everyone was out on the town for a good time, without a care in the world. Whatever troubles they might have in their day-to-day lives were forgotten, pushed into oblivion for a handful of hours.

And why not? This was New Year's Eve, when glasses would be raised to toast farewell to the old and welcome the new. The past and the present.

Andrew narrowed his eyes as he drove forward slowly, his grip on the steering wheel tightening to the point that his knuckles were white.

His mission, his purpose, on this night was to bring the past *into* the present. Events that had taken place forty years before were going to be brought into the now, and the piper paid.

Things were going to be set to rights at long last, the final chapter written for a story that had begun during a summer four decades ago. Before this night was over he would collect on a debt owed to a woman who was dead and gone, unable to receive what was undeniably hers to have.

Andrew glanced quickly at the piece of paper next to him on the seat, scanning the map he'd sketched showing the directions to his destination.

Two more blocks, he thought. The supper club in the large hotel he was seeking was just ahead, and inside that building was the man he sought, the one who was going to pay for what he had done. A man who had no right to raise his glass in a toast to the future until he had acknowledged his actions of the past and the woman who had suffered immeasurable heartache because of them.

"Final chapter and verse," Andrew said, a steely edge to his voice. "Tonight."

After what seemed an eternity, Andrew pulled into the parking lot of the hotel and drove to the far edge, ignoring the valet attendant by the front door of the large, brightly lit structure.

He locked his vehicle, smoothed the lapels of the dark suit he wore, then ran his hand down his tie. The knot in his gut twisted painfully, and he drew a steadying breath before squaring his shoulders and striding toward the entrance to the hotel.

The noise in the ballroom was nearly deafening as a multitude of guests talked and laughed while a band played on the opposite side of the crowded dance floor.

Tables stretched along one wall, displaying a vast array of food. Tables covered in linen cloths were set up in the area between the double doors leading into the room and the dance floor.

Crystal chandeliers cast a golden glow over the people, who were dressed in their very best for this special occasion.

Kara MacAllister looked up from where she sat at one of the tables when she felt a gentle tap on her shoulder.

"Is it my turn already, Richard?" she said, smiling at the man who had gained her attention.

"Yep, little sister, you're up. I've done my meet-and-greet bit at the door. According to the schedule, you're next. I swear, I didn't know anyone who came in during my stint."

Kara got to her feet, her full-length, mauve-colored dress falling in soft folds over her slender figure as she rose.

"Well, that makes sense," she said. "We each had a certain number of people we could invite to the party, so none of us could possibly know everyone." She laughed. "We could have gotten some of those sticky-paper name tags for the guests to fill out. You know, the ones that say 'Hi, I'm...,' and you write your name with a magic marker."

Richard matched her smile. "Oh, hey, that would be classy." He flapped his hands at her. "So, go, go. Tend to the door. I'm going to get myself some of that food before it's all gone. I'm hungry."

"You're always hungry," Kara said, then looked at the woman she had been sitting next to at the table. "Mother, I don't know how you managed to keep anything in the cupboards while Richard and Jack were growing up. They both still eat like there's no tomorrow."

"I was very well-known at several grocery stores," her mother said, smiling. "But as I recall, there was a certain young lady who held her own at the dinner table when she was a teenager."

"Gotcha, Kara," Richard said. "That's how I remember it, too."

"I'm outnumbered here," Kara said, laughing. "I'm off to do my smiling duty at the door."

Kara wove her way through the tables, smiling and waving at those who greeted her. She stopped at the closed double doors and realized instantly that she felt like some sort of security guard.

She clasped her hands loosely in front of her and tapped one foot in time to the peppy music floating through the air above the noise of the chattering, laughing people.

Ten long minutes passed and the doors didn't open.

Maybe everyone who had been invited had already arrived, Kara thought, glancing over the crowded room. It certainly appeared as though there were a hundred people here, which was the number that had been agreed upon.

She was beginning to feel rather silly standing there like a dressed-up soldier at the ready. Well, so be it. This meet-and-greet plan had been very important to her aunt Margaret, and everyone was being a good sport about it. She was the last one on the schedule to perform this duty, then a good time could be had by all.

Kara swayed slightly in tune to a waltz the band

was playing and hummed along with the lovely music. She jerked in surprise as one of the doors opened, snapping her out of her dreamy state.

My stars, she thought, as a frisson of heat rushed through her. What an incredibly handsome man had just walked into the ballroom.

Whose guest was *he?*

He was the epitome of the clichéd tall, dark and devastating. Wide shoulders, broad chest, long muscular legs, and rough-hewn features.

His hair was black and thick and fell just over the edge of his collar in the back. His skin was tanned by the sun, not by a booth in a salon, as evidenced by the crinkling squint lines beside his dark-brown eyes. He was, oh, maybe thirty-seven or thirty-eight.

Gorgeous. The man was drop-dead gorgeous.

And he was so intent on his scrutiny of the people in the room that he hadn't even noticed her standing there auditioning for the meet-and-greeter-of-the-year award. Chalk up one severe blow to her feminine ego. This would never do.

Kara cleared her throat.

The man continued his perusal of the room.

"Happy New Year," she said brightly and fairly loudly, "and welcome to the party."

The man's head snapped around and he frowned as he stared at her. She extended her right hand.

"I'm Kara MacAllister," she said, "and I'm the welcoming committee at the moment. May I ask your name and inquire as to whose guest you are?"

The man ignored Kara's outstretched hand, and she let it drop back to her side.

"I'm here to see..." he started, then cleared his throat. "Here to see...Robert MacAllister."

"Uncle Robert?" Kara said, smiling. "Why don't I take you to his table? I could be wrong, but I believe you're the last guest to arrive. I'm just standing here looking ridiculous."

No, she was looking beautiful, Andrew thought. Absolutely lovely. Her short curly black hair framed a face of exquisite features, including a smile that made her dark eyes sparkle.

She was fairly tall but small-boned, delicate, making him very aware of how big and bulky he was compared to her. And her lips. Man, there was a whole new meaning to the phrase "kissable lips" as of that very moment. She was—

Damn it, Malone, he thought, putting a halt to his rambling thoughts. Wake up. Did you catch the lady's name? *MacAllister.* She was Kara *MacAllister.*

She'd probably been in that group photograph he'd seen in the newspaper, but he'd zeroed in on another face, another person. The man he'd driven a hundred miles to confront.

"Where's Robert MacAllister?" Andrew said gruffly.

Kara frowned. "You don't exactly seem in a party mood, Mr.... I don't believe you mentioned your name."

"It's Malone. Andrew Malone."

"Well, Mr. Malone, please allow me to welcome you to the final event of the week-long MacAllister reunion," Kara said, smiling again.

Andrew nodded absently.

"But since you were invited to this shindig by

Uncle Robert, you no doubt know that we Mac-Allisters have been on the go since Christmas. It's been exhausting but wonderful, with so many special memories. We wanted to share this last night of the reunion with our friends.''

Good grief, she was babbling, Kara thought, feeling a warm flush of embarrassment stain her cheeks. What on earth was the matter with her? She was actually chattering like a magpie to keep Andrew Malone standing right where he was, instead of delivering him to his host the way she should.

She didn't do things like this. She didn't act like a giddy girl when in the presence of a good-looking man. Well, in all fairness to herself Andrew Malone was the *best*-looking man, bar none, she'd ever encountered in her entire thirty years but still... She really had to get a grip.

"Would you follow me please, Mr. Malone?" Kara said, with a sweep of one arm.

Andrew nodded, then fell into step behind Kara as she made her way through the maze of tables. His glance slid along Kara's back, and a jolt of heat slammed through him as he saw the sway of her hips and the way the soft material of her dress clung enticingly to her feminine curves.

Damn it, Malone, he fumed. She's a MacAllister.

Kara stopped, nearly causing Andrew to bump into her. She looked up at him and smiled.

"You're in luck," she said. "Uncle Robert and Aunt Margaret are heading back to their table from the buffet. I guess the others seated with them must be filling their plates. There's Uncle Robert over there. See?"

Andrew's heart thundered and a trickle of sweat ran down his chest.

There he was, he thought. Robert MacAllister. It was hard to believe that the man was only a few feet away and coming closer with every passing second.

He was much more dynamic in person than in the newspaper picture. He looked taller, his gray hair thicker, shoulders wider, and there was no sign of a belly inching over his belt. His suit was obviously expensive, custom-tailored, and he had brown eyes and an even tan.

Yes, there he was, in living, breathing color.

Robert and Margaret MacAllister reached the table, and Robert set down his plate to assist Margaret with her chair. She settled into place and spread her napkin on her lap.

"Uncle Robert?" Kara said before he had a chance to sit down.

"Oh, hello, Kara," he said, smiling. "Are you having a nice time this evening?"

"Delightful, thank you," she said. "I'm the meeter and greeter of the moment, and I've brought one of your guests to you so you can say hello." She glanced up at Andrew, then back at her uncle.

Robert frowned as he looked at Andrew. "*My* guest? I'm sorry, but Kara must have misunderstood you. I don't believe you and I have met."

"We haven't," Andrew said, his gaze riveted on Robert where he stood on the opposite side of the table.

"But you told me that..." Kara started, obviously confused.

"I said I was here to see Robert MacAllister,"

Andrew said, not looking at Kara. "I didn't say that he'd invited me."

"You crashed this party?" Kara said, planting her hands on her hips. "Of all the nerve. Are you a reporter? Is that it?"

"No," Andrew said, "I'm not a reporter."

"Then what do you want?" Kara said.

"Kara," Robert said, "I'm sure there's a reasonable explanation for why Mr...."

"Malone. Andrew Malone," Andrew said.

"Why Mr. Malone has come here," Robert said. "Would you care to clue us in, young man?"

"I'm here," Andrew said, a muscle jumping along his jaw, "because it's time. In fact, it's long overdue." He reached into his jacket and removed a folded piece of paper, which he tossed onto the table. "That picture made up my mind for me."

Margaret retrieved the paper and opened it. "This is the group picture of our family that was in the newspaper a few days ago."

"I don't understand," Robert said, frowning. "What does that photograph have to do with your arriving here uninvited, Mr. Malone?"

"The name doesn't ring a bell?" Andrew said. "Malone? It doesn't mean anything to you?"

"No, it doesn't," Robert said thoughtfully. "Should it?"

"I suppose not," Andrew said, a rough tone to his voice. "It didn't mean anything then, so why should it now?"

"Look, I'm afraid I'm going to have to ask you to leave," Robert said. "I have no idea why you're here, but this is a private party and—"

"For family only," Andrew said. "I know. That's why I'm here. You forgot to send me my invitation. The name Malone doesn't ring a bell? Okay, try this one. *Sally* Malone. *Sally.* Does that conjure up any memories, Robert? A summer a long time ago? An innocent young girl who fell in love with you? Hey, come on, Robert, surely you remember Sally."

The color drained from Robert's face as he stared at Andrew.

"Sally Malone," Robert said, hardly above a whisper. "I'd forgotten all about her."

"No joke," Andrew said, with a bitter sharp bark of laughter. "You forgot about her the minute she was out of your sight. But she never forgot you, Robert. That would have been really tough to do, considering her circumstances. Oh, no, she never forgot you."

"Robert, what is going on?" Margaret said. "Who is Sally Malone?"

"My mother," Andrew said, taking a step closer to the table. "My mother, who died when I was fifteen years old. My mother, who had your baby after you abandoned her that summer, MacAllister. Let me introduce myself again. I'm Andrew Malone. *Your son.*"

"What?" Kara said.

"Robert?" Margaret said, a frantic edge to her voice. "What is he saying? What does this mean?"

"My God," Robert said, his gaze riveted on Andrew. "You're...oh...oh...pain...I..."

Robert pressed both fists to his chest and in the next instant collapsed to the floor, knocking over his chair in the process.

It was bedlam. Margaret screamed Robert's name and jumped to her feet as people at other tables rose and turned in the direction of the commotion. Everyone seemed to be talking at once as Margaret dropped to her knees beside her husband.

"Get out of my way," Kara said, pushing past Andrew. "Move."

Andrew took a step backward as people began to hurry to where Robert lay on the floor, his eyes closed. Kara knelt beside her uncle, loosened his tie and undid the top two buttons of his shirt. She looked up and quickly scanned the crowd of people.

"Give him air," she yelled. "Ryan, I need help here with CPR. Forrest, call 911. Hurry up. We need an ambulance, paramedics. Tell them to contact Mercy Hospital where I'm on staff and tell those on duty in the emergency room to stand by for our arrival. I think Uncle Robert has had a heart attack!"

Hours later Andrew wandered aimlessly along a dimly lit hall in the hospital. He'd removed his tie, shoved it into his jacket pocket and opened three buttons on his shirt. A deep frown was on his face as he walked slowly, his hands in the pockets of his trousers.

A nightmare, he thought. He was in the middle of a nightmare *he* had created. He'd never be able to erase from his mind the image of Robert MacAllister crumpling to the floor.

What had followed was a blur, one scene slamming into the next in his mental vision.

The band had stopped playing. How strange that he should remember that. There had been no more pretty music floating through the air. Just shocked and panicked voices. People shouting. Margaret MacAllister crying. Kara MacAllister giving orders, telling everyone to move back, move back.

Kara was a doctor, that much was obvious. She'd assisted the paramedics when they'd arrived, told them what she wanted done. The guy who had helped her perform CPR on Robert—what was his name? Ryan. Yes, Ryan MacAllister. Someone had said that he was a cop.

Andrew dragged a restless hand through his hair and continued his trek.

Reporters had appeared in the ballroom at almost the same moment as the paramedics. Flashbulbs had gone off and questions had been asked of the people who were standing around with horrified expressions on their faces.

He'd kept backing up, backing up, until he'd reached the door, then hurried from the ballroom to the registration desk to ask directions to Mercy Hospital.

He'd managed to enter the hospital through a delivery door and had stayed out of view, not wishing to encounter any of the MacAllisters or the reporters. In the confusion he'd gone unnoticed, but had heard the grim bulletin that had been given to the press corps.

Robert MacAllister had suffered a severe heart attack and was being transferred to the cardiac intensive care unit.

His condition was critical.

"My God," Andrew said aloud, his voice ragged

with emotion, "what have I done?" He stopped in his tracks and swept his hands down his face.

He'd never intended to harm Robert. He'd only wanted what was rightfully due Sally Malone. He'd gone to the restaurant to confront Robert with his existence, to force the man to acknowledge that Sally had mattered, had been important.

That long-ago summer affair *had* taken place, and Robert would no longer be allowed to deny it, or the existence of the special and innocent young girl who had had her heart broken and her dreams shattered.

But he hadn't achieved his goal, Andrew thought, shaking his head. Instead? Robert MacAllister lay near death a floor above this one, while his family was gathered in a waiting area, clinging to one another, seeking solace from one another, waiting to hear whether Robert MacAllister would live or die.

And if he died, it would be Andrew Malone's fault. Robert's own son would be guilty of killing him.

Andrew closed his eyes for a moment and drew a shuddering breath.

He felt as though he was being crushed with the weight of his guilt, with the truth of what he had caused to happen. What kind of man was he? How had it come to this?

Confronting Robert MacAllister had seemed so right, a way of getting Sally Malone the recognition she deserved after all these years. But his mother would be appalled if she knew what he had done to Robert. She would be ashamed of the actions of her son.

Andrew opened his eyes again and stared down at the floor.

His life was completely out of control. During the past few months he'd felt strange, edgy, as though something was missing from his life, but not having a clue about what it was.

He kept telling himself he had everything he wanted and needed: a hefty bank account, classy apartment, an endless string of women who asked nothing more of him than he was prepared to give. His business was thriving and he knew he was respected, known as a man of integrity.

Despite everything there was a void, an emptiness within him that was chilling. And no, damn it, he wasn't falling prey to some midlife crisis because he was approaching his fortieth birthday. He didn't know what was wrong, what was plaguing him, but it would pass. He hoped.

And now? On top of his inner turmoil he had just created a hefty serving of guilt to heap on the pile.

"Malone," he said with a disgusted shake of his head, "you're a real piece of work."

Andrew started to walk slowly, turned a corner in the corridor, then was stopped in his tracks by a good-size wall that had glass installed from the ceiling halfway down to the floor.

The room beyond the glass was dimly lit, and Andrew stepped closer, his eyes widening as he peered into it.

Babies. A whole slew of tiny babies. As he'd traveled from one floor to the next in the hospital, using the stairs, he'd apparently ended up in the maternity wing.

What irony, he thought dryly. Here before him was life in its purest and most innocent form. And staring at these little miracles was a man who might very well have caused the death of his own father.

Andrew started to turn to leave the area when a sudden movement beyond the glass near the rear of the nursery caught his attention.

There in the shadows he could see…yes, she was definitely there. It was a woman in a rocking chair, holding a baby in her arms and feeding it a bottle. He couldn't see her face because from the shoulders up she was cast in shadow.

She wasn't a nurse. He could see the hospital gown she wore, but beneath it was a long dress that came to the tops of her high-heeled shoes.

Oh, man, Andrew thought, look at that. She was a mother, who had been out celebrating on New Year's Eve, then had come to the hospital to feed her baby before going home. She was bringing in the new year with her child, who apparently hadn't been able to be released from the hospital with its mother.

She was rocking slowly back and forth in the chair, holding that tiny infant tightly in her arms, safe from harm, as she fed it.

Andrew was unable to tear his gaze from the scene before him.

Mother and child. So beautiful together. So real, and honest, and perfect.

A foreign warmth suffused him as he stood watching the woman and child. With the strange warmth came a sense of fulfillment, of completeness, a startling realization that he had finally discovered what was missing in his life.

A wife. A soul mate. A partner. And a baby created with that woman, who would have vowed to stay by his side until death parted them.

That was what he wanted, needed, and he hadn't even known it.

He was tired of being a solitary man who came home to an empty apartment each night, having no one to talk to, to share with, to sleep close to in his big bed.

He wanted for his own what he was seeing beyond this nursery window.

But as the realization of his wants, his needs, really hit home, the warmth within Andrew was shoved roughly aside by a bone-deep chill.

He splayed one hand on the nursery window, feeling the hard surface, the wall that stood between him and what was within.

And the same was true of his heart. While still a teenager, he'd vowed that he would never love, never render himself vulnerable, be at the mercy of another who had the power to shatter his hopes and dreams. He would not be a victim of love as his mother had been.

If a woman he was dating began to make overtures about a permanent relationship or declared her love for him, as had happened on several occasions in the past, he ended things quickly, in a state of near panic as he registered a sense of being smothered, caught in a web he might not be able to escape.

The wall around his heart was as solid as the glass separating him from the babies, from the mother and child he could see in the shadows.

And he had no intention of lowering that wall. Not ever.

Andrew stiffened as the woman inside the nursery rose from the chair and disappeared into a deeper shadow beyond his view.

He should leave, he supposed. He had no business standing here in the middle of the night—he might frighten that mother when she came out of the nursery. But he just wanted to see her for a second, mentally thank her for revealing to him the truth about himself that he hadn't known, the inner yearning he would now be aware of and be on even greater guard against. He would do that in his mind while he bid her a happy New Year.

He heard a door open, then close, then the click of high-heeled shoes on the tile floor. He turned in the direction the sound was coming from along the side of the nursery, prepared to greet the mother from the shadows.

Andrew's heart thundered as Kara MacAllister came around the corner.

Chapter 2

Kara stopped so suddenly when she saw Andrew Malone standing before her that she teetered slightly, then steadied herself. She narrowed her eyes and wrapped her arms around herself.

"What are you doing here?" she said.

"I'm not following you, if that's what is going through your mind," Andrew said, frowning. "I was restless and went for a walk, that's all."

"I don't mean *here*," Kara said, flinging one hand in the direction of the nursery window. "I'm referring to your being in this hospital. How dare you come here after what you did?"

"It's because of what I did that I'm here," Andrew said, his voice rising. "I need to know that Robert MacAllister is going to be all right."

"Your needs, Mr. Malone, are very low on my priority list. I want you to leave, and as you're exiting the premises, keep your voice down if you speak to anyone. This *is* a hospital, you know."

"You may be on staff at this hospital, Dr. MacAllister," Andrew said, "but you don't own it. You don't have the authority to toss me out. I have every intention of staying put until Robert..." His voice trailed off.

"Until Robert what?" Kara said, shifting her hands to her hips. "Either dies or it's determined by his doctors that he'll live? Will that take care of your unfinished business so you can be on your way?"

"Look, I—"

"Oh, do tell me, Mr. Malone, because the suspense is more than I can bear. Which way are you voting? Do you want Uncle Robert to live? Or die? Which of those will meet your ever-so-important *needs?*"

"That's enough," Andrew said, his jaw tightening. "I never intended for anything like this to happen. How could I have known it would? I just wanted..." He shook his head. "Never mind. I'm not even going to attempt to explain it to you in the frame of mind you're in. You hate me. That's coming across loud and clear."

"Hating you would take more of my emotional energy than you're worth," Kara said. "But I truly despise you. How could you have done such a horrible thing? It was a family celebration and... My God, Andrew Malone, you're more of a MacAllister than I am, and you came to that party and..." She stopped speaking as her throat closed from the ache of unshed tears.

"What do you mean I'm more of a MacAllister than you are?" Andrew said.

Kara waved a hand in the air, dismissing Andrew's question.

"I owe the MacAllisters my life," she said. "But you'd better think about *this,* Malone. If what you claim is true about what happened between Robert and your mother all those years ago, you owe your life to a MacAllister, too.

"If it wasn't for that summer you made reference to at the restaurant, you wouldn't be here. You wouldn't even exist. As far as I'm concerned, that would be preferable to the person you are."

"I—"

Tears brimmed Kara's eyes. "I don't want to talk to you. I don't want to see you. I don't want to be anywhere near you after what you did to my uncle Robert tonight. You are the most despicable man I have ever had the misfortune to meet."

As tears spilled onto Kara's cheeks, she spun around and hurried away.

"You're right," Andrew said quietly as Kara disappeared from view. "Despicable? Ah, beautiful Kara, I can come up with a lot worse than that to describe me and what I did at that party."

Andrew sighed and shook his head. He looked at the nursery window again, attempting to recapture the fleeting sense of peace he'd had, the inner warmth and completeness, but it remained beyond his emotional reach.

He started slowly down the hallway, suddenly aware of how exhausted he was, how totally drained. Entering a waiting room that beckoned with the glow of a small lamp, he slouched into a chair, rested his head on the back and stared up at the ceiling.

If only...he thought. No, forget it. There was no purpose to be served by starting an "if only" list. But damn it, if only Clara, his drunk and bitter aunt Clara, hadn't shown up at his door with that newspaper in her hand.

He'd been sweaty, dirty and tired to the bone when Clara had arrived that night. He'd spent the day working with his men, instead of doing the suit-and-tie portion of his business, which was more the norm.

He hadn't slept well the previous night, had once again been plagued by the sense of restlessness, emptiness, of knowing something was missing from his life but not having a clue about what it was. A day of hard labor, he decided, would give him an opportunity to blank his mind and push his body to the maximum.

He was standing in his living room with visions of a long hot shower in his head when the intercom by the door had buzzed. He strode across the room and pushed the button with more force than was necessary.

"Yes, Roger?" he said.

"Ms. Malone is here to see you, Mr. Malone."

Ah, hell, it was Clara, Andrew remembered thinking, as his mind continued to travel back in time to that fateful night.

If Clara was using the name Ms. Malone again, it meant that her most recent divorce must be final. How many broken marriages did that make? Three? Four? Hell, he didn't know and really didn't give a rip.

"Tell her that I'm sorry, but I'm busy, Roger," Andrew said.

"Yes, well...um...she's rather...um...insistent, sir," Roger said. "She says it's imperative that she speak to you and won't leave until she does, sir."

Clara was drunk and giving Roger a hard time, Andrew thought. Damn it.

"All right," he said with a weary and disgusted sigh. "Send her up."

"Oh, thank you, sir," Roger said. "Thank you very much."

Andrew mentally tracked Clara's unsteady trek across the large lobby of the building and into the elevator. He ticked off the floors in his mind, and when he determined that Clara was now in the hallway leading to his apartment, he opened the door with every intention of not allowing her to enter his home.

Clara appeared before him and he frowned as the sickening odor of liquor reached him, along with a heavy dose of perfume.

Clara's bleached-blond hair was perfectly coiffured, her peach-colored suit and the jewelry she wore obviously expensive, but the class act stopped right there.

Her makeup was artfully applied, but even so wasn't able to cover the damage caused by years of excessive drinking. She had once been a beautiful woman, but now looked haggard and much older than she actually was.

"What do you want, Clara?" Andrew said, filling the open doorway.

"Is that any way to speak to your sweet auntie?"

Clara said, her speech slurred slightly. "Aren't you going to invite me in, darling?"

"No, I'm not," Andrew said, keeping a tight rein on his rising temper. "I've been on the job all day and I'm headed for the shower. I'm tired and dirty, and I don't have time to play games with you, Clara."

"I'm not here to play games," she said, her voice rising as she poked his chest with one manicured fingernail. "I have something to show you, and I definitely have an important announcement to make."

"Like what? You're getting married again? Fine. Have a nice life. Goodbye, Clara."

"Damn you, Andrew, listen to me!" Clara shrieked. "The time has come. I've kept Sally's secret all these years, but I don't intend to be silent one second longer." She waved a folded newspaper in the air. "This is the final insult, by God, the last slap in the face that he's going to get away with."

"What are you raving about?" Andrew said, frowning deeply.

"Your father! I was down in Ventura at a spa and... Damn him. Look at this newspaper, Andrew. See what your oh-so-important and filthy-rich father has that you don't. A family! A huge, warm and loving family surrounding him. But you and I are alone."

A sob caught in Clara's throat.

"We're so alone," she went on. "So alone. It's not fair. It's not. He walked out on your mother when she discovered she was pregnant with his child, with you, and it's time he paid his dues to you. And to me. No, to you, to you.''

Clara flung the newspaper to the floor of the carpeted hallway, and it opened as it landed. She pushed past Andrew and went into the apartment, weeping as she staggered forward.

Andrew stood still, hardly breathing, his heart pounding so wildly it was actually painful as it echoed in his ears. He stared at the newspaper and saw the full-color picture of a large group of people.

As though watching himself from a far distance, he saw his body bend, his shaking hands reach out and grasp the newspaper, then he straightened, his gaze riveted on the photograph.

Don't do it, Malone, his mind hammered. *Don't read the caption. Don't find out your father's name. Think about your mother's wishes. Sally didn't want you to know. She had always said that it would serve no purpose. Damn it, Malone, don't do it.*

Andrew drew a shuddering breath, then folded the newspaper, blocking the photograph from view.

"He should rot in hell!" Clara yelled, then sobbed. "He doesn't deserve to have what he does. He owes you, Andrew. It's time for Robert Mac-Allister to pay up.''

Andrew jerked as though he'd been struck.

Robert MacAllister.

His father's name was Robert MacAllister.

Robert...MacAllister...

Andrew forced himself to move, to step back, to shut the door, then to walk into the living room. He had to tell himself to put one foot in front of the other, to inhale, then exhale for each breath he took.

He opened the newspaper again, then gripped the edges so tightly they crumpled in his hands. Then slowly, so slowly, he lowered his gaze to read the caption beneath the photograph, to put the name with the proper face among the multitude of people in the picture.

And there he was.

Robert MacAllister.

His father.

The man who had broken the heart of a young and innocent girl so many years before. The man who had abandoned her when she needed him so desperately. The man who had shattered the hopes and dreams of Sally Malone.

Clara was slouched in one of the chairs, her head rocking back and forth.

"Not fair," she said, her eyes beginning to close. "All those children. Big family. Loving him, jumping at his command, thinking he's so wonderful. The mighty and powerful Robert of MacAllister Architects, Incorporated. So many people loving him. Not fair. I'm all alone…all alone…always alone.

"No, no, no, this isn't about me. I'm finally telling you who he is for *you*. You, Andrew. Make him pay for what he did to you and Sally. Make…him…pay…for…" Clara's head dropped forward and she fell asleep, her legs sprawled in an unlady-like fashion.

A bark of laughter escaped Andrew's lips, a rough, bitter-edged sound.

MacAllister Architects, Incorporated? he thought incredulously. He'd built more than one project following plans drawn by them for the contracting outfit. MacAllister Architects was a top-of-the-line company, highly respected and sought after.

Just as Malone Construction was.

Hey, hey, what a team they were. MacAllister Architects drew up the plans, and Malone Construction built the dynamite structure with perfection.

Oh, hell, yes, what a dynamic duo they were. Two pieces of a puzzle coming together, each with their hard-earned expertise.

The father. The son.

The son of Sally Malone, who had been swept off her feet by a young Robert MacAllister, given him her heart and her innocence, then was abandoned as though she never existed when she discovered she was carrying his child.

Andrew crushed the newspaper into a jagged ball and threw it across the room.

Well, he fumed, Sally Malone *had* existed, had mattered, had been a warm, loving, wonderful human being, the best mother any child could ask for.

He wanted nothing from Robert MacAllister for himself. Not a damn thing.

But for his mother?

Robert was going to stand before that large family, who no doubt worshiped the ground he walked on, and tell them what he'd done so many years before.

Robert was going to acknowledge that Sally had been a living, breathing person, who had deserved far better than what MacAllister had done to her.

Robert was going to be made to own up to what he had done forty years ago and admit that he had been wrong, a heartless uncaring slug, who had walked away from the responsibilities resulting from his reckless actions.

Robert MacAllister was going to reveal his feet of clay to the entire MacAllister family.

"Clara," Andrew said gruffly, "wake up. Wake up, damn it."

Clara's head snapped upward and she opened her eyes. She blinked several times, straightened in the chair, then smoothed the skirt of her suit.

"I wasn't sleeping," she said. "I was just resting my eyes, giving you a chance to come to grips with what you've just learned."

"Yeah, right," Andrew said. "I hope you came here in a taxi, that you weren't driving your car."

"Yes, as a matter of fact," Clara said, holding one hand out before her and examining her nails, "I didn't feel like dealing with traffic, so I called a limo service. I don't use smelly taxis. I prefer a private company. My driver is waiting across the street."

"Fine, then go home."

Clara looked up at her nephew. "Not until you tell me what you plan to do about Robert MacAllister. I broke my promise, my vow of silence, that I made to my poor dear sister. I did it on your behalf, Andrew. I put your needs before my own guilt for revealing the identity of your father.

"The least you can do is inform me what steps you plan to take to obtain what is due you from Robert MacAllister."

"Your mind is so twisted by booze, Clara," Andrew said, shaking his head. "Didn't you hear what you were saying when you were off on your tangent? You've got some sick idea that if MacAllister acknowledges me as his son, then you'll be welcomed into the MacAllister fold.

"You won't be alone anymore. That's it, isn't it? You're scared to death of being old and alone, with no one to love you. You brought that newspaper over here tonight for your own selfish reasons, Clara, for what you hoped to gain for yourself."

Clara got to her feet, swaying unsteadily for a moment.

"How dare you speak to me like that? Who took you in when Sally died and you were fifteen years old? Who put a roof over your head? Fed you when you ate more than three grown men at every meal?

"You would have been in foster care if it hadn't been for me, Andrew Malone. You owe me. Are you listening? *You owe me.*

"MacAllister won't be able to deny that you're his son. When you become a member of that enormous family, you will take me with you. Do you understand? Do you?"

"I don't want anything to do with MacAllister's family!" Andrew yelled. "There's only one thing I intend to get from that man. One thing."

"What is it?"

"It's none of your business, Clara."

"Money? No, that doesn't make sense. You have tons of money. His name? Yes, of course. You want to be recognized as a MacAllister, reap the rewards of his power, his status in society."

"Oh, Clara, give it a rest," Andrew said wearily. "You just don't get it. I'm Sally Malone's son and I'm very proud to be able to say that. I'm a Malone,

will always be a Malone. What I want from Mac-
Allister is for my mother and… Ah, hell, forget it."

"Your mother is dead!" Clara hollered. "What
can MacAllister possibly do for her now? You've got
to think of yourself, and think of me. Look at that
photograph again, Andrew. We deserve to be in-
cluded in that group. We're part of that family, don't
you see?"

"Clara, please, just go," Andrew said quietly. "I
need to be alone. I have to think about all of this.
Go home. Get some rest, something to eat. Don't
drink any more tonight, either."

"Yes, of course, you need to think," Clara said,
nodding. "Yes, yes, you do that. You'll sort it all
through and realize that I'm right. The time has come
for us…for you to take your well-deserved place
among the MacAllisters. I know you'll do the proper
thing, Andrew."

"Oh, yes," he said, a steely edge to his voice, "I
fully intend to do the proper thing, exactly what
needs to be done."

"Good, that's good," Clara said, starting toward
the door. "Plan it all out with that detail-oriented
mind of yours. I'll speak with you soon and you can
tell me what you are going to do. We're in this together, Andrew. Don't forget that. Don't forget me.
We're a team, have been ever since my dear little
sister died. Don't forget me, Andrew."

Clara left the apartment and a heavy silence fell
over the large expanse. Andrew drew a breath that
seemed to come from the very depths of his soul,
then he crossed the room and picked up the wadded
newspaper from the floor.

Sinking onto the sofa, he spread the paper out on the coffee table, smoothing it with his hands.

He stared at the tall, smiling gray-haired man in the center of the color photograph, saw his arm around the shoulders of the attractive older woman who was tucked close to his side.

Andrew shifted his gaze and read the entire article that told of the many accomplishments of the MacAllisters, the honors they'd received over the years.

"'This marvelous family,'" he read aloud, "'includes the senior MacAllister brothers, Ralph and Robert, who are now retired, and two generations, beginning with the eldest son, Michael, who is thirty-eight and a member of MacAllister Architects, Incorporated.'"

Andrew had leaned back and rested his head on the top of the sofa, staring at the ceiling.

"Oh, guess again, Daddy dearest," he'd said, his voice raspy with emotion. "Your eldest son isn't Michael. Your firstborn son is going to be forty in the spring and is the child you conceived with Sally Malone.

"I'll hear you say her name, MacAllister. You will acknowledge that she lived, that she loved you, that she mattered.

"And then? Then I never want to see you again. *Never.*"

A noise in the corridor of the hospital jerked Andrew back to the present and he lunged to his feet. He began to pace the waiting room, while he attempted to push the memories of that fateful evening in his apartment from his mind.

If only...his mind echoed. If only Clara hadn't brought him that newspaper. If only he hadn't allowed himself to examine the caption beneath the photograph. If only he hadn't driven to Ventura with his plan etched in stone, ready to be carried out.

But all those events had happened, and now Robert MacAllister hovered near death because of them.

Andrew stopped and hooked one hand on the back of his neck.

What had Kara MacAllister said? If it wasn't for a MacAllister, then Andrew wouldn't exist. What a strange, rather disconcerting thought. And, he had to admit, it was true.

And what had Kara meant by that other weird statement she'd made? He was more of a MacAllister than she was? That didn't make sense. Robert MacAllister was her uncle. She was Dr. Kara MacAllister. Why would *he* be more of a MacAllister than *she* was?

Andrew spun around and strode out of the waiting room. He had every intention of getting the answer from Kara MacAllister.

Chapter 3

Margaret MacAllister sat in a chair next to Robert's bed, her hand covering one of his. Various machines surrounded the head of the bed, humming, blinking, showing a jagged line on a green screen, all of them having wires that were attached to Robert's inert body.

Oh, Robert, Margaret thought, her eyes once again filling with tears. He was so still, hadn't regained consciousness since he'd collapsed at the party hours before.

Margaret glanced down at her full-length evening dress and shook her head.

It seemed like an eternity since they'd been celebrating New Year's Eve and the final event of the MacAllister reunion. It had been such a festive party and everyone there had been having a wonderful time.

And then?

That young man, that Andrew Malone, had appeared out of nowhere and shattered her world, destroyed her serene existence. Her beloved Robert was now hanging on to life by a thread, by the power of his will to survive the devastating heart attack he'd suffered when he'd heard what Andrew Malone had to say.

Dear heaven, Margaret thought, was Andrew Malone truly Robert's son? Who was Sally Malone in regard to Robert? And even more important, how old was Andrew?

Margaret closed her eyes, tears spilling onto her cheeks.

Oh, please, let Andrew be older than Michael. Let whatever had transpired between Robert and Sally have taken place *before* she and Robert were married. She couldn't bear the thought of Robert being unfaithful to her, having an affair after they had repeated their vows to each other, before their friends and families…and God.

Margaret opened her eyes and shook her head in disgust.

How selfish she was being. She was thinking only of herself, of how brokenhearted she would be if it came to light that Robert had actually been unfaithful to her.

She didn't know if Robert was going to live or die, and she was centered on her fears of learning the truth about him and Sally, instead of focusing on Robert, willing him to hang on, to live, to fight this catastrophe and win.

"I'm so sorry, my darling," she whispered. "I'm

behaving badly. Oh, Robert, please, don't die. I need you, love you so much. We have so many wonderful years left to spend together, so many memories to make."

Margaret dashed her tears away, then shifted so she could layer both of her hands on top of Robert's hand, which lay so still on the pale-green bedspread.

"Can you hear me, Robert?" she said. "Perhaps you can. I'm here for you and always will be." She paused. "I'm not going to dwell on what happened at the party. I'll just wait until you wake up and explain it all to me. Yes, that's what I'll do.

"So! Let's relive lovely memories, shall we? How about Christmas? Yes, that's perfect. It seems so long ago, but it has only been a week since we were all opening gifts at Jillian and Forrest's house. Oh, my, it was noisy, wasn't it? The children were so excited and...well, so were the adults."

A soft smile formed on Margaret's lips as she continued to speak.

"Remember how the triplets were dressed alike, confusing everyone because they're almost impossible to tell apart? Jillian and Forrest have never dressed them the same, but the girls wanted matching dresses for Christmas. I guess you'd have to be a five-and-a-half-year-old girl to understand why.

"Jessica came running over to us, remember, Robert? You played your game with her, pretending you didn't know which triplet she was, and she was so indignant, informing you that you were the only one who had been able to tell them apart from the moment they were born and you knew she was Jessica. She wasn't Emily or Alice, she was Jessica.

"Your brother is finally a grandpa, and Mary is a grandma, because Jack showed up with his new bride, Jennifer, and her son—their son—Joey. My goodness, we were all so surprised. Mary is thrilled and already talking about where and when to have a baby shower because Jennifer is pregnant."

Margaret squeezed Robert's hand gently.

"I truly believe you can hear me, because you've always listened to whatever I've said, given me your undivided attention whenever I spoke. Such a lovely gift that has been all these years. I thank you for that, Robert."

She drew a shuddering breath.

"I'm getting gloomy again. Back to nice memories. Oh, I know, remember how Jessica told us on Christmas how Patty had a new six-month-old brother because Uncle Ted and Aunt Hannah had 'dotted' baby Ryan from Korea?

"You told Jessica that baby Ryan was 'adopted,' and she informed you that she had just told you that very thing—baby Ryan was 'dotted.'

"Oh, we're blessed with so many wonderful grandchildren. Andrea was such a tomboy while she was growing up, never wanted to play with her dolls. Remember? And now here she is, the mother of two sets of twins. She and John are very busy parents, aren't they?

"I forgot to tell you that Jenny confided in me a few weeks ago that she and Michael are stopping at two children, that our namesakes, Bobby and Maggie, are it. But one never knows. Bundles from heaven sometimes have a way of showing up in our lives when we least expect them."

Like Andrew Malone, Margaret thought suddenly, a shiver coursing through her.

No, no, she wasn't going to dwell on Andrew, on how old he was—not now. She was concentrating totally on Robert. Her darling Robert, who was going to make it through this, would open his eyes and smile at her. He was going to be fine, just as good as new.

He had to be.

Oh, dear God, he just had to be.

"Aunt Margaret?"

Margaret jerked in surprise at the sound of a voice and a hand being placed on her shoulder. She looked up to see Kara frowning at her.

"It's close to 2 a.m.," Kara said. "You need to go home, get some rest, Aunt Margaret. Uncle Robert is stable. I'll call you if there's any change in his condition."

"I can't leave him, Kara," Margaret said, fresh tears filling her eyes. "What if he woke up and I wasn't here? No, I'm staying."

"You'll need your strength to get through all of this," Kara said. "I just spoke to Michael and he said he'd drive you home. Please. Take a nap for a few hours, at least. You can shower, put on clean clothes, have something to eat, then come back to the hospital. Come on. Michael is waiting for you."

"I wonder where Andrew Malone is right now," Margaret said, "and how he feels about causing Robert to have a heart attack."

"Andrew is here at the hospital," Kara said. "I've spoken to him, but he's staying away from the family. He...he appears to feel very badly about what took place when he announced that he was Robert's son.''

"This is all so unbelievable," Margaret said. "Think of what's happened because of an article in a newspaper. This is a nightmare."

"I know," Kara said. "But in all fairness, Aunt Margaret, I believe that when tests are run, we'll discover that Uncle Robert had a problem with his heart long before tonight. I'm not defending Andrew Malone or what he did, but—"

"I understand." Margaret sighed as she nodded. "Several times during the past week I saw Robert rubbing his chest and asked him what was wrong. He said he was simply having indigestion from all the rich food we were eating during the reunion. We didn't heed the warnings his body was giving us."

"Don't dwell on that," Kara said. "What's done is done, and the important thing now is to see Uncle Robert through this. He wouldn't want you sitting here totally exhausting yourself, Aunt Margaret. You know that."

"Yes, I know." Margaret got to her feet, then leaned down to kiss Robert on the forehead. "I'll be back soon, my love." She straightened again. "All right, Kara, deliver me to my chauffeur. I'll go home for a little while, but promise me you'll call if—"

"Yes, yes, I will," Kara said, placing an arm around her aunt's shoulders.

After one last lingering look at her husband, Margaret left the intensive care unit with Kara. They walked down the quiet hallway toward the waiting room.

"I have clothes here I can change into," Kara said.

"I just haven't taken the time to do it. I can bunk in the residents' sleep room, and I'll leave instructions that I'm to be notified if there's any change in Uncle Robert's condition."

"It's awfully good of you to spend the night here, Kara."

"I love Uncle Robert. Besides, since I'm on staff here, I'm the one who's in the best position to do it. I don't have any patients scheduled at my office tomorrow, either. Now all we have to do is convince the guys to go home."

"Have any of them spoken about the scene between Andrew Malone and Robert at the party before Robert collapsed?" Margaret said.

"They haven't said anything to me about it," Kara said. "I know they all heard the confrontation because they were close by at the time, but they might very well be putting it on an emotional back burner for now and just concentrating on Uncle Robert. I really don't know."

Margaret nodded.

They entered the waiting room, and Margaret swept her gaze over the tall handsome men who rose immediately to their feet.

Michael, Ryan, Forrest, John, Richard, Jack and Ted—she looked at each in turn. Even dear Ted had stayed because he considered himself a true member of their family. Such fine men they all were. She was so proud of all of them, loved them so much.

And Andrew Malone? What words would those who knew him use to describe him? Was he honest, hardworking, a man of integrity and other admirable values? If so, how could he have come to that restaurant and done what he had with a clear conscience? What had he hoped to gain? Was Andrew really Robert's son? And, dear heaven, if he was, how old was he?

Margaret sighed and shook her head.

Stop it, she admonished herself. She kept coming back to those frightening questions. She was so selfish, so—

"Exhausted," Michael said. "You should see yourself, Mom. You're out on your feet. You and I are leaving right now."

"We're all going home," Margaret said, lifting her chin. "Kara is staying here and will telephone if there's any change in Robert's condition. You all need your sleep, just as I do. We have a long way to go before this nightmare is over."

"But—" Ryan started.

"Don't argue with me, Ryan," Margaret said. "I'm in no mood for it. Just do as you're told—all of you. Pretend that you're as young as your children and that I'm in charge."

"She has spoken," Forrest said.

"Indeed I have," Margaret said.

"Hey," Michael said, raising both hands as he frowned at the other men, "don't look at me. Just because I'm the oldest doesn't mean I'm willing to take her on when she gets like this." He paused and his frown deepened. "Well, I think I'm the oldest."

"Don't go there, Michael," Ryan said, narrowing his eyes. "Not now."

"No, not tonight," Margaret said. "The issues raised by Andrew Malone will be addressed when Robert is able to explain what we need to know."

"Well, Mom," Forrest said, "for what it's worth, we figured out to a point who Malone is."

"What do you mean?" Margaret said.

"We've had a lot of hours to sit here," Forrest said. "We were talking earlier, and Michael and I thought the name Andrew Malone sounded familiar, that the guy even looked like someone we'd seen before."

"And?" his mother said, hardly above a whisper.

"It finally hit us," Forrest went on. "He's Andrew Malone of Malone Construction. He's built quite a few projects from plans we drew up. I even talked to him last year on a site. He's from Santa Maria, but his outfit works all over the state, and he's got a top-of-the-line reputation."

"He's also a nutcase," Richard said, frowning. "He's Uncle Robert's son? Give me a break. He's after something. Money, probably."

"He doesn't need money," Ryan said. "Ted and I ran a check on him through our resources at the police department. Malone is well-set financially, and is squeaky clean as far as the law goes. I guess I should have told you that earlier, but we were all walking on eggs around the subject of Malone and what he accused Dad of. I don't know what Malone wants, but I'll find out. Oh, yeah. Guaranteed."

"Ryan MacAllister," Margaret said, "you are *not* to do your macho cop thing with Andrew Malone. This will be handled in a mature and nonviolent manner. Am I making myself clear?"

"No," Ryan said.

"Ryan," Margaret said, a definite warning tone to her voice.

Ryan sighed. "Yeah, okay, Mom—for now."

"I'll deck him for you, partner," Ted said. "Your mom didn't yell at me."

"I just did, Ted Sharpe," Margaret said, "and that goes for all of you. Michael, I'd like to go home, please. All of you go to your families and I'll see you tomorrow...well, later today, considering the hour."

Hugs were exchanged and the group left the waiting room.

Kara pressed fingertips to her aching temples, then walked slowly from the room with the intention of going to the locker area in the lower level of the hospital and changing out of her party dress.

After stopping at the nurses' station and explaining that she was staying at the hospital and would have her pager turned on in case she was needed, she walked slowly down the hall, aware suddenly of how very weary she was.

As she approached the entrance to the intensive care unit, she halted. Andrew Malone had his back against the wall near the doorway. His arms were folded loosely over his chest and his eyes were closed. A dark shadow of a beard appeared on his face, and his hair was tousled slightly as though he'd been dragging a hand through it.

He looked so tired, Kara thought, and so very very alone. The MacAllister family was banded together, supporting each other, standing close as a unit to weather this storm that was threatening them.

But Andrew had no one.

She knew—oh, yes, she truly knew—how chilling

that feeling was. There had been a time in her life when she'd had no one, had been frighteningly alone.

But then she'd been drawn into the warm loving embrace of the MacAllister family, had become one of them, had belonged, had been loved and made to feel special and wanted.

If what Andrew Malone claimed was true, if he was Robert's son, then he deserved that warmth and caring, too, more than she ever had.

Kara sighed and shook her head.

She felt as though she was being pulled in two directions.

A part of her was still angry at Andrew for what he had done at that party. It was cold, and cruel, and ugly, and the ramifications were almost more than she could bear.

Yet another section of her being felt an ache in her heart for Andrew's isolation, his aloneness.

The fact that he was still in the hospital said he was riddled with guilt about the outcome of his actions. He was standing vigil, waiting to learn what would happen to Robert, just as the entire family was.

Only, Andrew was all alone.

Kara sighed, decided that she was losing what was left of her exhausted mind, then walked forward slowly, stopping by Andrew's side.

"Andrew?" she said softly.

He jerked away from the wall, blinked several times, then met Kara's gaze. In the next instant he gripped her shoulders.

"Is he dead?" he said, his voice choked with emotion. "Did I kill him? Oh, God, please don't tell me that Robert died."

"No, no," Kara said quickly. "Uncle Robert is holding his own. I saw you standing all alone and..."

Kara's words trailed off as she lost her train of thought. She was suddenly aware of the incredible heat that was rushing through her from Andrew's hands where they were still gripping her upper arms. Her breasts were heavy, achy, yearning for a soothing touch that only Andrew could provide.

Dear heaven, what was this man doing to her? She should step backward, force him to remove his hands, but she was pinned in place by the mesmerizing depths of his dark-brown eyes.

MacAllister eyes.

Oh, yes, those were MacAllister eyes. Andrew Malone was, indeed, Uncle Robert's son. The more she looked at Andrew, the clearer the resemblance became. Andrew was a MacAllister.

"You...you should get some rest, too, Andrew," she said, hearing the thread of breathlessness in her voice. "There's no purpose to be served by your staying, pushing yourself beyond the point of exhaustion. Go get a few hours' sleep."

Take your hands off her, Malone, Andrew ordered himself, but didn't follow his own directive. He *needed* to touch her, to be connected to her like this, just for another moment. She was filling him with warmth, chasing away the chill of his loneliness. But that warmth was rapidly becoming heated desire, churning and coiling low in his body.

"Kara," he said, his voice raspy.

He wanted to nestle her close to him, to wrap his

arms around her, to kiss those delectable lips of hers, then make sweet love with her for hours. Ah, man, he was going up in flames.

"Andrew, I..." Kara said. *Want you to kiss me, hold me.* "We're both very tired. We've been through an extremely stressful ordeal and we're not thinking clearly."

"You're feeling what I am, aren't you?" he said. Andrew shook his head and let his hands drop to his sides. "We're related, for crying out loud. What am I doing?"

"No, we're not, but that's beside the point," Kara said, wrapping her hands around her elbows.

"You don't believe me, do you? You don't believe I'm Robert MacAllister's son."

"Yes, I do," she said. "You have the MacAllister eyes. When I look at your features, I can see Uncle Robert in you. But we're not related, because *I'm* not a MacAllister."

"I don't understand what you mean. I also don't understand why you're speaking to me, expressing concern for me. You made it perfectly clear that you despise me for what I did. Believe me, I'm not crazy about myself at the moment, either."

"I *do* despise you for what you did at that hotel, but...oh, I don't know. I'm so confused. I was very quick to pass judgment on you," Kara said, "because I was so worried about Uncle Robert. I'm still upset about his condition, not knowing if he'll make it through the critical next twenty-four hours. But I'm the last person in the world who should be censuring another person's actions."

"Why? What do you mean? And if you're not a MacAllister, then who are you?"

Kara sighed. "I guess I'm not making much sense. Perhaps…perhaps we can discuss this after we've had some rest."

"No, Kara, please. Can't we talk now? Just for a few minutes at least? This place…" Andrew glanced around. "This place is getting to me. I know I don't have the right to ask for your company but…"

"I understand," Kara said. "A hospital can be very overwhelming when you're in the midst of a crisis and especially…especially if you're alone. I…yes, all right. A few minutes. Why don't we go to the cafeteria and get a cup of coffee, or some juice? Then we both need to get some sleep."

Andrew nodded and they walked to the elevator, each reaching out to press the button on the wall at the same time. Their fingers brushed and they pulled their hands back quickly, feeling as though they'd been singed by an incredible heat.

When the doors opened, Kara waved Andrew into the elevator ahead of her, wanting to see where he would choose to stand so she could keep as much distance between them as possible.

Andrew entered the elevator and turned to face Kara. As she stepped forward her heel caught in the grating and she stumbled, gasping as she felt herself falling. With a natural instinct Andrew gripped Kara's shoulders to steady her, his elbow hitting the panel of buttons. The doors closed and the elevator began to move, but Andrew did not release his hold on Kara.

"Thank you," she said, looking up at him. "I…"

Kara forgot what she was going to say as she was pinned in place by Andrew's mesmerizing eyes. Her heart raced and her breathing quickened. The heat from Andrew's hands was rushing though her, churning low and deep within her.

Let her go, Andrew thought. Kara was steady on her feet now and he was going to take his hands off her and—

"Ah, hell," he said, then captured Kara's mouth with his.

Kara encircled Andrew's neck with her arms as he wrapped his arms around her, pulling her close to his heated body.

Desire rocketed through him as he parted her lips to delve into the sweet darkness of her mouth with his tongue, seeking and finding *her* tongue, stroking, dueling.

Passions soared and reason fled.

The elevator bumped to a stop and they jerked apart as the doors swished opened.

"Oh, dear heaven," Kara said breathlessly, then rushed out of the elevator, vaguely aware that they were on the floor where the cafeteria was located.

"Kara..." Andrew said, then hurried after her as the doors began to close.

"That didn't happen," she said, not slowing her step. "That...did...not...happen."

"Oh, yes, it did," Andrew said, drawing a much-needed breath. "It *definitely* did."

Kara glared at Andrew as they entered the cafeteria. A short time later they were seated at a small table. Kara took a sip of her orange juice, then stared into the glass as though it was the most fascinating thing she had ever seen. Andrew ignored the cup of coffee in front of him as he looked at Kara.

"There's something happening between us, Kara, and I want to know what it is."

Why? he asked himself in the next instant. What difference did it make? Why was it so important? Hell, he didn't know.

Kara's head snapped up. "What happened, what it is, is the product of fatigue, worry, stress and... It didn't mean anything, Andrew."

"Didn't it?" he said, his voice low and rumbly as he looked directly into her eyes.

She couldn't breathe, Kara thought frantically. Andrew had stolen the very breath from her body with that kiss, and she wasn't able to refill her lungs with air when he looked at her like that. She was going to pass out cold right into her orange juice.

"Don't," she whispered. "Oh, please, Andrew, just...don't."

He leaned toward her. "Don't what? Don't desire you? Don't want to kiss you again? Don't want to make love with you?"

"Stop it," she said, looking quickly around the room, then meeting his gaze again. "None of this is real. We're exhausted, not thinking clearly. This has been a night of nightmares, and we're trying to escape to somewhere we don't have to face what has taken place."

"Nice speech," he said, leaning back in his chair. "But I'm not buying it for a second. You're turning me inside out, lady, and nothing like this has happened to me before. I want—for some reason I can't fathom—to know what this is."

"You're just full of questions that *you* want the answers to, aren't you, Mr. Malone?" Kara said, lifting her chin. "You want to know what is happening between us. You want to know why I'm concerned about your lack of sleep after making it clear earlier that I'd be more than happy to strangle you with my bare hands. You want to know why you're more of a MacAllister than I am."

Andrew nodded. "That covers it pretty well, I'd say. Which one of those questions would you like to address first, Dr. MacAllister?"

Kara's shoulders slumped. "You're a very exasperating man, do you know that? You want. You want. You want. Do you always get what *you* want?"

"If I put my mind to it, yes." Andrew reached over and drew his thumb gently across Kara's lips. "Do you?"

Kara shivered from the feel of Andrew's callused thumb caressing her lips, and she moved her head back. She was torn between the urge to smack his hand away and the desire to press it to her lips.

"Don't you want to know what this is that's taking place between us?" Andrew said, wrapping both hands around his coffee cup.

"There is *nothing* happening between us," Kara said. "You'll realize that yourself after you've had some rest. Just forget about what happened in that elevator, Andrew. In the light of the new day it will be clear that it meant nothing."

"Fair enough. We'll discuss it in the light of the new day."

Kara rolled her eyes heavenward, then took another sip of juice.

"So, why am I more of a MacAllister than you are?" Andrew said.

"It's very simple. I'm a MacAllister in name only. I was adopted by Mary and Ralph MacAllister. You're Uncle Robert's son, so you're a MacAllister by birth, or blood—however you want to put it."

"Oh, I see," Andrew said, nodding. "They adopted you when you were a baby?"

"Well, no, I... Actually, I didn't become a MacAllister until I was eighteen years old. Mary, Ralph, Jack and Richard invited me to become an official MacAllister when I was old enough to legally make my own decisions. I had been their foster child since I was sixteen and come to love them with my whole heart."

"They waited until you were a legal adult, then... Whew. That is a class act."

"That's the caliber of people the MacAllisters are, Andrew. All of them. That's your heritage, your roots. I assume that you loved your mother, Sally Malone, very much, but you're a MacAllister, too, and you can take a great deal of pride in that."

"Yeah, right," he said, dragging a hand through his hair. "After what Robert did to my mother? There isn't a rubber stamp of excellence on these people, Kara." He shook his head. "Let's not get into all that now. I want to know about you." He smiled. "Uh-oh, there I go again with *I want*."

Kara's heart did a funny little two-step as she stared at Andrew.

Andrew Malone smiling was more than she could

handle in her exhausted state, she thought frantically. His smile softened his features, revealed straight white teeth and changed his brown eyes to liquid depths a woman could drown in. Oh, this man just didn't quit.

"Yes, well..." she began, then cleared her throat. "I've told you about me. I was Ralph and Mary MacAllister's foster child, then adopted by them when I was eighteen. End of story."

"I'll wait," Andrew said quietly.

"Wait for what?"

"For you to feel comfortable enough with me— even more, to trust me enough—to share the complete story of why you were a foster child, why you didn't have a home at sixteen. I'm not normally the most patient of men, but for you? I'll wait."

Andrew covered one of Kara's hands with one of his on the table. Heat danced along Kara's arm, then across her breasts to finally settle low and intense in her body.

"Because, Kara MacAllister," Andrew said, "I know, I just somehow know, that you are most definitely worth waiting for. When you're ready to tell me the whole story, I'll be here. I'll listen to every word. I just hope you'll come to trust me that much, Kara, I truly do. I don't know why it's so important to me, but it is."

She was going to cry, Kara thought incredulously, drawing a shaky breath. Andrew's softly spoken words were touching her in a place deep within her.

He wasn't pushing, wasn't crowding her, wasn't demanding an explanation about her past, wasn't doing his *I want* routine.

He was simply waiting—waiting for her to trust him because…because she was worth waiting for. Oh, good grief, she was going to start blubbering like a baby if she didn't get out of here.

She was overreacting to *everything* due to her exhaustion. Everything, including that kiss shared with Andrew in the elevator.

Kara slipped her hand from beneath Andrew's and got to her feet.

"I have to get some sleep," she said. "I strongly suggest that you do the same."

"I doubt there's a hotel room free in Ventura on New Year's Eve," Andrew said, looking up at her. "I hadn't planned on staying over." He ran his hand across his chin. "I didn't pack a bag, don't even have a razor."

Kara folded her arms beneath her breasts. "Oh? You just intended to drive into town, destroy as many MacAllister lives as you could, then leave?" She closed her eyes and shook her head. "I'm sorry. That was uncalled for." She looked at Andrew again. "I'm beyond rational thought. Maybe I can arrange for you to get some sleep in an empty room here in the hospital."

"Don't worry about me. I'll figure out something. I'll see you in a few hours, Kara. Maybe you'll have news about Robert's condition by then."

"Yes, yes, perhaps I will. Good night, Andrew."

"Kara? Think about trusting me. Will you do that? Think about it?"

Kara nodded jerkily, then turned and hurried away. Andrew watched her until she disappeared from view, then drew a weary breath as his exhaustion seemed to slam into him like a physical blow.

He glanced around the nearly empty room and felt the chill of loneliness consume him once again.

Chapter 4

"No, I'm not sure how long I'll be away," Andrew said into the telephone receiver. "You have the number here at the hotel, so call and leave a message for me if something comes up that you can't handle... Yes, have the foreman on each job site check in with you daily there at the office... Yeah, you're right. You'll get fat and lazy playing executive. Okay, Harry, I'll talk to you later. Thanks for stepping in for me like this... See ya."

Andrew replaced the receiver, but didn't remove his hand as he stared at the telephone.

He'd begun calling hotels at dawn, using the pay telephone in the lobby of the hospital, and had finally managed to book a room. He'd left the hospital, then discovered to his surprise that a great many open-twenty-four-hours stores were ready for business despite the holiday.

After purchasing some clothes and personal items, he'd driven to the hotel and stretched out on the bed, falling into a deep sleep before he'd even removed his shoes.

Andrew glanced at his watch.

One o'clock in the afternoon. He'd showered, shaved, put on fresh clothes, then called Santa Maria to give his top foreman instructions on running Malone Construction.

Now? He was starving, should order some food from room service. But first he had to know how Robert MacAllister was doing. Should he call the hospital and pretend to be a reporter? No, they probably had a pat answer that divulged very little to the members of the press.

Andrew's hold on the receiver tightened, but he still left it in place.

Kara. He needed to speak to Kara about Robert. Kara was his link, his only source of real information. Kara, who had also been front and center in the tangled and confusing dreams he'd had when he'd crashed onto the bed and slept.

Kara MacAllister, Andrew thought. The kiss they'd shared in the elevator had been dynamite. He could vividly recall her taste, her aroma, the way her delicate body nestled so perfectly against him. He wanted her. He wanted her with a driving force, a need, the intensity of which defied description.

Kara was a complex and intriguing woman. She was intelligent. She had spunk, a temper that rose to the surface when she was provoked and made him understand where the phrase "beautiful when angry" had come from. She was fiercely loyal to her adopted family. She loved deeply and completely.

Loved deeply, Andrew mentally repeated, releasing his grip on the receiver and getting to his feet. Was there a special man in Kara's life? Someone she loved deeply?

He began to pace around the large room.

He didn't like that idea, not one little bit. Another man, other than him, kissing Kara? Touching her? Making love to her? No. No way. He didn't know why, but the mere thought of another man being with Kara caused a painful knot to tighten in his gut.

There was no man in Kara's life, he reasoned, because if there was, he would have been at the party with her, then stayed by her side during the crisis the MacAllisters were facing. Fine. Good. Kara was not in a committed relationship.

Andrew stopped pacing and shook his head.

He was losing it. It was none of his damn business who Kara might or might not be involved with. And heaven knew, he sure wasn't intent on becoming seriously entangled with her.

But then again, facts were facts. Kara had returned that kiss in the elevator in total abandon, had melted against him, holding nothing back. She had wanted him, desired him, as much as he did her. Damn it, he knew she did.

Yeah, okay, so she'd attempted to dismiss what had taken place between them as the product of their fatigue and stress. Well, he wasn't buying that. This was the light of the new day she had spoken of, and he wanted Kara MacAllister every bit as much as he had last night.

Kara, who had secrets in her past.

Would she come to trust him enough to tell him about her life, what had happened to cause her to be alone, a foster child with no family of her own? Lord, he hoped so. Why, he didn't know, but he wanted, needed, her to trust him, believe in him, know he would never do anything to hurt her.

"Yeah, right," Andrew said, sinking back onto the edge of the bed. "I've *already* hurt her by causing her uncle to have a heart attack. Sure, Malone, the lady will trust you without a second thought. Hell."

Andrew took a deep breath and let it out slowly.

He was going nuts thinking about Kara. What was of utmost importance right now was the condition of Robert MacAllister. He was doing everything but stand on his head to postpone calling the hospital, because he was scared out of his shorts that Kara would tell him that Robert had not survived the massive trauma to his heart.

"Do it, Malone," he said, picking up the receiver and looking at the piece of paper where he'd written the telephone number of the hospital.

A sudden vision of another hospital from years ago flashed in Andrew's mind, and he replaced the receiver with a trembling hand.

He was fifteen years old and had come directly from school to see his mother in the hospital where she was dying of cancer.

He'd been six feet tall already, but hadn't filled out, was all arms and legs and enormous feet on a skinny frame. He'd folded himself into the small chair next to his mother's bed and held one of her hands with both of his, watching her sleep. A few minutes later she'd opened her eyes and smiled at him.

"Hello, my darling," Sally Malone said, her voice weak. "How was school today?"

"Fine. Good. Okay," Andrew said. "How are you feeling, Mom? Are you in a lot of pain?"

"No, no, they keep me very comfortable, and have ever since I had to come here last week. I'm just very tired, Andrew. So very tired." She paused. "Did you see your aunt Clara when you arrived?"

"Yeah, she was going outside for a cigarette. As soon as she saw me, she hightailed it for the elevator so she could get her nicotine fix. She probably needs a drink, too. It wouldn't surprise me if she carries a flask in her purse."

"Oh, Andrew, don't be so hard on Clara. She's a very unhappy person. She's never known the joy, the wonder, of what you and I have together."

"No one forces her to drink too much or to hook up with one loser after another. She makes her own misery, Mom. I don't feel sorry for her. She's loaded with money from when that guy she married died and left her everything, but she just hangs around her fancy house drinking and—"

"Shh. Be patient with your aunt Clara. You're going to be living with her after…after I'm gone, and I hate the idea that you two will be at odds."

"No, I'm not living with Aunt Clara. I can take care of myself. I look older than I really am and I'll get a job and—"

"Andrew, please, stop it. Promise me you'll go with Clara. I know you don't want to leave your school and all your friends, but you're to move up the coast to Santa Maria and live with Clara. The only other alternative would be for you to go into foster care, and I can't bear the thought of your being with strangers. Promise me that you'll finish high school while under Clara's roof. Promise me, Andrew, please."

Andrew sighed. "Okay, I promise. I'm not going to act like a son living with his mother, though. It will be a place to eat and sleep, nothing more. I don't like Aunt Clara, Mom, and I don't trust her. She always has a...a plan, a scheme or something. She looks out for herself and doesn't give a rip about anyone else."

"She just sees things differently than we do." Sally drew a shuddering breath. "Oh, I'm so tired. I've fought this menace within me for as long as I could, but... Oh, my darling Andrew, I'm so sorry to be leaving you. You've brought me nothing but happiness from the moment you were born. I'm not afraid of dying. I just wish I could watch you finish growing up, see you marry, hold your babies."

"Don't wear yourself out, Mom. Take it easy," Andrew said. "I don't intend to ever marry. Loving someone gives them a power over you, the ability to destroy you, break your heart and... Never mind."

"You're wrong, Andrew. Love can be glorious, like a miracle, when you find the right person. Don't deprive yourself of that just because I chose the wrong one. Sweetheart, do you resent the fact that I've never told you who your father is?"

"I don't care who he is," Andrew said firmly. "You said that you loved him, but he didn't love you. That's it. End of story. The guy broke your heart and I have no use for him. We've done just fine without him, whoever he is. You've said for years that it would serve no purpose for me to know his identity. That's fine with me."

"Thank you, Andrew. I would be upset if I thought you'd been angry all these years because I wouldn't divulge your father's name." Sally closed her eyes for a moment, then looked at her son again. "Andrew? Please hold my hand. Please?"

"I am, Mom. I have your hand in both of mine. I'm right here."

"I can't feel...your hand. I..."

"Mom? Mother?"

"Forgive me for leaving you. Forgive me. Don't grieve for me, my sweet baby boy. I want...you to...be happy. You deserve...to be happy because...you've brought me so much...joy. I'm so...tired. I love...you. I...love...you. I...love..."

"Mom!" Andrew said, tightening his hold on her hand. "No! Don't go. Don't leave me. Not yet. Mom! Oh, God, no-o-o."

Andrew had buried his face next to his mother's head on the pillow and wept.

The feel of tears on his cheeks jolted Andrew back to the present, and he stared up at the ceiling of the hotel room for a long moment, struggling to regain control of his raging emotions.

He dragged his hands down his face, then propped his elbows on his knees and skimmed his thumbs over the tips of his moist fingers.

He hadn't cried since that day in the hospital when his mother had died, he thought. He'd wept then, until there were no more tears to shed.

And these tears? They weren't for Sally Malone or for the lonely fifteen-year-old boy who had been forced into an early manhood. No, they were for Kara, and Robert, and for all the MacAllisters who were going through the horror of a long hospital vigil now just as he had experienced so many years ago.

They were suffering immeasurable pain because of what he had done. He had set off on a mission that his mother would not have approved of.

He'd been so determined that Robert MacAllister would acknowledge the existence of Sally Malone. But if she had truly wanted that recognition, what was rightfully hers, she would have approached Robert herself and demanded he take responsibility for her and his child.

"Ah, man, Malone," Andrew said aloud, shaking his head. "You went off half-cocked, didn't think it through, just reacted to Clara's rantings and ravings, and that photograph in the newspaper, and..."

And now? An entire family was in pain because of what he had done. He couldn't reverse it, couldn't fix it, couldn't do anything, except wait to find out if Robert MacAllister was going to survive.

Andrew snatched up the telephone receiver and dialed the number of Mercy Hospital. When someone answered, he asked to speak to Dr. Kara MacAllister.

"I'll need your name before I page her, sir," the woman on the telephone said.

"Malone. Andrew Malone."

"Thank you, sir. Please wait on the line while I page Dr. MacAllister."

Yes, he'd wait, Andrew thought. He'd wait for Kara to answer the page. He'd wait for Kara to trust him enough to tell him about her past, reveal her innermost secrets to him.

But for the life of him, he couldn't think of one good reason she would even consider doing that.

"Oh, Kara," Margaret whispered, "Robert looks so much better. See? There's even a little color in his cheeks now."

"Yes, there is," Kara said. "He's sleeping peacefully, Aunt Margaret."

"Did you see the smile he gave me before he dozed off?" Margaret said, her eyes filling with tears. "That was my Robert."

"It was a beautiful loving smile," Kara said, nodding. "It hasn't been twenty-four hours since Uncle Robert's heart attack, but the specialists feel he is going to make it through this. Now that he's out of intensive care, they're discussing what tests they want to run and when they think he'll be up to going through them. I'm so happy that—"

The pager in the pocket of her white medical coat buzzed. She took it out and looked at the tiny screen on the top.

"I have to call the hospital operator," she said. "I'll go out to the nurses' station so I won't disturb Uncle Robert."

"I'll just sit here and watch him sleep," Margaret said. "Will that be all right?"

"Yes, that's fine," Kara said. "I know some of the family is here, but you're the only visitor Uncle Robert is to have for now. The doctors were very emphatic about that. The others will have to be patient. It probably won't be too long before they can see him. I'll be back soon.''

Kara hurried from the room and went to the nurses' station. She lifted the receiver to the telephone and pressed a button.

''Dr. MacAllister,'' she said.

''There's an Andrew Malone holding on the line for you, Dr. MacAllister,'' the woman said. ''Shall I put his call through?''

Andrew, Kara thought, a vivid image of him forming instantly in her mental vision. She'd dreamed about Andrew Malone. Sensual dreams. Dreams of being held in his arms, kissed and caressed by him. Dreams that had caused her to toss and turn in the narrow bed in the residents' room. Dreams that had finally jolted her awake to discover that heated desire was pulsing low in her body.

''Dr. MacAllister?'' the operator said. ''Are you still there?''

''Oh. Oh, yes, I'm here. I'm sorry. Please put Mr. Malone's call through. Thank you.''

Kara depressed the button on the telephone and an instant later it rang. She lifted her hand again and saw that it was trembling slightly.

''Dr. MacAllister,'' she said, hoping her voice was steadier than it sounded to her own ears.

''Kara? This is Andrew. How are you? And how is Robert?''

''Uncle Robert regained consciousness early this morning,'' she said. ''He's in a private room now and sleeping peacefully. His doctors are very optimistic about his surviving the heart attack and are conferring as to what tests to run and when.''

"Thank God," Andrew said, his voice husky. "Oh, man, what a relief. I can't begin to tell you how…well, I can only hope you know that I'm grateful that he's going to be all right. You believe me, don't you?"

"Yes. Yes, Andrew, I believe you. I'm aware of how distressed you were about what happened. Uncle Robert has a long way to go here, but things certainly look brighter than they did last night." Kara paused. "Where…where are you, Andrew?"

"I managed to get a hotel room."

"Oh, I see. Well, that's good. You got some sleep, then?"

Yes, and dreamed about you, Andrew thought.

"I slept," he said. "Did you?"

A warm flush stained Kara's cheeks as she remembered the dreams she'd had of Andrew.

"Oh, yes, I was snug as a bug in the residents' room. I'm as good as new."

"I'm glad to hear that. Listen, I'm going to have something to eat, then come over to the hospital. I'll stay in the shadows, keep out of your family's way, but I'm not going back to Santa Maria until I know what the tests show about Robert's condition. I'd like to see you while I'm there."

"I…well, yes, of course, you'll want to be kept up to date on Uncle Robert's condition. Just so you know, I'll be checking on my patients who are here, doing my rounds. I'll watch for you…in the shadows."

"Kara, being kept apprised of Robert's condition isn't the only reason I want to see you. You know that, don't you?"

"I..."

"Don't you?"

"Yes, Andrew, I know that."

"Good. Until later, then. Goodbye."

"Goodbye," Kara said softly, then replaced the receiver slowly.

"You were talking to Andrew Malone?"

Kara spun around to see her brother, Richard, frowning at her.

"Yes, Richard, I was," she said. "He called to check on Uncle Robert. He's been extremely concerned that—"

"That we'll sue the pants off him probably," Richard said. "Some fancy lawyer would no doubt find a way to file a suit of some kind against Malone for what he did to Uncle Robert."

"Richard, Andrew is sincerely sorry for what happened at that party."

"Andrew? It's Andrew now? Jeez, Kara, how can you be so cozy with the guy? He nearly killed our uncle, for crying out loud."

"Richard, that's not fair. It wasn't Andrew's intention to hurt Uncle Robert. Andrew simply wanted..." Kara paused. "Well, I don't know exactly what the purpose of that confrontation was, but it certainly wasn't to cause Uncle Robert any physical harm."

"You're defending what Malone did?" Richard said, his frown deepening. "Are you aware that reporters were at that party? Have you seen the newspapers? They're having a field day with this. The secret son of highly respected, powerful and wealthy Robert MacAllister crashes family party and...

That's just an example of what is in the papers. The press have picked up Malone's lie and are running with it.''

"Richard, what Andrew said is true. He *is* Uncle Robert's son. When you look at Andrew up close, you can see the same MacAllister eyes that all of you have. His features, too, are Uncle Robert's. There's no denying the truth, and you're going to have to accept it.''

"Just how 'up close' to Malone have you been, little sister?'' Richard said, folding his arms over his chest. "If that guy is making a move on you, there is going to be hell to pay, believe me. He better stay away from you, or he'll hear from me—personally.''

"Oh, Richard, stop it,'' Kara said. "I'm not sixteen years old anymore. I don't need you and Jack defending me against everyone walking around in a pair of pants. I'm all grown up, remember?''

"Okay, you're all grown up,'' Richard said, nodding. "So, all-grown-up sister, where is your family loyalty? You're standing there pleading Andrew's case, saying he didn't mean to cause Uncle Robert any harm. What's next? Guess who's coming to dinner?''

"Who served you a nasty pill for breakfast?''

Kara turned to find Brenda Henderson glaring at Richard.

"Hi, Brenda,'' Kara said. "Are you here to collect Mr. Congeniality—I hope?''

"Cute,'' Richard said, glowering at Kara, then directing his attention to Brenda. "What are you doing here?''

"I came to see how your uncle is, Richard,''

Brenda said. "I was your date at the party when all this happened, you know. I adore your uncle Robert. I've come to like all your family—except you at the moment. You're a grump."

"I am not," Richard said. "I'm simply questioning why Kara is being so damn nice to Andrew Malone. She's getting up close and personal with the jerk."

"Richard MacAllister," Kara said, planting her hands on her hips, "I never said that I—"

"Children, children," Brenda said, raising both hands. "Peace among siblings, please."

"Knock it off, Brenda," Richard said. "Just because you're my best friend, that doesn't give you license to get pushy and mouthy."

"Sure, it does," Brenda said, smiling brightly. "As your best friend, I can say anything I want to. Therefore, I go on record as saying that you are acting like an overprotective, obnoxious big brother. And I doubt seriously that you have all the facts regarding Andrew Malone."

"Amen and thank you, Brenda," Kara said.

"You're welcome," Brenda said, nodding decisively. "I heard the good news about Robert. That is so great. Come on, Richard, you can buy me lunch in the cafeteria before I go back to work."

Richard threw up his hands in defeat and laughed.

"You're on, bossy Bren," he said. "For being such a smart aleck, you deserve to eat the crummy food in this place." His smile faded as he looked at Kara. "I'm sorry I jumped on your case. Just be careful around Malone. Okay? He's after something, I'm sure of it. And remember where your loyalties lie. You're a MacAllister.''

"Leaving now," Brenda sang out, taking Richard's arm. "Ta-ta, Kara. See you later. Give your uncle Robert a big smooch from me when you see him.''

"I will, Brenda. Bye," Kara said quietly as the pair walked away.

It was a good thing Richard couldn't peer into her mind, she thought, to see just how disloyal she'd been to her family with Mr. Malone.

Chapter 5

Kara smiled as she lifted the baby, being extremely careful to move him in a slow steady motion without the slightest jiggle. Inching him closer until his little head was resting on her shoulder and his blanket-wrapped body was nestled against her, she inhaled his sweet baby-lotion aroma.

"Hello, my love," she whispered. "I've missed you. Do you remember me? Do you know that I'm your mommy?"

"You picked him up perfectly that time," a nurse said, glancing over from where she was tending to another baby in the hospital nursery. "You're becoming a real pro, Mom. Those poor little crack babies can't tolerate any jerky movements, or loud noises, for that matter. By the way, don't you think it's time you gave your son a name?"

Kara settled into the rocking chair. She accepted

the bottle another nurse handed her, eased the baby into the crook of her arm and began to feed him. "I'm not going to name him until I hear that my application to adopt him has been approved. I'm trying to convince myself that it won't hurt so badly if I can't be his mother if I'm not the one to give him a name."

"Oh, fat chance of that," the nurse said, laughing. "That little guy has well and truly stolen your heart, Kara. Besides, I can't think of one reason why you wouldn't be approved to adopt him. Everything is in your favor, as far as I can see."

"I'm single, remember?"

"And that is a drug baby you're holding," the nurse said. "People aren't beating down the doors to adopt those kiddies. I'd hate to know the total number of them who are in the foster-care system. Oh, I forgot to tell you. Your son gained almost a whole ounce. At two weeks and two days old, he weighs four pounds, six and a half ounces."

"My goodness," Kara said, then dipped her head to kiss the baby on the forehead. "Aren't you the little piggy? I'm so glad he's eating well now. Is he sleeping any better, Judy?"

The nurse crossed the room to stand next to the rocking chair.

"No, he's still very restless. He's withdrawing from drugs and it's not an easy road to go."

Kara frowned as she nodded.

"Even after his system is clear, he won't like being moved too quickly or disturbed by noise," the nurse went on. "He may or may not outgrow that." She smiled. "Why am I telling you this? I know you've read tons of material on drug babies. You realize what you're possibly in for.''

"Oh, yes, I know. Years of happiness being his mother," Kara said, smiling. "We'll face whatever comes when it gets here, and we'll be fine." Her smile faded. "Oh, Judy, what if my application to adopt him is denied?"

"Don't be a gloomy Gus. You'll be approved. In the meantime give the kid a name, for Pete's sake. There you go—Pete. Peter MacAllister. Yes? No? Have you even started a list of possible names for him?"

"No," Kara said. "I know it's silly, but I just won't allow myself the luxury of doing that."

"New mommies have been known to be a tad weird at times," Judy said, laughing. "I remember the mother of a preemie we had in here a few years ago. The baby had an underdeveloped gag reflex. She couldn't swallow and was being fed intravenously.

"Then one day she spit up on Mom's blouse, which meant what comes up, can go down, and she was on a bottle after that. The mother was so thrilled, albeit superstitious, that she wore that blouse every time she visited until the baby went home. Mom would wash the blouse out by hand each night and put it back on the next day. What a hoot."

"I think that's sweet," Kara said. "I'm in good company with the nutsy new-mommy crowd." She paused. "Don't you love his hair? It's like black silk capping his head. And his nose. Isn't that the cutest nose you've ever seen? I just adore his nose."

"Save me from gushing mothers," Judy said, rolling her eyes heavenward. "Okay, let's see. Yes,

Kara, his hair is gorgeous, his nose is cute, his toes are adorable, his lips are like rosebuds, his…''

Kara laughed, then looked quickly at the baby to be certain the sudden noise hadn't startled him.

"Okay, okay, I'll shut up," she said. "But then again… No, I'm just kidding. I'm sure every mother believes that her baby is the most perfect, most beautiful one ever born."

"Giving birth to a baby doesn't automatically make a woman a good mother. That bundle in your arms is evidence of that. Imagine taking drugs while you're pregnant, not caring what it's doing to your baby when you… Oh, don't get me started on that. Change the subject. Rumor has it that your Uncle Robert is improving."

Kara nodded. "He regained consciousness this morning and has been moved into a private room. His doctors are running some tests. The entire family is so relieved. Uncle Robert isn't out of the woods by any means, but things are looking brighter at this point."

"Kara, is all that stuff in the newspapers true?" Judy said. "You know, about the secret son showing up at your family reunion?"

"I refuse to read what's been written," Kara said, "but one of my brothers told me about the stories they're printing. And, well, yes, Andrew Malone did come to the party and confront Uncle Robert, but Andrew didn't intend to harm anyone. He's terribly upset about what happened."

"Burp your kid," Judy said. "I take it from what you're saying that you've talked to Malone."

"Yes," Kara said, moving the baby upward so she

could rub his back. "Let's change the subject again."

"Okay, but it sure sounds like a big mess. I wonder what Malone wants? You know what I mean?" Judy laughed. "You're ignoring me. Okay. Shift of topic. Have you told your family about the baby yet?"

Kara sighed. "No, I had it all planned. I was going to tell them on New Year's Eve at the party.

"I realize that sounds like I'm contradicting myself. I won't give him a name until I know he's going to be mine, yet I was going to tell the MacAllister clan about him now. But everyone was going to be together at the same gathering *without* the kids.

"I felt that was the best time because if I wasn't approved to adopt him, then the little ones wouldn't be asking me over and over where my baby was.

"Well, so much for that. We're all concentrating on Uncle Robert, so I'll just tell them about this sweetie pie later."

"I hope that pie has reached five pounds by the time your adoption is approved so you can take him home straight away. Have you bought a crib?"

"No," Kara said.

"Got it," Judy said, nodding. "A crib falls into the same category as a name. Lucky you, little No-Name MacAllister, you're going to sleep in Mommy's dresser drawer."

"Well, I've been looking at cribs, changing tables, dressers. And clothes. Oh, Judy, you should see the darling clothes they have for babies. Little baseball suits and overalls and...I bought a bib. It says 'I love my mommy' on it."

"Whoopee," Judy said, laughing. "The kiddo actually owns a bib." She paused. "So tell me this much. Do you believe this Malone guy is your uncle's son?"

"Yes. Yes, I do."

"Why did he wait this long to come forward, Kara? That doesn't make sense at all. Is he broke? After the MacAllister money?"

"No, Andrew owns a very successful construction company. I honestly don't know why he waited until now, or why he came forth at all. It's very confusing."

"No joke," Judy said. "I sure want to know the next installment of this story. Don't you, little No-Name MacAllister?"

The baby burped.

And Kara MacAllister's heart nearly burst with love for her precious little son.

The hotel where Andrew was staying was only four blocks from the hospital, and he decided to walk, get some fresh air. He cut through a pretty little park in the midst of the business district, slowing his steps to enjoy the lush green grass, tall trees and to watch a mother duck with her babies, swimming on the manmade pond.

He filled his lungs with the crisp clean air and realized he felt the best he had since that awful moment Robert MacAllister had clutched his chest and collapsed to the floor.

Robert was going to live, Andrew thought. Thank God for that. He wasn't completely out of harm's way, but he was certainly much improved from his unconscious state in the intensive care unit. According to Kara, they'd now run tests and figure out what needed to be done to insure that Robert's road to recovery was successful.

Andrew stopped walking and sank onto a wooden bench beneath a tall elm tree.

So now what? he asked himself. Should he finish what he'd started once Robert was completely out of danger? Demand that MacAllister acknowledge Sally Malone's existence? Make Robert take responsibility for his actions of so many years ago?

No.

There was nothing to be gained by that. Sally was gone, would not have wanted Andrew to pursue this mission he'd set in motion. He'd been wrong, so damn wrong, to confront Robert in the first place, and he sure as hell wasn't going to repeat that mistake.

Once he knew that Robert MacAllister was truly going to be all right, that would be that. He'd return to Santa Maria and pick up his life where he'd left off, go on as he'd been before.

Andrew frowned as an image of his big empty apartment flashed before his mental vision. He saw himself entering the living room after a day at the office, with the long hours of the evening stretching silently before him.

No one was waiting for him to come home.

No one gave a rip whether he even arrived there safely.

No one cared.

"Oh, give it a rest," he muttered under his breath.

Where was this pity-pot junk coming from? He was alone by choice, preferred it that way.

Yeah, okay, okay, he'd discovered a deep inner yearning for a wife and child to share his life with when he'd seen the mother and baby in the hospital on New Year's Eve. The woman in the shadows who had turned out to be Kara MacAllister.

But that seed of need was minuscule compared to his determination never to love, never to render himself vulnerable, at the risk of having his heart smashed to smithereens as his mother's had been. That newly found want would disappear in time because it wouldn't be nurtured or paid attention to.

He'd return to Santa Maria, get back into his busy routine, and everything would be fine. He'd put all that had happened here in Ventura out of his mind and forget it in time as though it had never taken place.

And he'd never see Kara MacAllister again.

Andrew lunged to his feet as he felt a chill sweep through him. He started off again, ignoring the cold fist that had tightened in his gut at the thought of walking away from Kara without a backward glance.

His attraction to Kara, his strange need to have her trust him enough to reveal her innermost secrets to him, the intensity of his desire for her, were all unsettling, raised questions that plagued him unmercifully. Questions he was determined to have the answers to.

Why did Kara have this hold over him? He didn't know. He didn't know. He didn't know.

Andrew turned a corner on the cobblestone path

and bumped into a woman coming from the opposite direction.

"Oh, I'm sorry," he said. "I wasn't watching where I was going."

"Nor was I," the woman said. "I was deep in thought and... Oh, dear heaven, you're...you're Andrew Malone, aren't you?"

Andrew stared at the woman for a long moment, then his heart began to beat in a wild tattoo.

"Yes, I am," he said finally, "and you're Margaret MacAllister."

Margaret nodded, her gaze riveted on Andrew. The color drained from her face and her breath caught.

"You have his eyes," she whispered. "The MacAllister eyes and...and your features... Oh, God, it's true. You're Robert's son."

"Yes," Andrew said, "but please believe me when I say how sorry I am about what I did at that restaurant. I'd give anything if I could turn back the clock. I don't expect you to accept my apology, to forgive me, but I am truly sorry about what happened."

Margaret nodded slowly. "Yes, I believe you are, but the clock can't be turned back. What's done is done. Many lives will never be the same again."

"I know," Andrew said, dragging a hand through his hair.

"I can't embrace any emotions about you, Andrew," Margaret said. "Not now, not yet. I need to concentrate completely on Robert. The doctors decided he was strong enough to run tests this afternoon, and I came over to this little park for some private time. I never expected to see you here.''

"I'll leave you in peace.''

"Peace?" Margaret said. "I wonder if I'll ever have that again. It depends, I suppose, on what Robert tells me about him and your mother.''

"I—"

"No," she said, raising one hand. "Don't say anything and, please, I beg of you, don't tell me how old you are. I need to hear all this from my husband.''

"I understand," Andrew said, nodding.

"How strange it is, so very strange, to be looking at you, someone I don't even know, and see my Robert's eyes, his features. You're a MacAllister and I don't know...I don't yet know how to deal with that.''

"I shouldn't have come to Ventura. There was no purpose to be served by the rest of you being made aware that I existed. Robert knew, has always known about me, but...it felt right at the time, seemed so important that I... But I'll be leaving as soon as I'm certain that Robert will be all right. You can forget that I was ever here.''

"Oh, Andrew, if only that was true," Margaret said with a sigh. "You can't be erased like chalk on a blackboard. You exist. You're Robert's son. You're also obviously very angry about something. That was apparent at the restaurant when you spoke to Robert.''

"Yes, I was angry, have been for many years, but now I realize that it was misplaced anger. I wish I could disappear without your ever knowing that I'm alive.''

Margaret smiled slightly. ''So do I, as cruel as that sounds, but it's too late for that. Just remember, Andrew, there are two sides to every story. You've only heard the words spoken by your mother. You have yet to hear what your...what Robert has to say. Now if you'll excuse me, I'd like to go sit down and be alone for a while.''

''Yes, of course,'' Andrew said, then watched until Margaret disappeared from view around the bend in the sidewalk.

He started off again in the direction of the hospital, Margaret's words echoing in his mind.

You've only heard the words spoken by your mother.

No, he thought, that wasn't true. The only thing that Sally Malone had ever said on the subject was that she had loved deeply but had not been loved in return.

The ugly details of Robert's abandonment of pregnant Sally, of turning his back on that frightened and desperate young girl, had come from Clara.

He'd overheard so many arguments between his mother and Clara as his aunt hammered away at his mother, telling her how foolish she was not to demand child support from her son's father, how gullible and unsophisticated she had been in the first place to have been taken in by that smooth-talking liar.

After he'd moved in with Clara following Sally's death, he'd heard it all over again, time after time. Sally had been deserted, discarded like yesterday's newspaper, by a man who had used Sally for his own selfish purposes.

She'd been disowned by parents who were furious and ashamed that their teenage daughter had gotten pregnant, had forced Sally to leave the house, declaring that they never wanted to see her again.

Clara would sneak out to visit her sister in the shabby room where she was barely managing to exist, telling her each time that it was asinine to live hand-to-mouth as Sally was. Make him pay up, Clara told Andrew she had urged Sally. Make him be accountable for what he had done.

Just remember, Andrew, there are two sides to every story.

Again, Margaret's words echoed in Andrew's mind, and a headache began to throb painfully in his temples.

What other side to this story could there be? Andrew asked himself. Facts were facts. Sally had gotten pregnant the summer she had been with Robert and had raised her baby alone with no financial or emotional assistance from Robert MacAllister, who had walked away from Sally and their child.

There just wasn't a flipside of the coin to examine.

Yes, he'd learned the gory details from his aunt, not his mother, but that didn't change the truth of what had taken place so long ago.

So long ago.

That was the kicker. That was what he should have focused on before working himself into a rage and driving down to Ventura. He should have let the past lie as it was, leave it alone, let his mother rest in peace.

But it was too late for that.

Now he had to wait and be certain that Robert would be all right.

And he had to figure out how to free himself of the unsettling hold Kara MacAllister had on him.

Andrew pulled himself from his troubled thoughts as he approached the hospital. He saw several reporters standing by the front entrance chatting with one another. He'd heard a nurse say that the press had been banned from going farther than the lobby in search of MacAllister news to feed to the public, a public always hungry for a scandal connected to people with power and money.

Andrew stopped walking and stayed by the side of the building, out of view of the reporters.

What if he walked right up to them, he thought, and told them that he'd been out partying on New Year's Eve, had been drunk when he'd crashed the MacAllister party and everything he had said in that ballroom wasn't true, was simply the product of his having had too much to drink?

No, of course he wasn't Robert MacAllister's son. Get real. He was just a man named Malone, who owned a construction company upstate and had over-indulged in liquor on a holiday. Sorry, folks, but there really wasn't a juicy story here, after all, so why not pack it up and shuffle off to Buffalo?

The idea had merit—to a point—but it would never work.

Because every one of those reporters had a camera hanging around his or her neck. Every one of them would probably take a picture of him. Every one of them would examine that photograph very very carefully.

And he had been told by Kara and now by Margaret that he had the one feature that could not be denied in regard to his identity.

He had the MacAllister eyes.

Chapter 6

Much to Andrew's frustration, he was unable to get Kara alone after he reached the hospital. Each time he caught a glimpse of her, she was with one or more of the MacAllisters, who were there in force again while Robert was undergoing his tests.

Some people, he supposed, would consider him a coward for skulking in the shadows and making certain that he didn't come face-to-face with any of the MacAllister family.

In actuality he was attempting to avoid what would undoubtedly be a nasty and loud confrontation, perhaps even a physical one, between him and the MacAllister men.

A hospital was not the place for that to happen, nor did the press need any more juicy tidbits to serve to the gossip-hungry public.

So for now he would remain out of sight and hope he could somehow speak to Kara alone.

As three of the MacAllister wives he'd come to recognize emerged from the elevator, Andrew pushed open the door leading to the stairs and made a hasty exit from the floor where Robert's private room was. Robert was somewhere else in the building being put through the battery of tests the council of doctors had agreed was necessary.

Andrew sighed and leaned against the wall, folding his arms over his chest.

He'd never run from a fight in his life, he thought. He'd taken on the bullies in school who'd singled him out on occasion for reasons only they knew. He'd learned early on how to defend himself with his fists, and once he'd grown to his full height and filled out, there were none left who wished to take him on.

In the business arena he stepped up and presented bids on projects right along with the big outfits while Malone Construction was hardly more than a hope and a dream. Little by little he'd established himself as a force to be reckoned with, a man owning a competitive company that would always produce what it promised.

He'd earned the respect he had. He'd earned the money he possessed. He'd earned his place in the high-society scene in Santa Maria. What he had not earned, and never would, was a place in the Mac-Allister family.

To have Robert MacAllister's blood running through his veins meant nothing. The MacAllister family had been built on a foundation of years of love, loyalty and dedication. He knew, somehow just knew, that each one of them would be willing to lay his or her life on the line for one of their own.

He couldn't appear in their lives at nearly forty years old and expect to receive the warmth and caring they willingly gave to each other.

No, he was a Malone, and his entire family consisted of an alcoholic aunt named Clara and his gentle mother, Sally, who was now only a memory. That was it. That was all there was.

Man, Andrew thought, shaking his head. He was doing it again—feeling sorry for himself. Ridiculous. He'd only known he was a MacAllister for a handful of days. He didn't belong in the loving embrace of that family. Hell, no. He hadn't paid his dues, hadn't earned the right to be there.

Besides, he reasoned, he'd go nuts in a family that big. They probably popped into one another's homes without warning, dropped off cakes and kids, and delivered opinions about every aspect of their lives.

Considering the total number of children, which he didn't remember, plus the adults, there was probably a birthday party for someone on the calendar every time they turned around.

They'd storm the gates of one of the MacAllister houses, and it would be bedlam—kids running everywhere, babies crying, balloons to be blown up and a pile of presents to be opened and gushed over.

They'd barbecue. Yeah, that would be the best way to handle a mob like that. Everyone would bring a dish or two, do a potluck thing, then have a picnic dinner in the backyard.

They might play horseshoes, or volleyball, or

maybe touch football. Yeah, touch football. The MacAllister men were good-size guys, would play a rough game of ball, while the wives and kids and grandparents cheered from the sidelines.

They'd take that game seriously, give it their all, and when it was over they'd slap one another on the back and compare scrapes and bruises as trophies. They'd slug down cold beer, laughing and talking as they wiped the sweat from their faces with their grass-stained shirtsleeves.

The wives would shoo them off to clean up before hamburgers and hot dogs were placed on the grill, creating a mouth-watering aroma that would float through the air, tempting the neighbors to wander over and join the boisterous party.

As dusk crept in, a tired whining child would be scooped onto the nearest lap and hugged in loving arms, which that kid would welcome without question, knowing he was safe there even though it might not be his own mother or father who held him.

When there was a crisis in the MacAllister family, as there was now, everyone would drop what they were doing, put their lives on hold and rally around. They would comfort one another, know when to listen and when to keep silent, were prepared to do whatever was needed.

Despite the huge number of bona fide MacAllisters, they apparently felt there was always room for more. Beneath the photograph in the newspaper, the caption had listed a guy named…what was it? Oh, yeah, Sharpe. Ted Sharpe, his wife, Hannah, and a couple of kids, one being a cute baby of Asian descent.

He'd seen Ted Sharpe earlier that day when the man had arrived with Ryan MacAllister for what had been a brief stop at the hospital. Both men had been wearing police uniforms and, Andrew guessed, had ducked into the hospital while on duty to check on Robert.

Sharpe wasn't a MacAllister; he was obviously Ryan's partner on the police force. But Sharpe and his family were welcomed into the fold, the circle, and had no doubt earned their place there.

And Kara. Kara had been a foster child, who hadn't been a cuddly little baby when she'd gone to live with Mary and Ralph MacAllister. No, she'd been sixteen years old. Most teenagers were tough enough to deal with, let alone one who had been through heaven only knew what.

Yeah, there was always room for one more in the MacAllister family.

But not for him.

"Hell, Malone," he said, dragging both hands down his face, "give it a rest."

His overloaded mind was taking him all over the map, into territory where he didn't even want to be.

He'd feel smothered in a family like the MacAllisters. He'd never be able to handle all those people being in his face, minding his business.

Caring what happened to him.

Showing up at his door with chicken soup when he had the flu.

Listening to him, really hearing him, when he shared what was going on in his life.

Singing "Happy Birthday" to him when he blew out the candles on his cake on his special day.

Making him part of the team when they played touch football.

"Malone, damn it, knock it off," Andrew said, pushing himself away from the wall.

He stiffened as the door leading to the stairs opened suddenly. Then his heart seemed to skip a beat when Kara appeared and allowed the door to close behind her with a hush.

"Hello, Andrew," she said, smiling slightly. "I saw you come out here. This is the first chance I've had to get away so I could speak to you."

"I know," he said, looking directly into her eyes. "The whole family, *your* family, seems to be here again."

"They're your family, too," she said softly.

Andrew closed the distance between them and framed her face in his hands. A frisson of heat slithered down her back at the feel of Andrew's strong, callused, but gentle hands on her soft skin.

"No, they're not," he said. "I've just been thinking about that, about how I'm not a MacAllister, not really, and never will be."

"But you are. You're Robert's son."

"Technically I'm a MacAllister. DNA testing would prove that I'm a MacAllister. But, Kara, it takes more than that to belong, really belong, to a family like yours. You're not just a bunch of people getting together once in a while to go through the motions of celebrating a holiday.

"The MacAllisters are an unbeatable force, a unit, a seamless circle that is bonded together, ready to take on whatever comes—good, bad, in between. Each one of you has earned your place within that circle. Me? I'm the cause of one of the members of that family nearly dying. No, I'm not a MacAllister.''

"But—"

"Hey, it's okay. It really is. I could never measure up, anyway, wouldn't know how to act, what to do. I'm a loner, a private solitary man and...and I prefer it that way. My life as it is suits me just fine. It does. I...ah, hell, forget it."

Andrew lowered his head and captured Kara's mouth in a kiss that was nearly rough in its intensity. In the next instant the kiss gentled, as he drank in the sweet taste of Kara, allowed the very essence of her to push aside the turmoil raging in his mind.

He just wanted to feel, to savor, to fill his senses with her.

Kara returned the kiss in total abandon, splaying her hands on Andrew's muscled chest, feeling the rapid tempo of his heart beating beneath her palm.

It had been an eternity since he'd last kissed her. She'd missed him. She'd missed this ecstasy, this acute awareness of her own womanliness compared to Andrew's blatant masculinity.

Oh, she felt so vitally alive and feminine. The heat of desire was swirling within her, growing hotter, pulsing low in her body. She wanted him. She wanted to make love with Andrew Malone.

What was happening to her? And why? She didn't know. She just didn't know.

Andrew broke the kiss as he reached the edge of his control, then slowly and so reluctantly dropped his hands from Kara's face and took a step backward.

"Do the MacAllister men," he said, his voice

raspy with passion, "play touch football at birthday parties?"

Kara blinked, bringing herself back from the sensual haven she'd floated to.

"Pardon me?" she said.

"Never mind," Andrew said, then drew a much-needed breath. "It was a dumb question, wasn't important."

"Touch football? Do the guys play touch football at birthday parties?" Kara said, frowning. "It's not a dumb question, just a strange one. But the answer is yes, they do. It's a tradition at all family gatherings, birthday party or not. Andrew, why did you ask that?"

"I don't know," he said with a sigh. "Please, just forget it." He paused. "Do you have any news about Robert yet?"

"Yes. Uncle Robert is going to have double-bypass surgery tomorrow morning. The doctors don't want to wait any longer because there's too great a chance of him having another heart attack if they do."

"I see," Andrew said, frowning. "How's Margaret holding up?"

"She's frightened, but she knows Robert is in the best of hands. I guess that sums up how everyone is feeling at the moment.

"The doctors said that Uncle Robert can't have any visitors between now and the surgery. He's very tired from going through the tests, and they're going to keep him slightly sedated until morning.

"Aunt Margaret isn't happy about that, but she has

no voice in the matter. Everyone is getting ready to leave for home.''

Andrew nodded.

"I have patients scheduled at my office tomorrow who I must see,'' Kara went on. "I'll be calling over here for updates, and I'll come as soon as I can. I'm not quite certain how to keep you informed tomorrow, Andrew, because I won't be here at the hospital until at least the middle of the afternoon.''

"Could I telephone your office?''

"Well, yes, that would be fine. I'll tell my receptionist, Lucy, to expect your calls. If I'm with a patient, Lucy will tell you whatever information I have at that moment.''

"What kind of doctor are you?'' Andrew asked. "A specialist? Most doctors are these days.''

"No, I'm an old-fashioned general practitioner. A family doctor.''

"Somehow that doesn't surprise me,'' Andrew said, "considering the family you come from. It makes sense that you'd want to be available to treat your patient's whole family if they needed you.''

"Yes, that's exactly why I went into family practice. But you said 'the family I come from.' Remember, Andrew, I didn't even know the MacAllisters until I was sixteen, didn't legally become one until I was eighteen.''

"I realize that,'' he said, "but you've earned your place in the circle.''

"But you don't want to,'' Kara said, frowning. "Earn your place in that circle you keep referring to.''

"No.''

"Are you so very certain that's true, Andrew?" she said, reaching out and placing one hand on his cheek. "Or are you attempting to convince yourself it is?"

Andrew's jaw tightened. "I know who I am, Kara, what my needs are, what I can handle, deal with, and what I can't. I didn't confront Robert at that party with the idea of being welcomed into the family.

"I couldn't...breathe in the big crowd you people create when you're together. I'd feel smothered, drained dry, be expected to give more than I would be able to and... This is all moot, not worth discussing, because no one is going to open the door to that circle for me, anyway."

"Exactly why *did* you come to that party?" Kara said. "What did you hope to achieve by confronting Robert? Why did you keep silent all those years, then suddenly appear?"

"None of that is important now."

"I'll wait," Kara said, lifting her chin.

"What?"

"Tit for tat, Mr. Malone. I'll wait until you trust me enough to share that information with me. That's fair, isn't it? You're waiting to hear my life story, waiting for me to trust you enough to tell you about my past. As I said, tit for tat."

Andrew smiled and shook his head. "You're a tough cookie, Dr. MacAllister."

"Yes, I am, when I need to be. All the Mac-Allisters are. And like it or not, Andrew, you're a MacAllister, too. Now I really must go. I have a bottle to feed to a hungry baby."

"The baby you were feeding in the nursery last night?"

"Yes," Kara said. "That baby."

"Is he a patient of yours? Well, yes, he must be to be getting such special treatment from you."

"He's...very important to me," she said. He's my son. Oh, please, God, let that hope and prayer come true. All the paperwork was completed; the required visits to her home by the social worker had been done. All she could do now was wait for the decision by the judge. "He's very special."

"Lucky kid," Andrew said. "Listen, are the doctors saying what Robert's chances are of surviving the surgery tomorrow?"

"All they'll say is that they're optimistic."

"Which says nothing." Andrew paused. "May I see you later? Would you like to have dinner away from this place?"

Oh, dear, Kara thought, what should she do? Say? Yes? No? To go out to dinner with Andrew away from the hospital was dangerous. And disloyal.

But to be with Andrew in a restaurant, sharing a meal like all the other people there? It would make them simply a man and a woman. Oh, right. There was nothing *simple* about her reaction to Andrew, her desire for him that was like nothing she'd known before.

She was continually drawn to him, and each time he touched her, kissed her, her passion soared. She wanted him with an intensity that was nearly frightening. Oh, yes, going out to dinner with Andrew Malone was very very dangerous.

"Kara?" Andrew said. "Dinner? It wouldn't be a

fancy deal.'' He glanced down at the jeans and sweater he was wearing. "I'm not dressed for five-star dining. We could get a hamburger or a steak at a family restaurant or whatever.'' He chuckled and shook his head. "Now I'm talking about *family* restaurants. That word has been everywhere I've turned since I came to Ventura. Well? Do you want to go or not?''

"I...um...'' Kara said.

Everyone was leaving the hospital now, she thought. They would all be safely away before she'd finished feeding the baby and wouldn't see her with Andrew. Richard was already angry at her for even speaking with Andrew, let alone going out to dinner with the man.

Remember where your loyalties lie, Richard had said, and he had a point, she supposed. Yes, Uncle Robert had been unknowingly suffering from heart problems before the confrontation at the party, but it had been Andrew who had pushed him over the limit of what Robert's heart could handle.

But Andrew hadn't intended any harm to come to Uncle Robert. Still, that didn't erase the fact that because of the confrontation between Andrew and Robert, her uncle had had a life-threatening heart attack. But then again...

"My mind is a jumbled mess,'' Kara said, pressing her fingertips to her temples.

"There's a lot of that going around,'' Andrew said dryly. "I'm a charter member of that club. Back to the question. Do you want to get something to eat after you feed that baby? Actually, you don't have to feed him, do you? I mean, that's not part of your duties as his doctor.''

"I *want* to give him his bottle."

Andrew shrugged. "Fine."

"All right. I'm making a decision about dinner. My answer is... Give me a minute here."

"Am I missing something? What's the problem?" Andrew said, frowning. "It's not as though I'm asking you to run off to the Bahamas with me. We're talking about a meal here."

"Well, for one thing, Andrew, you have to understand that some members of the family are not thrilled that I am communicating with you on a regular basis. My brother Richard, for one, is very upset with me about it, feels I'm not being a loyal MacAllister."

"Ah," Andrew said, nodding, "I see. That makes sense. Richard and the other guys would no doubt like to take me apart, which also makes sense."

"Yes, well, I told Richard that I'm all grown up now and I make my own choices." Kara drew a steadying breath. "So, yes, I'd like to have dinner with you."

"Good. That's good. Where shall I meet you?"

"Well, why don't you come to the maternity wing with me and we'll leave from there. Just give me a minute to say goodbye to everyone. I'll be right back."

Andrew nodded and Kara left the landing, the door once again closing behind her with a soft swish.

So, Kara was catching flak for talking to him, Andrew thought. Was being accused of not having MacAllister loyalty. He was the bad guy in this scenario, and Kara was assumed to be sleeping with the enemy.

Bad choice of words, he thought as a flash of heat rocketed through his body. Sleeping with the enemy. With him. Making love with him through the night. No, knock it off. His body couldn't handle the images he was creating in his mind. He was going up in flames.

He shouldn't have kissed Kara again. He couldn't stop himself from kissing her again. And Kara had welcomed his kiss, had returned it with the same heated desire that had consumed him. Kara wanted him as much as he wanted her.

The question at hand was, what were they going to do about it?

Kara hugged Margaret, then swept her gaze over the others who were assembled in the hallway outside the closed door to Robert's room.

"All of you should try to have a relaxing evening if you can," Kara said. "You know my schedule for tomorrow. I'll be calling in, then I'll get back over here as soon as possible."

"I still don't see why I can't sit with Robert this evening," Margaret said. "I'm his wife, for mercy's sake. I'm not going to upset him or cause him any stress or... This is ridiculous."

"You're pouting, Mother," Forrest said. "Orders are orders, and doctors are very big on giving them. Right, Kara?"

"It's a power trip we thrive on," Kara said, smiling. "Tomorrow will be a long day, Aunt Margaret.

You need to rest and Uncle Robert has to be kept very quiet until his surgery."

"Yes, yes, so they said," Margaret said with a click of her tongue. "So be it. Well, we still have to eat dinner. Should we pick up the children and go somewhere? Or maybe take pizzas back to someone's house?"

"Pizza sounds good," Jack said. "All the kids are with Jillian and Jennifer at Forrest and Jillian's house. We can take pizzas there. Okay, Forrest?"

"Let's roll," Forrest said. "Coming, Kara?"

"Oh, I...um...have something I have to do here at the hospital before I can leave," she said.

"Okay," Forrest said, nodding. "We'll save you some pizza, then."

"No," she said quickly. "What I mean is, thank you, but I believe I'll pass."

Richard looked at Kara intently. "Have other plans, little sister?"

"Don't start anything with me, Richard," Kara said, narrowing her eyes. "You've made your point, I heard it, now drop it."

"What point?" Jack said. "I'm obviously missing out on a sibling battle here. Shame on me. Whose side am I on? What's the scoop?"

"The scoop, big brother," Richard said, glaring at Kara, "is that our little sister has become very oozy with Andrew Malone."

"Ho-boy," Jack said, raising his eyebrows. "This isn't a battle, it's an entire war."

"What it is," Kara said, planting her hands on her hips, "is none of anyone's business if I choose to keep Andrew Malone informed of Uncle Robert's condition.

"Andrew feels very badly about what happened. It was never his intention to harm Uncle Robert. He... Oh, never mind. None of you are going to believe a word I say about Andrew, anyway. I'm wasting my breath trying to talk to you."

"I believe you, Kara," Margaret said quietly. "I'm aware that Andrew feels badly."

"*You've* talked to the jerk, too?" Richard said incredulously. "I don't believe this. Cripes, Aunt Margaret, the guy nearly killed your husband."

"No, Richard," Margaret said wearily, "that's not entirely true. Robert and I have been ignoring the signals his heart was giving him. He should have had a complete physical examination long before now. Granted, Andrew's arrival triggered the heart attack, but while we're on the subject of Andrew Malone," Margaret continued, changing tack, "there's something that all of you should know. I'm going to say this once, then I don't wish to discuss it further until Robert is well enough to explain things to me.

"Andrew Malone *is* Robert's son. He has the MacAllister eyes, plus features I see in my own children. Yes, Andrew is Robert's son."

"Oh, hell," Michael said, shaking his head. "How old is he?"

"I said there would be no more discussion on the matter, Michael," Margaret said, looking at him sternly.

"'Kay," Michael said, nodding quickly. "You bet, Mom. Whatever you say."

"I'll be damned," Forrest said. "Malone is really my...what? Half brother?"

"Put a cork in it, Forrest," Jack said. "Your mom said the subject is closed for now."

"Oh, right," Forrest said. "Sorry. But...whew. This is a heavy trip."

"Enough said," Margaret said, lifting her chin. "Who is going to stop and get the pizzas?"

"I will," Forrest said. "There's plenty of soda and stuff at our house to drink."

"Are you coming over later for pizza or not, Kara?" Richard said.

"No, Richard, I'm not," Kara said, looking directly at him.

Richard shook his head in frustration and the group started toward the elevator. Jack let the others pass him, then kissed Kara on the forehead.

"Be careful, sister mine," he said, smiling at her. "That's all I ask. Just be careful. I don't want to see you get hurt. Not ever. I love you, kid."

"I love you, too, Jack," Kara said softly, feeling the tears stinging the backs of her eyes. "Thank you."

As Jack walked away, Kara closed her eyes for a moment to regain control of her emotions. When she opened her eyes again, she was completely alone in the quiet empty hallway of the hospital, and a chill coursed through her.

She didn't want to be alone, she thought. Not right now. There were times when she sought privacy and solitude, but this wasn't one of those times.

She just didn't want to be alone.

And she didn't have to be.

Because Andrew was waiting.

Chapter 7

Kara entered the nursery and sought out the nurse on duty.

"Hi, Peggy." Kara said quietly. "Are you here alone? Where are the other nurses?"

"Having dinner," Peggy said, smiling at her. "I'm holding down the fort. So far everything is quiet." She laughed. "I shouldn't have said that out loud. Now all the babies will start to wail at the same time. Guaranteed."

"I hope not." Kara smiled, then became serious. "I'm going to feed my baby."

Peggy nodded. "Sure. He's been fussing for a few minutes, so he's probably figuring out he's hungry and is getting ready to cut loose with an air-raid siren. Go ahead. Enjoy."

"Yes, I will, but... Do you see that man standing outside the nursery window there?" Kara said. "I'm going to invite him in to sit with me while I feed my son. However, I'd appreciate it if you wouldn't say anything about my plans to adopt the baby."

Peggy looked across the nursery and her eyes widened. "Oh, my gosh, is that your baby's father? What is he doing here? The birth mother signed the release forms to allow the baby to be adopted and left the day after she gave birth. Why is the father suddenly showing up?"

Kara frowned in confusion. "He's not the baby's father. What made you think he was?"

"Look at him. He and the baby have the same black hair, tawny skin, high cheekbones and…oh, yes, he could pass for your baby's father." Peggy paused. "Why are my lips sealed about your wanting to adopt the baby?"

"Because I haven't told anyone yet. Only the nursery nurses know and, of course, the social worker."

"Oh, I see," Peggy said, nodding. "Got it. Well, I'll heat a bottle for your munchkin. When are you going to name that little darling?"

"I've been through this with Judy," Kara said, laughing. "She thinks I'm nuts, so I don't think I'll repeat my reasoning on the subject."

"Okeydokey," Peggy said. "I'll bring you a bottle in a second."

"Peggy, wait," Kara said. "That man…is Andrew Malone."

Peggy's eyes widened again. "*The* Andrew Malone? From the newspaper stories about how your uncle's secret son showed up at the big bash you

MacAllisters were having and... *That* Andrew Malone?''

"Yes," Kara said. "So could you not react to that fact when I introduce you to him?"

"Oh. Right. You bet." Peggy leaned closer to Kara. "Is Andrew Malone really Robert MacAllister's secret son from a past affair?"

"Peggy, please," Kara said. "I don't want to discuss it."

"Well, darn, you're no fun. I'm off to heat your kiddo's bottle."

Kara left the nursery by the side door and went to the front of the window, where Andrew was looking through the glass at the babies.

"Andrew?" she said.

"Hmm?" he said, his gaze still riveted on the infants in the bassinets.

"Would you like to come inside and sit with me while I feed the baby?"

Andrew's head snapped around. "Me?"

"Well...yes," Kara said, smiling at him. "The baby eats very slowly, and we could chat while I'm giving him his bottle. I just thought it would be nicer for you than being out here all alone or reading old magazines in the waiting room."

"Oh, well, sure, okay," Andrew said. "I guess. The closest I've ever been to a tiny baby is standing here looking at this bunch through the window. Are you certain I should be inside the nursery? Maybe I have germs or something."

Kara laughed. "It'll be fine. Come on. My—the little guy I'm going to feed is getting antsy for his dinner.''

"You're the doctor," Andrew said, shrugging. "Lead on and I'll follow, complete with germs."

"Oh, for heaven's sake," Kara said, laughing again.

Man, oh, man, Andrew thought as they walked along the side corridor by the nursery. Kara's laughter would bring bright sunshine to the cloudiest day. And...jeez. That was one of the corniest things his beleaguered brain had ever produced. But damn it, it was true. He really did like Kara's laughter.

And her smile. And the way her dark eyes sparkled when she was happy. And how she felt when he was holding her close to him. And her taste, her aroma, her silky curly dark hair that framed her delicate lovely face so perfectly and—

"Here we go," Kara said, bringing Andrew from his rambling thoughts.

They entered the nursery, and Peggy appeared to hand Kara a bottle. Kara made the introductions, Peggy looked at the notorious Andrew Malone a tad too long, then finally headed back across the room.

"Would you hold this please?" Kara said, extending the bottle toward Andrew.

He stared at the baby bottle, Kara's face, the bottle again, then finally grasped the bottle between his thumb and index finger, holding it out in front of him.

"It won't bite you," Kara said.

"Give me a break," Andrew said, smiling. "Put a hammer in my paw and I'm comfortable. But this?" He nodded toward the bottle. "I'm afraid I'll smash it if I wrap my whole hand around it."

"Baby bottles don't shatter that easily," Kara said,

"and besides, you...you have a very gentle touch when it's needed."

Their eyes met and desire licked through them instantly, like a match being set to dry leaves. Kara tore her gaze from Andrew's and walked to a bassinet set against the far wall. Andrew took a steadying breath, then followed her, the bottle at arm's length in front of him.

"Hello, sweetheart," Kara said, reaching into the bassinet. Mommy is here, my love. Mommy is here. "Are you hungry?"

She lifted the baby slowly and so very carefully, then shifted him to the crook of her arm.

"He's a crack baby," she said, her voice hushed as she looked up at Andrew. "His birth mother was on drugs, and this little guy is paying the price. He's going through withdrawal. Crack babies can't handle sudden movement or loud noises. He's had a very rough start in life, I'm afraid."

"No joke," Andrew said, his gaze focused on the baby. "He's so small. I have never in my life seen such a tiny human being."

"He only weighed a little over four pounds when he was born," Kara said, "but he's gaining steadily. He's doing very well, considering the circumstances. Don't you think he's beautiful, Andrew?"

"Yes, I do," Andrew said, nodding. "I really do. He's amazing. He has everything he's supposed to have, only it's in miniature. You know what I mean? Eyes, nose, mouth... Look at those tiny hands, those fingers. I have pencils twice as wide as those fingers. Amazing."

The baby blinked, drew a shuddering breath, then began to cry. Andrew jerked in surprise.

"What's the matter with him?" he said. "Do something, Kara. Wow! How can so much noise come out of such a small person?"

Kara laughed and settled into the rocking chair. She extended her hand toward Andrew and he slapped the bottle into it. She popped the nipple into the baby's mouth and he began to suckle hungrily. Andrew glanced around, then reached for a stool on wheels, which he pulled close to the rocker.

"Way to go, sport," he said, seating himself to watch the baby eat. "Polish that off and we'll buy you a hot-fudge sundae for dessert."

This, Kara thought, had been a major mistake. Very very foolish. She was soaking up Andrew's endearing reactions to the baby like a thirsty sponge. She was sharing her son with him before anyone in her family even knew that she hoped to adopt him, to make him truly hers.

And it felt so right, so very warm, and rich, and wonderful to have Andrew sitting right next to her and the baby while she tended to him.

The next time she came to the nursery to feed the baby, she'd envision Andrew being there with her, she just knew she would. Oh, yes, this was a very foolish mistake.

"How could someone take drugs while they were pregnant?" Andrew said. "That blows my mind."

"I know," Kara said, nodding. "But it happens a lot, I'm afraid. It will be a while before I...they know if any long-term damage was done to this little guy. He didn't deserve to start life this way."

"Mmm," Andrew said.

"Andrew," Kara said, glancing at him, then redirecting her attention to the baby. "My aunt Margaret told the family that she had spoken with you and that she knows you're Robert's son. She said you have the MacAllister eyes, and she could also see Robert in your features."

"Dandy," Andrew said dryly. "I bumped into your aunt—literally—in that little park near here. She's a classy lady. She really is. So she dropped that bombshell on the troops, huh? I bet that went over like a dull thud. What did everyone have to say on the subject?"

"Aunt Margaret didn't allow anyone to comment," Kara said. "She said it wasn't open for discussion and she was waiting until Uncle Robert could explain things to her. Believe me, when Aunt Margaret speaks in a certain tone of voice, she is listened to." Kara paused. "Your age, how old you are, is going to have a major impact on this whole situation."

Andrew nodded. "I realize that. Your aunt asked me not to tell her how old I was. She wants to hear it all from her husband, not from me."

"Yes."

"Do *you* want me to tell you how old I am, Kara?"

"No," she said, shaking her head. "It's not my place to know before Aunt Margaret does."

"There's that family loyalty again," Andrew said, sitting straighter on the stool. "Does your family know that you're having dinner with me tonight?"

"They reached that conclusion without my telling

them. It got mixed reviews. My brother Richard is being grumpy about it, and my brother Jack was concerned but very sweet. The others wisely kept silent on the subject.''

"I'm sorry I'm causing you problems," Andrew said, frowning.

"I make my own choices, Andrew. I have the right to do that. I—"

A sudden loud buzzing noise reverberated through the air, and the baby stopped suckling on the nipple. He shuddered, then began to eat again.

"Uh-oh," Kara said.

"What is that?" Andrew said. "What's going on in here?"

"Kara," Peggy called from across the room. "I have a preemie in distress. Can you help me?"

"I'm coming," Kara called, causing the baby to jerk at the increased volume of her voice. She stood, then bent down toward Andrew. "Here, take him."

Before Andrew actually realized what was happening, he had the baby in the crook of one arm and the bottle in his other hand. The baby screwed up his little face and cut loose with an earsplitting wail.

"Kara, wait," Andrew said. "Hey, come back here. You can't... Kara!"

"Feed him," she yelled.

"Holy hell," Andrew said, then placed the nipple of the bottle in the baby's mouth, slowly, tentatively.

The baby hesitated, then began to suckle.

"Oh, thanks, kid," Andrew said, his shoulders slumping with relief. "Go for it." He frowned. "Why are you staring at me? Okay. Whatever. I'll stare right back at you. How's that?"

Andrew began to feel his tightened muscles relax as the baby continued to eat, his eyes riveted on the man who was feeding him.

He was holding a miracle, Andrew thought incredulously. Feeding him. Taking care of him. He had power tools that weighed more than this little guy. Man, he was small, so tiny, so perfect.

Andrew eyed the rocking chair, looked at the baby again, then got to his feet slowly, hardly breathing. He settled onto the chair and began to rock gently back and forth.

"This is better, don't you think?" he said to the baby, who was still staring at him. "Comfy, huh? You know, sport, you drew a lousy hand coming into this big old world, but you're going to be fine. You're tough, a fighter, I can tell.

"You'll grow up to be an honorable man, who follows his dreams. And remember this—you can be anything you want to be if you work hard enough. Settle on a dream and hang on to it. Don't let anything or anyone stop you from achieving what you've set out to do. Okay? Good."

The baby stopped eating and his eyes began to close as Andrew continued to rock, talking to the infant in a low rumbly voice.

"When I was a kid...oh, maybe seven years old," Andrew said, "I wanted a bike. That's all I could think about. Man, did I want a bike. But my mother couldn't afford to buy me one, so I shut up about it so she wouldn't feel bad. You know what I mean?

"Anyway, I hung on to that dream of having a bike and I worked my tail off. I mowed lawns, went to the park every day and collected cans, walked the neighbor's dog, did all kinds of stuff. Every night before I went to bed I counted my money, watched it grow higher in the jar I kept it in.

"Then guess what happened? My aunt Clara showed up out of the blue and she bought me a brand-new, candy-apple-red bike. But you know something, sport? I never liked that bike. Never felt like it was really mine. It didn't make sense to me at the time, but when I was older I realized that I'd really wanted to earn enough, on my own, to buy myself a bike.

"That's an important lesson to learn. If you work hard for what you want, it will mean a lot more than if someone just hands it to you. Got that? No? I bored you right to sleep, huh? That's all right. I'll just hold you. You're safe. Nothing can hurt you, because I've got you right here in my arms."

Kara blinked back her tears as she stood listening to Andrew as he talked quietly to the baby. She drank in the sight of the big strong man holding the helpless tiny infant, took every word Andrew said into her heart, her very soul.

Oh, dear heaven, she thought frantically, she was falling apart, could feel fresh tears threatening to spill onto her cheeks. But Andrew and her son looked so perfect together, so wonderful, and what Andrew was saying was so wise and so…so fatherly. Andrew was a natural-born daddy, he truly was. He—

Oh, Kara, stop it, she ordered herself, taking a deep steadying breath. She was indulging in a silly fantasy, envisioning Andrew as the baby's daddy and…what? As her husband? Good grief, that was insane. She hardly knew the man and here she was imagining the three of them as a family and...

Yes, all right, she cared for Andrew. In the short time she'd known him he'd somehow had a major impact on her life, on her sense of self, on her womanly desires, wants and needs.

It was probably due to the circumstances under which they'd met. The confrontation at the party, then the crisis of Uncle Robert's heart attack, which had pushed everything into high gear, heightening emotions on all levels.

That made sense. Yes, it certainly did. She wasn't acting normally in regard to Andrew, because these weren't ordinary events they were involved in.

Once things calmed down, she'd be capable of viewing Andrew in the proper light, as she would any man she had just met. She would once again be in control of her mind, her heart and—oh, please— her body that was betraying her at every turn.

Kara nodded, squared her shoulders, lifted her chin and walked to the rocking chair.

"Well," she said quietly, "you two seem to be doing just super. Thank you, Andrew, for stepping in like this. The little preemie is fine now. My—the baby didn't finish his bottle? That's all right. Sometimes he doesn't because he runs out of energy and... He's sleeping so peacefully in your arms."

And she was babbling like an idiot, she admonished herself. Andrew was sitting there, looking at her son, not at her, calmly rocking back and forth as he held the baby, as though he did this every day of the week, while she was coming unglued. *Kara MacAllister, get a grip.*

"I'll change his diaper and put him back in the bassinet now," she said.

No! Andrew thought, his hold on the baby tightening slightly. Not yet. Not as long as this little guy was still filling him to overflowing with that same foreign warmth he'd felt last night when he'd seen Kara feeding him in the shadows. He wanted to savor the warmth, just for a while longer, store it away somewhere so he could remember it in the future.

Oh, man, this was nuts. He knew, he'd discovered, that deep within him was a want and need to have a wife and child. A baby just like this one, a wife and mother just like—ah, hell, okay—just like Kara.

But it wasn't going to happen. Because to have those things, he had to strip himself bare, fall in love and be vulnerable to heartache and betrayal and... No way. No. He'd never do that. Not ever.

Andrew looked up at Kara.

"Sure, take him," he said, striving for a casual tone of voice. "He's zonked out, sleeping like a—" he shrugged "—baby. I don't imagine these little guys care who holds or feeds them, as long as somebody gets the job done."

"You're wrong, Andrew," Kara said, reaching for the baby. "It matters."

Kara bent lower to retrieve the infant from Andrew, bringing her face just inches from his. He placed the baby in her arms, and she turned her head to gaze directly into Andrew's eyes.

"Thank you," she whispered, "for taking such good care of him."

Andrew's heart thundered as he resisted the urge to lean forward and claim Kara's lips with his.

"It was my pleasure," he said, his voice husky. "Believe me."

Kara smiled slightly, then straightened and walked across the room with the baby to a changing table. Andrew reached over and placed the bottle on the stool, but didn't release his hold on it for a long moment. He sighed and got to his feet.

A few minutes later Kara went to the side door of the nursery and smiled back at Andrew.

"Ready to get something to eat?" she said.

Andrew glanced at the bassinet where Kara had placed the baby, then looked at her again.

"Sure," he said. "I'm a starving man."

He'd nurture his body with good wholesome food, Andrew thought, as he left the nursery with Kara. But his inner yearnings he would ignore until they faded, then were finally gone, never to return.

Then his life would be back on track, the way he wanted it, the way it had always been.

He'd be alone.

And the chill that had just swept through him as he envisioned his dark solitary future could go straight to hell.

"Andrew?" Kara said as they stepped into the elevator.

"What!" he said sharply, then shook his head. "I'm sorry. I didn't mean to bark at you. It's been a long day, that's all."

"That's what I was just thinking," Kara said. "I'm exhausted and I'm sure you are, too. The family is having pizza at Forrest and Jillian's house so they can sit back and relax, rather than go to a noisy restaurant.

"I...I was wondering if that sounded like a good idea to you, We could pick up a pizza and go to my apartment, just...chill out."

Andrew nodded. "That definitely appeals. I believe we could both use some quiet time. Things have been rather hectic, to say the least."

"Okay."

The elevator bumped to a stop and the doors opened on the main floor of the hospital, which was a hubbub of activity. They started across the lobby, then Andrew placed his hand on Kara's arm to stop her.

"Yes?" she said, looking up at him questioningly.

"I was just wondering," he said, "who will feed the baby the next time he's hungry?"

"The nurses will tend to him."

"Do they know not to jiggle him, not to make any sudden movements or loud noises?"

"Yes, Andrew," she said, smiling at him warmly. "They know."

"Right. Okay," he said, nodding. "Let's go. What do you like on your pizza?"

Andrew Malone, Kara thought as a strange warmth tiptoed around her heart, *if you make me fall in love with you before you walk out of my life, I'll never forgive you for as long as I live.*

Chapter 8

Andrew felt comfortable in Kara's apartment the moment they entered. Her home *looked* like her, he decided, as he glanced around the large living room. It was decorated with a feminine touch without going overboard to the point that a man would feel he didn't belong there.

The furniture was warm oak. The sofa was upholstered in a big bright floral print, and two easy chairs were done in fabric that picked up colors from the bouquet on the sofa.

There was a round, glass-top coffee table, matching end tables, and one wall held a tall bookcase that was filled with a wide variety of books, plus a multitude of framed photographs. On another wall was a home-entertainment center with a television, VCR and stereo.

She used the second bedroom as an office, Kara

said, as she prepared glasses of soda in the kitchen, which had gleaming white appliances. She had a computer and research books in there, as well as a desk that had belonged to her father, Ralph, before he retired from MacAllister Architects.

She explained that her parents had moved to Florida when her father retired, as her mother, Mary, knew that Ralph would continually find excuses to head for the office if they stayed on in Ventura.

Kara put some easy-listening music on the stereo, then they settled onto the carpeted floor next to the coffee table and began to eat the delicious take-out pizza that was, amazingly, still hot.

Kara launched into a story about the MacAllister family's "baby bet business." She told him that for several years her cousin Forrest was the undefeated champion to the point that his on-the-mark predictions of the new arrivals were becoming a tad eerie.

"I was in medical school in Boston at the time," Kara said, "but my aunt Margaret kept me posted on the baby bet. Then Forrest made a prediction that everyone felt would be his undoing." She took another bite of pizza.

Andrew leaned toward her. "Chew fast. What did Forrest predict?"

Kara swallowed, then sipped her soda. "Well, the whole family was gathered—at a pizza parlor, if I recall right—and Forrest arrived with his wife, Jillian, and a big paper shopping bag. No one could figure out what he was up to."

Andrew laughed. "You're killing me here. What was in the bag?"

"Three pink stuffed-toy bunnies. Forrest predicted

that Jillian was going to have triplet girls. The guys were rubbing their hands together, totally convinced that at long last Forrest was going to pay out money, instead of collecting a fistful.''

"And?"

Kara laughed and shook her head. "Jillian had identical triplet girls."

"You're kidding," Andrew said, whooping with laughter. "Man, that is something."

"I know. The girls are so adorable. They're five years old already. No, pardon me, they're five and a half years old. They'll correct you immediately if you don't tack on that half year."

"So is Forrest *still* the baby bet champion?" Andrew said.

"No. Hannah, who is married to Ted Sharpe, was expecting a baby when Ted met her. Forrest made his prediction, but Ted made his own, different from Forrest's. Ted said that Hannah would have a baby girl on Christmas Day. Not only did she do exactly that, but Ted delivered the baby before the paramedics could arrive. Forrest was dethroned as the baby bet champion, big time. But the story doesn't end there."

"Go on," Andrew said eagerly.

"Ever since Ted won the baby bet about his daughter, Patty, the daddies have been the ones to predict every single baby born into the family. Isn't that weird? When a pregnancy is announced, everyone looks at the daddy-to-be and says 'Well?' and— shazam—Dad nails it. What a hoot, huh? I love it."

"That's a great story," Andrew said, smiling at

her warmly. "It really is. I've...I've never known a close-knit family like the MacAllisters."

"They're very special," Kara said, matching his smile. "Oh! Now there's a bachelor bet going on. Can you believe that? Jack told us about it when he arrived here from visiting his friend, Brandon, in Arizona.

"Jack was a confirmed bachelor, as Brandon had once been, and Jack told Brandon to bet all he wanted to, but Jack MacAllister wasn't doing the marriage bit.

"By the time Jack left Prescott, Arizona, he was married to Jennifer, became father to Jennifer's son, Joey, and now there's a little Jack on the way. Jack has already said that Jennifer is having a boy. There's no doubt in anyone's mind that it will be a baby boy.

"Someone in Prescott—the sheriff, I think—is targeted for the bachelor bet and so is my brother, Richard. Jack said he tried to throw me into the pool, but he guessed they weren't including bachelorettes. Oh, my, being a MacAllister is such fun. I'm so blessed to be able to call them my family." Kara paused. "They're your family, too, Andrew."

"Don't go there, Kara," Andrew said with a sigh. "Not tonight. I'm enjoying being with you. I've even laughed out loud, which is the first for that since I hit town. Thank you for inviting me here into your home, sharing this evening with me."

"You're very welcome," Kara said softly. "I'm glad you're here."

Without being totally aware that he'd done it, Andrew covered one of Kara's hands with one of his own on the coffee table and began to stroke her soft skin with his thumb.

Kara looked away from Andrew, then drew a wobbly breath. "Do you want the last piece of pizza?" she said.

"The what?" Andrew said, releasing Kara's hand and frowning slightly. "Oh! The pizza. Last slice. Yes, it is, isn't it? The last... Damn it, Kara, you're turning me inside out here. I have never...never in my entire life desired a woman the way I do you." He stared up at the ceiling for a long moment, then looked at her again. "That sounded as phony as a three-dollar bill. I sure as hell wouldn't buy into that line."

"But it isn't a line, is it?" Kara said, more a statement than a question. "I...I just can't believe you'd lie to me, Andrew, try to seduce me."

"Of course I wouldn't," he said, his voice rising. "I'd never do that to you. You're too important to me, too... Ah, hell, what a mess. You're looking at a very confused man, Kara MacAllister."

"And I'm a very muddled woman, Andrew Malone," she said, then sighed. "I tell myself that I'm overreacting to you, to how much I want you, how much I...care about you because of the circumstances under which we met.

"We're in a volatile situation where emotions are running in high gear, and nothing is quite like it normally would be. I'm hanging on to that theory like a lifeline, because otherwise I would be totally overwhelmed by..." She stopped speaking and shook her head.

"Well, aren't we a pair?" Andrew said, smiling slightly. "Nuts and nuttier or whatever."

Kara laughed. "That about sums it up, I think. Eat that last piece of pizza. It's calling your name. Would you like some more soda?"

"No, I'm fine, thanks," Andrew said, picking up the slice of pizza. He polished it off in short order, then drained his glass. "Fine meal. Good company." He paused. "Kara, you said you believe that I wouldn't lie to you. That implies you are coming to trust me. It that true?"

"I know where you're going with this," she said, looking directly into his eyes. "You're waiting for me to tell you why I was a foster child."

"You said the key word, Kara—waiting. I'm not pushing you. It may sound like I am from what I just said, but I'm not."

"And that means a great deal to me, Andrew, it really does." Kara diverted her gaze from his and fiddled with her napkin. "Of course, I'm *waiting* for you to share with me, too. To tell me why you confronted Uncle Robert now, after all these years, and what you hoped to accomplish by doing that."

Andrew began to trace the letters on the pizza box that spelled the name of the parlor. One minute passed, then two, with the only sound in the room being the dreamy music coming from the stereo. Andrew finally raised his head slowly and met Kara's gaze.

"I didn't know the identity of my father," he said quietly, "until just before I came to Ventura, to that party at the hotel. My mother told me early on there was no need to know my father's name, and I accepted that.

"I realized years ago that Clara, my aunt, knew what my father's name was, but I never asked her, nor did she divulge it. Then the article about the MacAllister family reunion came out in the newspaper, accompanied by the photograph of all of you."

Andrew got to his feet and settled onto the sofa, a deep frown on his face as he stared at the far wall. Kara's gaze was riveted on him, and when she felt a sudden pain in her chest, she reminded herself to breathe.

"Clara arrived at my apartment drunk," Andrew said, "ranting and raving and waving that newspaper in front of my face. She went on and on about how my father had a large family, who no doubt worshiped him, and how unfair it all was.

"She dropped the newspaper on the floor, and when I picked it up, I thought of my mother, her wishes to keep my father's identity a secret, and I folded the newspaper closed over that picture. I didn't allow myself to read the caption beneath that would tell me all the names of the people in the photograph."

"That…that must have been a very difficult thing to do," Kara said softly.

Andrew shifted his gaze to meet hers. "Yeah, well, the willpower it took was all for nothing, because Clara, who was still raging on, yelled out my father's name. There it was. After all these years. *Robert MacAllister.*"

"Oh, my," Kara said, her eyes widening.

"Something came over me, Kara. I don't know how to explain it, really. So many emotions were coming at me at once. I managed to send Clara on her way, then I looked at the photograph in the newspaper and read the article that accompanied it.

"Memories from my childhood were slamming against me. The shabby places we were forced to live in, how hard my mother worked to make ends meet. I didn't appreciate until I was older how difficult it all was for her. She'd drag herself out of the apartment, bone tired, to play ball with me or to take me to the park or whatever. She was a wonderful mother, but she was attempting to be a father to me, too, and it was a rough road to go."

Kara nodded, then shook her head slightly to dispel a sudden image of the baby boy she hoped to adopt, which flashed before her mental vision.

"Anyway," Andrew went on, dragging a hand through his hair, "I guess I sort of lost it as I stared at that newspaper photo. I was filled with hot fury at the way Robert MacAllister had treated my mother, how he abandoned her when he found out she was pregnant with his baby, just turned his back and walked away."

Andrew narrowed his eyes, looked into space once more, and when he spoke again, there was a steely edge to his voice.

"I didn't want anything from Robert MacAllister, not one damn thing. Not his name, not his money, not his social status, nothing.

"But, by God, he was going to accept responsibility for what he had done. In front of his whole family, he was going to admit that he had deserted my mother when she needed him most. He was going to say the words that I was determined to hear—*Sally Malone mattered.*''

Tears filled Kara's eyes and she pressed trembling fingertips to her lips. Andrew turned his head to look at her again, pain radiating from the depths of his dark-brown eyes. MacAllister eyes.

''My mother was a beautiful human being,'' he said, his voice rough with emotion, ''both inside and out. Robert was going to acknowledge her existence.

''I became obsessed with the need to hear him say that my mother mattered, that she... Ah, hell, this sounds so damn crazy. It made sense to me at the time, but...I nearly killed a man because of what I had to hear Robert MacAllister say. No one in your family will understand why it was so important to me.''

''*I* understand,'' Kara said, as tears spilled onto her cheeks. ''I truly do, Andrew, because—'' a sob caught in her throat ''—because when I was sixteen years old, when Mary and Ralph took me home as their foster child, I didn't feel, I didn't believe, that I...that I mattered to anyone in the world.

''I know what you wanted from Uncle Robert for your mother, because it was what I received from Mary, Ralph, Jack and Richard for myself. Oh, yes, Andrew, I really do understand why you went to the party and confronted Uncle Robert. I...'' Kara stopped speaking and shook her head as tears closed her throat.

''Ah, man,'' Andrew said, lunging to his feet. ''I didn't mean to upset you, Kara. I'm sorry.'' He closed the distance between them and drew her up from the floor and into his arms, holding her tightly. "I'm so damn sorry that I made you cry."

"Oh, no, please don't apologize," she said, her voice muffled as she buried her face in Andrew's shirt. "It's just that what you were saying brought back so many painful memories."

Kara lifted her head to look at Andrew, and he nearly groaned aloud as he saw the tears glistening on her cheeks and in her dark eyes.

"Some of the MacAllisters will understand why you were compelled to do what you did, Andrew," she said. "Maybe they won't all be able to grasp it, to realize how important it is to know that you matter, that you count, but some of them will, I'm sure of it."

"Maybe," he said. "But if I could turn back the clock, I wouldn't have gone to the party. My mother has been dead since I was fifteen. I was hell-bent on collecting on a debt that *I* felt was owed to her, not one that she ever expressed a need to have satisfied. What I did was wrong, very very wrong."

He sighed and tightened his hold on Kara.

"But I'll tell you this," he said, his voice raspy. "The fact that you understand why I did it, forgive me in a way for my actions, means more to me than I can ever begin to tell you. Thank you. Thank you so damn much."

Kara nodded, then sniffled.

"Come on. Sit down next to me on the sofa," Andrew said. "It's my fault that you're upset, that you were flung back in time to a painful part of your life. Let me hold you, just hold you, give you the comfort you've just given me."

They settled onto the sofa, Andrew's arm snugly around Kara as she nestled her head on his shoulder. Kara began to gather her courage, feeling as though she was drawing additional strength from Andrew's solid powerful body. She shifted finally so she could sit upright but still remain in the circle of Andrew's arm, as she looked directly into his eyes.

"My parents…" she started, then cleared her throat and lifted her chin. "My parents left me in a movie theater in Chicago when I was three years old. I was found curled up asleep in a chair with no one else around me in the row. There was a note pinned to me that said my name was Kara and that they didn't…didn't want to be parents any longer."

"Ah, man," Andrew said, tightening his hold on her. "I'm going to say that I'm sorry, but I realize that doesn't come close to cutting it. Do you remember them at all? Your parents?"

"Not really. They're just vague blurry shapes in my mind. I remember that I had a favorite teddy bear, but I didn't bring it with me that day, and later when I was placed in a foster home, I cried and cried for my bear. I don't believe that my parents were very loving, nurturing people, because I cried for my teddy bear, not for them."

Andrew frowned as he nodded.

"So, there I was, just one more of a multitude of case numbers in the foster-care system. I was given the last name of Smith, then shuffled around a great deal. As the years passed, I grew angrier and angrier, had no self-esteem, covered my inner pain and feelings of inadequacy by acting out, being a very difficult child, then an even more rebellious teenager."

"That's understandable," Andrew said.

"When I was sixteen, I met a boy while I was hanging around a mall with my friends from school. He was cocky, very sure of himself, and all the girls were crazy about him. I was thrilled when he singled me out to be his girlfriend. He picked *me* over all the others, wanted *me*."

Kara shook her head and sighed. "I was so pathetic, was willing to do anything he asked of me, so he would continue to love me. He took drugs. I can recall hesitating when he told me to take some drugs he offered me and how angry he became over my initial reluctance. Was I his girl or not? Was I part of his scene or wasn't I? I was terrified of losing him, of not being loved by him, so I started taking drugs.

"Rick—that was his name—became very excited about the fun we could have in California. He'd go on and on about how great the party scene was out here. That's what we would do, he told me, we'd drive to the Coast in the car he'd saved up to buy. I ran away from the foster home where I was living and off I went with Rick."

"What did you two live on?" Andrew said. "I mean, did Rick even have a high-school diploma?"

"No, neither of us did, and we soon ran out of money. We did odd jobs. I was a waitress for a while, but I was fired because I went to work high on drugs. We ended up sleeping in parks, watching out for the police. It was a nightmare. I was torn, a part of me wishing I'd stayed at the foster home in Chicago and the other part of me holding on to Rick any way that I could. Then…"

Kara stopped speaking and stared into memory-filled space. Andrew waited, not speaking, his heart thundering in his chest.

"Then," Kara continued finally, "Rick started talking about the money we could make if I would go on the streets, sell myself to men who were willing to pay for what I could offer them."

"What?" Andrew said. "He...he wanted you to become a..."

"Prostitute, yes," Kara said, forcing herself to look at Andrew again. "I knew I couldn't do it, I just couldn't. But before I told Rick that, I discovered I was pregnant with his baby. He was furious, said I had wrecked any chance I had of being attractive to men. To make a long grim story shorter, he demanded that I get rid of the baby. I refused and he left me. I never saw him again."

"Damn him," Andrew said, a pulse beating wildly in his temple. "What did you do then?"

"Well, I certainly didn't take any more drugs, as I was determined to have and keep my baby. I would have someone who *really* loved me and who I could love in return—my child. I kept on the move so the authorities wouldn't find me, going to free clinics for checkups, staying a night here and there in community shelters, spending other nights in parks."

"Ah, Kara," Andrew said, taking her hand with his free one.

"I was here, in Ventura, when I went into labor six weeks early," she continued, speaking very softly. "I gave birth to a beautiful little girl. I held her in my arms once, in the delivery room, and I'll never forget..." Her eyes filled with tears. "I'll never ever forget her tiny face, how exquisite she was. But—'' a sob caught in her throat ''—oh, Andrew, she died.

''My baby died the day after she was born. I had taken drugs before I knew I was pregnant, hadn't been able to eat properly in the following months, she was born too early and... She didn't have a chance, *I* didn't give her a chance to live and she...she died.''

''Oh, God.'' Andrew dropped Kara's hand and wrapped his arms around her, pulling her close to him as she cried. ''I don't know what to say to you. I'm sorry, so sorry, you went through all that.''

Kara raised her head again and Andrew shifted enough to take a clean handkerchief from his back pocket. He dried her tears slowly, gently, then pressed the soft linen into her hand.

''I named her Gloria,'' Kara said, tears echoing in her voice. ''That's what she was—glorious, a miracle, so precious and—''

''Kara, stop,'' Andrew said. ''You don't have to do this, relive this. Don't do this to yourself.''

''No, no, I'm all right. I need to finish telling you this. You trusted me, shared with me about why you sought out Uncle Robert, and I'm returning that trust in kind, Andrew.''

He had never in his life felt so humble, so special, so... Man, he couldn't even put a name to all the emotions tumbling through him, one into the next. What an incredible gift this woman was giving him. And what a rare and wonderful woman was Kara MacAllister.

Kara drew a trembling breath before continuing her story.

"I was still in the hospital and I couldn't stop crying about my daughter's death. I just wept on and on. I was so alone, in such pain, felt there was no purpose to my life. I was worthless and evil and… No one would miss me if I wasn't there, because I didn't matter to anyone. I just didn't matter."

"Which is why you understand what I was trying to do for my mother by confronting your uncle."

"Yes," Kara said, nodding. "Oh, yes, I truly do understand." She paused. "Then Mary MacAllister walked into my room, introduced herself, said she was a volunteer at the hospital and sat down next to my bed. She told me to go ahead and cry until I had no more tears, then she wanted to tell me something. She just settled back, folded her hands and smiled at me.

"Oh, I was hateful. I bit her head off, wanted to know what do-gooder mission she was on. Mary just kept smiling, then reached over and took one of my hands. She said I was coming home with her and explained that her husband's name was Ralph, and that my two older brothers—that's how she put it right from the start—my older brothers were Richard and Jack.

"Then she said that on the way to the house we were going to stop at a place and order a proper headstone for my daughter's grave, because Gloria deserved that and, she said, so did I."

"Unbelievable," Andrew said, awe ringing in his voice.

"I know. The first few months I lived with the

MacAllisters I put them through hell. I was nasty, refused to carry on a decent conversation with them, stayed in my room when I wasn't in school. They all just acted as though my behavior was perfectly fine. Little by little, I began to trust them and came to love them all so very very much. They saved my life, they honestly did."

"Then when you were eighteen, they asked you if you would do them the honor of allowing them to adopt you, make you a MacAllister legally," Andrew said.

"Yes," she said, nodding. "They put me through medical school, too. I've tried and tried to pay them back the money they spent on my education, but each time I attempt that, they shoo me away. They say that Jack and Richard didn't pay back what had been spent on them for a higher education, so why would they take money from their daughter, when they didn't get or expect any from their sons?

"Oh, Andrew, do you realize how blessed I am to have the family I do? All the MacAllisters are like that, all of them. They're open and honest, giving and loving people. If you need it and they have it, it's yours, no questions asked.

"I know you loved your mother, Andrew, but please remember that you're a MacAllister, too. That family is yours, just as much as it's mine, if not more.

"A few years ago I had a new headstone made for Gloria's grave. It now reads Gloria MacAllister." Tears filled Kara's eyes again. "It was a gift I wanted her to have—the MacAllister name. Then she would be a little angel in heaven who knows she would have been loved unconditionally if she had lived, by the finest people I have ever known.''

Andrew pulled Kara close again and held her almost too tightly, wishing he could somehow, *somehow,* erase the horror of her youth, take her pain into himself to free her of its burden on her. He wanted to protect her from any future heartache, keep her safe here in his arms, out of harm's way.

Nothing and no one, by God, he vowed fiercely in his mind, would ever hurt Kara MacAllister again.

Kara eased back a bit against Andrew's hold, making him aware of how tightly his arms were encasing her. He loosened his grip, but kept his arms around her. She met his gaze directly.

''Thank you for listening,'' she said. ''You have every right to stand in harsh judgment of what I did all those years ago, but I'm hoping you won't. The MacAllisters taught me how to forgive myself, to believe in myself, to know in my heart, my mind, my very soul, that I do—oh, yes, I do—matter.''

''More than you know,'' Andrew said, his voice gritty with emotion, then his mouth captured hers in a searing kiss.

Kara raised her arms to encircle Andrew's neck, and she leaned into him, receiving his kiss, returning his kiss, savoring the healing power of his kiss.

Then the memories of past pain began to fade, were finally swept into oblivion. There was only the present, the moment, the heated desire that was consuming them with hot flashing flames.

Andrew raised his head a fraction of an inch to speak close to Kara's lips.

"I want you, Kara," he said. "I want to make love with you."

"And I want you, Andrew," she whispered. "I don't want to analyze it, think it through, argue with myself about the right or wrong of it. I just want to make love with you in a world wc'rc creating at this very second, where no one exists but the two of us. Oh, yes, this is our night to be together."

In one powerful motion Andrew slid an arm beneath Kara's knees and rose from the sofa with her held in his embrace. She clasped her hands behind his neck and laid her head on his shoulder as he strode down the short hallway to her bedroom.

Chapter 9

Andrew Malone, Kara thought dreamily, was the most magnificent man she had ever seen. He was standing before her, obviously comfortable with his nakedness and with the knowledge that she was visually tracing every masculine inch of him.

His body was perfectly proportioned. He had wide shoulders, long muscular legs, a flat belly and a broad chest, which was covered in curly black hair. He was fully aroused, his body announcing the intensity of his desire for her.

"Oh, Andrew," Kara said, meeting his heated gaze. "You are everything and more than I imagined you would be. You truly are."

"So are you," he said, his voice gritty. "You are beautiful, Kara, exquisite."

Kara pressed one hand on her flat bare stomach. "I still have faint stretch marks from being pregnant with Gloria. They're not very visible, I guess, but I know they're there, and I imagine they always will be."

"They're badges of honor that only a woman can earn," Andrew said, smiling. "Don't cover them up." He opened his arms to her. "Come here...please."

Kara closed the distance between them and sighed with pleasure as she melted into Andrew's embrace. The small lamp on the nightstand next to the double bed cast a soft glow over the room, encasing them in a golden hue of subdued light.

Andrew kissed Kara deeply, then they tumbled onto the mint-green sheets on the bed. When he broke the kiss, he lay beside her, propped on one forearm, his other hand splayed on her stomach. He looked directly into her eyes for a heart-stopping moment, then lowered his head to claim her lips once more.

They were on fire, burning with want and need that seemed to have been tormenting them forever. At last, at long last, the moment had come, the time to share this most intimate act that had somehow, surely, been created just for them.

Andrew shifted his mouth to one of Kara's breasts, drawing the nipple deep inside to lave it with his tongue. She closed her eyes to fully savor the sensations sweeping through her. He moved to her other breast, and a soft smile formed on her lips as she gloried in the pleasure being given to her by this magnificent man.

Kara opened her eyes again as her hands fluttered over Andrew's moist strong back. She could feel his muscles bunch and move beneath her feathery touch, and marveled at the pure masculinity of him. There had been very few men in her life, but Andrew was far and beyond anyone she had ever known.

On this night, she thought hazily, Andrew was hers. He would bring to her all that he was, and she would receive him into her body, giving of herself in total abandon. She knew, just somehow knew, that their joining would be like nothing she had ever experienced before.

Andrew trailed a ribbon of kisses down Kara's stomach, then lower, and lower yet. She tossed her head restlessly on the pillow as the heat within her threatened to consume her, dissolve her.

"Andrew," she whispered, "please. I... Oh, please, come to me."

Never, Andrew thought. Never in his entire life had he wanted a woman as much as he did Kara. And never before had he felt such a driving need to assure a woman's pleasure. But then, never before had there been Kara.

He traveled upward again to claim her mouth in a searing kiss, then spoke close to her lips.

"I'll protect you," he said, his voice a hoarse whisper. "I'll be right back."

"Hurry," Kara said, then flicked her tongue across his lips.

Andrew left the bed to retrieve a foil packet from his wallet. Moments later, an eternity later, he returned to Kara's outstretched arms, which were welcoming him back into her embrace.

He moved over her, catching his weight on his

forearms and looking directly into her eyes, which shone with a smoky hue of desire.

"This means more to me than I can begin to tell you, Kara," he said. "I have to know...I just have to be certain that you won't have any regrets that this happened."

Kara framed Andrew's face in her hands and smiled. She drank in the very sight of him, filled her senses with his male aroma, savored the taste of him that lingered on her lips.

"No regrets, Andrew," she said. "I promise you that. This is our night, and I'll cherish every precious memory of it."

"Ah, Kara," he said, a groan rumbling deep in his chest.

He kissed her, then entered her, filling her, encasing himself in the dark heat of her femininity. He began to move, slowly at first, then increasing the tempo, his body nearly beyond his control as he took them both higher and higher in a pounding rhythm.

Kara matched him beat for thundering beat, raising her hips to meet him, clinging tightly to his shoulders. She felt his muscles tremble beneath her hands and realized that he was holding himself back, being certain of her pleasure before seeking his own release.

She had never felt so special, so cared for. Oh, yes, yes, it was true—to Andrew Malone, she mattered.

The tension built within her, coiling tighter, taking her nearer to the place she sought. Close now...so very close...

"Oh, Andrew," she said, digging her fingers into his shoulders. "Be with me. Together. Andrew!"

Andrew granted her plea as he threw back his head and joined her in ecstasy. It was an explosion of senses. It was rich and real, honest and earthy. It was theirs.

Andrew collapsed against Kara, spent, sated. Mustering his last ounce of energy, he rolled off her to keep from crushing her, then nestled her close to his side. She trembled and he stroked her back until she fully returned from the glorious place they had gone to—together.

Neither spoke. Hearts slowed and bodies cooled. Andrew reached for the blankets and covered them, tucking the soft material around Kara with exacting care. He laid his head on the pillow again, his lips resting lightly on Kara's forehead.

"I'm not a man who is great with words," he said finally, breaking the silence in the room. "Even if I was, this was beyond description in its beauty, its importance, its... All I can say to you is...thank you."

"And *I* thank *you*," Kara said softly. "I've never... What I mean is...it was all so beautiful, so...well, words are failing me, too. But that's all right, because we both know how...how rare and wonderful this was, what we shared. We know."

"Yes." Andrew paused. "No regrets?"

"I promised and I meant it. No regrets."

"Good. That's good."

"I'm so sleepy, Andrew."

"Then sleep, lovely Kara. I'll hold you right here

in my arms. You're safe from harm. Nothing can hurt you, not while you're with me.''

''Just like when you held the baby in the nursery,'' she said, her lashes drifting down. ''He was safe in your arms, too. I want to tell you about the baby, about my hope to…'' Kara's voice trailed off as sleep claimed her.

Andrew sifted his fingers through her silky curls as he listened to Kara's even breathing.

She wanted to tell him *what* about the baby? he thought. She hoped to what? Forget it. He was beyond the capability of thinking. He was going to go to sleep, right here, with Kara in his embrace.

He was at peace, contented, and that warmth, that foreign warmth, was filling him to overflowing. No, this wasn't the time to think. All he was going to do was savor, then sleep.

Andrew allowed the hovering somnolence to float over him and claim him. He slept, his head resting on the same pillow as Kara's.

Andrew stirred, inhaled the enticing aroma of coffee, then in the next instant realized he didn't have a clue where he was. He sat bolt upright in the bed, blinked, then sank back against the pillow.

Kara, he thought, glancing at the empty expanse of bed next to him. Beautiful, giving, sensual Kara. What an incredible night it had been. Their lovemaking was sensational, unbelievable, had been… Well, there he was again, unable to find the words to describe it.

Andrew laced his hands beneath his head and

stared up at the ceiling, a small smile tugging at his lips.

Oh, the lovely Dr. MacAllister was something. She'd woken him in the night with feathery kisses on his lips, then down his chest. She slid on top of him, feeling like heaven itself as she wriggled against him.

Then…oh, man, then she'd settled over him, taking him fully inside her, and they'd ridden the sensuous wild waves until they exploded, seconds apart, flung into mindless oblivion.

Andrew cleared his throat and shifted on the bed as his body began to respond to the lovemaking he was vividly reliving in his mind.

A moment later the subject of those mental pictures entered the bedroom.

"Coffee delivery," Kara said, smiling as she approached the side of the bed.

Andrew bunched the pillow behind him and sat up, allowing the sheet to fall across his hips. He accepted the coffee mug from Kara, then she sat down on the bed next to him.

"Thank you," he said, then took a sip of the hot coffee. "Mmm. Perfect. This is what I call service. I could get used to being spoiled rotten." He paused and frowned. "You're all dressed. You look very pretty, but I get the distinct impression that it means you're about to go somewhere."

"I have patients to see at my office," Kara said. "Remember?"

Andrew nodded, then met her gaze directly.

"Kara, are you all right? I mean, this being the ever-famous morning after, you know."

Kara placed one hand on Andrew's beard-roughened face.

"I'm fine, Andrew. More than fine," she said. "It was a beautiful night. I have no regrets, if that's what you're worrying about. None at all."

"Good," he said. "That's good. And, yes, it *was* a beautiful night."

Kara dropped her hand from Andrew's face, then leaned forward and kissed him deeply. When she finally broke the kiss, her cheeks were flushed.

"What time is the first patient due at your office?" Andrew said, his voice husky with desire.

"Too soon," she said, getting to her feet. "I've got to go. Where will you be later so I can report to you the results of Uncle Robert's surgery?" Kara looked at her watch. "His operation is scheduled for an hour from now. I imagine the whole family is already at the hospital."

Andrew sighed. "Skulking in the shadows at that place is getting old, but I don't want to upset the applecart by coming face-to-face with a MacAllister. Maybe I'll go back to my hotel and wait there to hear from you."

"Or you could..." Kara laughed and shook her head. "I can't believe I'm being so forward. This isn't like me at all." She shrugged. "What can I say? Nothing I've done in regard to you is remotely close to familiar. I was going to suggest that you just stay here and wait for my call if you wanted to."

"Whew." Andrew grinned at her. "Racy lady. I like your plan, but I need to shower, shave, put on fresh clothes."

"Okay. Give me your hotel number and I'll contact you there."

"I'd like to see you later," Andrew said.

"Let's wait until we see how Uncle Robert's surgery goes," Kara said. "I have no idea what this day will bring. I just pray that my uncle will come through the surgery with flying colors. If only he'd had a complete physical months ago so his heart condition could have been discovered early on and... Well, that's a bunch of useless thinking."

"Hey, I'm an expert on the 'if only' trip. All it does is wear out your brain." Andrew paused. "I'll be thinking about you today, Kara, and about Robert."

"Thank you," she said, smiling at him warmly. "Now I really must dash."

Andrew gave Kara the name of his hotel and his room number. They kissed goodbye—once, twice, three times—then she hurried from the room, calling over her shoulder that the door to her apartment would lock automatically when Andrew left.

As Andrew sipped the remaining coffee, he swept his gaze over the bedroom.

Nice, he thought. Admittedly he hadn't paid the least bit of attention to the bedroom decor last night. The room was fairly large, done in mint green and pale yellow, and looked...well, nice. It was very feminine and pretty—like Kara.

He drained the mug, set it on the nightstand, then began to drum the fingers of one hand restlessly on the sheet.

The morning after, he thought. He had been assured by Kara that she was emotionally fine about what had taken place between them. But for the first time in his life he felt the niggling need to ask himself the same question.

How did *he* feel about the previous night's chain of events in the light of the new day?

Like a man who was skating on very thin ice, he thought dryly. He was moving at breakneck speed into territory where danger signals were flashing like neon signs.

Kara was becoming so important to him so quickly and with such intensity it was overwhelming, and very *very* unsettling.

When she'd told him the history of her childhood, then the tragic story of the death of her baby daughter, he'd wanted to make a list of everyone who had hurt her, then seek them out, deliver a very physical message that they were paying up for what they had done.

His heart had ached, actually hurt, when he'd envisioned Kara as the confused and sorrowful teenager who had only held her baby once before she died. She had been a scared lonely sixteen-year-old girl who didn't believe that life was worth living, didn't believe that she mattered.

When he'd held Kara as she wept for that infant daughter of long ago, he'd been consumed with protectiveness, possessiveness, had silently vowed that no one would ever hurt Kara again because, by damn, *she was his now.*

"Oh, hell," Andrew said, dragging both hands down his face.

That was crazy thinking. Ridiculous, too. Kara wasn't his, because to entertain ideas like that spelled commitment, meant falling in love, meant forever and ever, for Pete's sake.

Marriage. Babies. A mortgage on a house that had a lawn to mow and trash cans to take to the curb on the designated day.

And trees. Trees with leaves that would fall off in autumn and have to be raked and stuffed into plastic bags. Big piles of leaves that a kid would have a helluva fun time running and jumping into, scattering, burrowing deep into, then jumping up with a laugh of pure innocent joy.

The dog would follow the kid into the piles of leaves, barking, wiggling with excitement and wagging its tail, and licking the face of the little boy when he suddenly reappeared.

Or maybe it was a girl. Girls jumped into mounds of leaves, didn't they? Sure, they did. They probably didn't get all prissy and do the don't-get-me-dirty thing until they hit adolescence. Yeah, sure, the little girl would play in the leaves *with* the boy and the dog.

The day would be crisp with a hint of winter in the air, and Kara would prepare the perfect meal to match the weather—grilled cheese sandwiches and tomato soup, which they all would consume hungrily in front of a roaring fire in the hearth.

The kids—hey, even the dog—would be tired from the hours of playing in the leaves and would be bathed and put to bed early, after prayers were said and a story read.

Then he and Kara would be alone in front of the romantic fire and they'd—

"That's it. That's all. I have no intention of ever

raking leaves for kids to jump into,'' Andrew said, throwing back the sheet and blanket on the bed.

His feet hid the floor with a thud, and he strode across the room toward the bathroom.

''Besides that,'' he fumed, ''there aren't piles of leaves and a freezing-cold winter to hint at in Ventura. Ventura? Hell, I don't even live in Ventura. I'm losing it. I've lost it. I'm out of my mind.''

Andrew slammed the bathroom door behind him, erecting a barrier between him and the fantasies his wandering mind had created.

Kara's office was in a row of buildings that formed a small strip mall just off one of the main streets of Ventura. It had been converted to a doctor's office years before by a physician who had chosen to retire just when Kara was searching for a place to open her practice.

It was fate, Kara had decided, when she signed the lease. The retiring physician was also a general practitioner, so she inherited many of his longtime patients. Her own reputation for excellence, as well as her genuine caring, increased her caseload and the number of appointments scheduled each day.

Lucy, Kara's receptionist, had worked for the previous doctor for thirty years, and was now a plump smiling grandmother in her late fifties, who ran the office like a well-oiled machine.

Kara greeted Lucy upon arriving and accepted the cup of coffee Lucy handed her. Kara then hurried to her private office at the end of the corridor. She closed the door, took a sip of the cinnamon-flavored coffee, then set the mug on her desk.

After changing into a pale-blue medical jacket, Kara glanced at the mirror hanging behind the closed door. She hesitated, then crossed the room tentatively, finally standing in front of the mirror and leaning forward to scrutinize her reflection.

That, she thought, a warm flush creeping onto her cheeks, is the face of a woman who has been well and truly, exquisitely and wondrously, made love to.

Her eyes were clear and sparkling. Her skin had a dewy glow and a slight telltale pink strip of tender skin that had been close, very close, to a beard-roughened face.

Oh, heavens, she might as well shout from the rooftops that she had made beautiful love with Andrew Malone.

"Don't be silly," she told her image in the mirror. "No one will be able to tell. Your imagination is working overtime."

Shaking her head at her own foolishness, she sank into the creaky leather chair behind her desk that the old doctor had left behind for her use. She cradled the coffee mug in both hands and settled against the soft leather, staring into space.

Andrew, her mind hummed. She'd hated to leave him, missed him already, had used all her willpower to walk out of the bedroom this morning as he'd gazed at her with desire radiating from his eyes, and his naked body beckoning to be touched.

Heat consumed her like a rushing current, and she could feel the pulse of desire begin to throb low in her body. She glanced quickly at the closed door, ordered herself to get a grip, then drank some more of the delicious coffee.

Andrew was definitely front-row center in her mind, she admitted to herself, and it wasn't just because of the lovemaking they had shared. No, oh, no, it was due to much more than that.

They had trusted each other with their innermost secrets, had revealed painful memories of the past. They had listened to what the other was saying, to what was most important to them. They had given each other a rare and special gift; they'd cared about the other's sorrows, had let the other know that they mattered.

"Oh, Kara," she said, shaking her head, "what are you doing? You're treading in dangerous waters, madam, and you'd better slow down and watch your step."

Andrew had become so important to her so very quickly, was such an intricate part of her life and her...her fantasies.

She would never forget how she'd felt as she'd stood in the nursery at the hospital watching Andrew holding the baby she hoped would become her son, talking to the infant, telling him about the bike that he had worked so hard for and how having it handed to him by his aunt Clara had diminished his enjoyment of the bicycle.

In that moment she had envisioned Andrew as a loving father to that baby, a wonderful daddy. And she would be the baby's mother and and Andrew's wife.

And that was ridiculous.

And those were very dangerous fantasies to indulge in.

In her ever-increasing unguarded moments, An-

drew was chipping away at the protective wall she
had built around her heart many many years before.
She'd lowered that wall as a teenager to embrace the
love of the MacAllister family, to bask in their
warmth and honesty and genuine love for her.

Over the years she'd begun to yearn for more,
wanted to create a family unit of her own. But each
time she envisioned trusting a man with her heart and
happiness, a chill would course through her as dark
images of Rick would surface from deep within her.

She'd skittered around the issue of a special man
in her life and begun to dream of being a mother,
providing a home for a child no one wanted, just as
no one had wanted her when she was small. She
would attempt to adopt this baby, not to replace
Gloria, never that, but to reawaken her maternal instincts that had been snuffed out before they could
fully blossom.

Kara set the mug on the desk and sank back in the
chair again, staring at the ceiling.

She was terrified of loving, falling in love, because
of a poor choice she made at sixteen? She was still
allowing Rick to rule her life all these many years
later?

This was the first time she'd taken a really close
look at her determination not to commit herself to a
serious relationship with a man. She'd just known it
wasn't right for her, that she needed to protect herself
against that type of entanglement. She had accepted
that knowledge without question. Because of what
she had done as an unhappy, angry, confused teenager?

Kara wrapped her hands around her elbows and frowned deeply.

Why hadn't she examined her innermost feelings on this subject long ago, dealt with it, put the ugly memories to rest?

She sighed and closed her eyes.

Because, she thought dismally, there had been no reason to. There had never been a man in her life who even gave her a fleeting thought of marriage, never a man who caused her to fantasize about hearth and home, and forever and ever.

Until now.

Until Andrew Malone.

"Oh, Kara," she said, shaking her head, "you are in deep, deep trouble here."

The intercom on the desk buzzed, causing Kara to jump. She leaned forward and pressed the button on the small box.

"Yes, Lucy?"

"Duty calls. Your first patient is here."

Thank goodness, Kara thought. Now she could concentrate on someone else's problems and escape from the turmoil in her own mind.

"I'll be right there," she said. "Oh, Lucy, please remember that you're to interrupt me no matter what if there is a call from the hospital about my uncle Robert." She paused. "And, Lucy? I'll take any calls from a Mr. Malone, too."

"Got it," Lucy said. "Over and out."

Kara got to her feet and smoothed her jacket. She squared her shoulders, lifted her chin and headed for

the door, wondering if in addition to appearing like
a woman who had engaged in fantastic lovemaking,
it would also be apparent that she was teetering on
the edge of her sanity.

Chapter 10

Andrew strolled through the busy mall, allowing the bustling shoppers to move around him as he glanced absently into the store windows he passed.

Kara had telephoned him at his hotel earlier, and in a breathless, excited voice, had told him that Robert's surgery had been a success and that the doctors were extremely pleased with her uncle's vital signs.

"Uncle Robert is going to be all right, Andrew," Kara had said. "He'll be put on a strict diet, which will probably make him as grumpy as a bear, and will have a program of exercises set up specifically for him, but if he behaves himself, he'll be as good as new. Oh, I'm so relieved. The whole family feels as though a tremendous weight has been lifted from our shoulders."

"I feel the same way," Andrew had said quietly. "Believe me, I really do."

"I know you do," Kara said. "Listen, I still can't say when I'll be free. I'll call you later, okay?"

"Sure, that's fine."

"Bye for now."

And that had been that, Andrew thought, stopping in front of a sports-equipment store and staring at the display in the window.

A part of him had registered a tremendous sense of relief that Robert MacAllister was going to survive the heart attack and subsequent surgery.

But another section of him had felt a letdown of sorts.

Andrew sighed and continued on his way, halting next in front of a store that sold gourmet food in fancy boxes, tins and various other containers.

He now knew why he'd been bummed, he thought. He'd paced restlessly around his hotel room long enough to figure it out, then had gotten cabin fever and headed for the door to escape from the four walls and the realization he'd made.

The truth of the matter was he no longer had a legitimate reason to stay in Ventura. He had no intention of pursuing his original mission of demanding that Robert MacAllister acknowledge his abandonment of Sally Malone so many years before. He didn't plan to see or speak to Robert again.

He'd caused enough damage and wasn't about to repeat his performance. There was nothing to be gained by it. He never should have come to Ventura in the first place.

But if he hadn't, he never would have met Kara.

And Kara, Andrew thought, frowning as he trudged through the mall, was why his euphoria at the good news regarding Robert had shifted so dramatically to bleak emptiness in practically the next breath.

It was time to return to Santa Maria, get on with his life, step back into the role of owner of Malone Construction and get caught up on all the appointments he'd had his secretary cancel.

It was time to go.

And he'd never see Kara MacAllister again.

A vivid image of Kara flashed before his mental vision, and Andrew's breath caught. He saw her laughing, smiling, then gazing at him with eyes radiating a depth of desire that matched his own. The picture in his mind was so vivid, it was as though she was there with him, was about to fling herself into his arms to receive his kiss.

Heat rocketed through Andrew's body, and he glanced around quickly, certain that everyone passing could read his passion-laden mind. But no one was paying one bit of attention to him. He was just a guy who probably appeared to be killing time while his wife shopped somewhere in the busy mall.

Wife, his mind echoed. No, he didn't want one of those, thank you very much. He didn't want a wife, or kids who played in piles of leaves, or a dog. He didn't want to fall in love, be expected to make a commitment to forever, have to live each day wondering if the happiness would last.

He didn't want to be Kara's husband.

He wanted to be her lover, her friend, have a special place in her life for...well, a while. He wasn't ready to walk out of her existence yet. Not yet. Eventually, sure, just as he did with any woman he became involved with, but damn it, not yet.

Still, facts were facts, and his stay in Ventura was at an end.

"Well, hell," Andrew said aloud, causing an elderly lady who was passing to glare at him.

Andrew moved to the next store window and found himself looking at a display of baby clothes.

Man, he thought, look at that stuff. It was so small it was incredible. There sure was a bunch of it. There was a frilly pink dress that had tiny bows, and a miniature baseball suit, complete with a cap.

A small smile tugged at Andrew's lips.

That baseball outfit would be perfect for that little baby he'd held in the nursery. That kiddo was fighting the battle of his life, and he was going to make it, by damn. Rough start or not, that scrapper would be just fine.

He hoped.

Yeah, he really did want that baby to be all right, have a chance at a decent life, be the recipient of a huge serving of happiness and love.

He'd like to buy the little guy that baseball suit, Andrew thought, as a symbol of stepping up to the plate and meeting life head on. And winning. Beating the odds, making it—big time.

Forget it, Andrew thought, shaking his head in self-disgust. Kara would think he was completely nuts if he showed up at the hospital with a baseball suit for a baby he didn't even know.

But, damn it, he *did* know him. He'd held him, fed him, told him about the bike, that long-ago, yearned-for bike, which Clara had diminished in value and meaning. He hadn't even realized he remembered that bike until he'd started telling the story of it to the baby.

If you want something, work hard for it, earn it yourself, deserve to have it, and it will mean more to you in the end. That was what he'd told the baby, who had slept through his sermon on the subject. But it was true, was the philosophy he'd lived by ever since he'd been old enough to understand it.

He'd waited, worked hard for patience, kept silent when he would have urged Kara to speak, to divulge her innermost secrets. And when she'd finally come to trust him enough, she had shared with him the sad and poignant tale of her youth. She'd given him that gift, and it meant more to him than he would ever be able to put into words.

Andrew nodded.

That minuscule baseball suit represented a lot of important messages about life—at least to him. It didn't even matter if anyone else understood the meaning of those inches of cloth. *He* would know, and he wanted that baby in the nursery, the first baby he'd ever held, fed, interacted with, to have it.

"Forget it, Malone," he muttered, then spun around and strode away.

After Andrew had gone about twenty feet, his step slowed, then stopped. He swore under his breath, turned again and retraced his path. After one more long look at the little striped suit in the window, he pulled open the door and entered the store.

Nature was painting the heavens in sunset colors of pink, purple and gold when Kara hurried across the parking lot toward the front doors of the hospital.

She was a study in frustration, she admitted to herself, and would have to work on a cheerful attitude, complete with beaming smile, before she saw Uncle Robert.

But, darn it, the day had started out so marvelously, so exceptionally, when she'd wakened at dawn to see Andrew sleeping peacefully next to her in her bed.

Except for the fantastic news that Robert was going to be just fine, the day had gone downhill after she'd left her apartment with the taste of Andrew lingering on her lips and desire thrumming low in her body.

A multitude of her patients had apparently taken personal inventory of their bodies as part of their New Year's resolutions and had decided they just didn't feel up to par. They had to see Dr. MacAllister today, not tomorrow. Today.

Lucy had squeezed as many extra patients as she could into an already busy schedule, and Kara had operated at top speed the entire day. She'd spoken to Andrew briefly to tell him of the success of Robert's surgery, but when she grabbed a moment to telephone him later, he hadn't been in his room at the hotel.

She had no idea where he was, and so was unable to confirm plans to be with him later that night. She was weary, hungry and most definitely pouting because seeing Andrew was not etched in stone.

"Smile, Kara," she told herself. "Put on a happy, happy, happy face."

The doors to the hospital swished open, and her brother Richard stepped out into the crisp evening.

"Richard," Kara said, her smile genuine as she stopped directly in front of him. "Talk about timing." She frowned in the next instant. "Why am I smiling at you? You're off the Richter scale angry at me."

Richard gripped Kara's shoulders and planted a loud smacking kiss on her forehead.

"That is part of my apology," he said. "The other is my saying I'm sorry I was such a pain about your talking to Andrew Malone."

"Oh," Kara said, surprised. "What changed your stand on the issue?"

"A stern lecture from our fierce aunt Margaret," Richard said. "Whew. She really gave me what for. She said we all had the right to our own feelings and opinions regarding Andrew Malone, but none of us had license to stand in judgment of anyone else's choices on the matter. Oh, yeah, and I'd better shape up or she'd smack my butt."

"Awesome," Kara said, laughing. "She'd do it, you know."

"Oh, believe me, I know. Anyway, I really am sorry I came down so hard on you about Malone. Brother Jack also informed me that I was being a jerk. I was headed over to your office right now to say all this, since you hadn't shown up here at the hospital. I have a plane to catch and didn't want to leave town without setting things to rights between us."

Kara stood on tiptoe and kissed Richard on the cheek.

"All is forgiven," she said. "Where are you winging off to?"

"Anchorage, Alaska," he said, frowning. "Is that grim or what? I was supposed to be there first thing this morning. I postponed leaving until I knew that Uncle Robert was going to be all right, but now I've really got to haul myself up there.

"When the computers in a major company crash, the big boys get a tad hysterical. I'll ride in on my white charger and save the day—if I don't freeze to death first. Alaska." He shook his head. "Cripes."

"Don't you get tired of all the traveling you do as a computer troubleshooter, Richard? It would drive me nuts. You live out of a suitcase, instead of enjoying your lovely apartment." Kara picked an imaginary thread from her brother's jacket. "And your schedule certainly doesn't give you much time to spend with Brenda."

"Oh, here we go," he said, rolling his eyes heavenward. "I don't know what it's going to take to convince this family that Brenda and I are just friends. Where is it written that a man's best friend can't be a woman?

"Brenda lives in the apartment next to mine. We share meals on occasion, go out together if we're in the mood and... Forget it. I've been over this turf at least a hundred times."

"Yes, Richard," Kara said, smiling. "I'm sorry, Richard. I won't bring it up again, Richard."

He rapped his knuckles lightly on the top of Kara's head.

"Remember that statement," he said. "I have to

go. I saw Uncle Robert for a few minutes. He looks great, he really does."

"That's good to hear," Kara said, "but not surprising. Patients are usually much improved after that surgery. Of course, Uncle Robert has to recuperate from the original heart attack, too, but he's going to be fine. Are the MacAllisters still here in force?"

"No. Everyone got to say a quick hello to Uncle Robert, then Aunt Margaret sent them packing. She's still upstairs, though."

"All right. How long will you be gone?"

Richard shrugged. "I never know until I get to the job and see what the situation is. I only stay at hotels that have laundry service, that's for sure." He kissed her on the forehead again. "Bye for now, little sister. And, well, as far as Andrew Malone goes, just stay alert. Okay?"

"You bet," Kara said, then turned to watch her handsome brother stride away.

Stay alert, her mind echoed. Be continually aware of the sensual impact Andrew had on her? Realize that she had shared her innermost secrets with Andrew, allowing him to know of the existence of Gloria, her precious daughter?

No, of course, that wasn't what Richard was referring to, because he had no idea of what had transpired between her and Andrew. Despite Richard's apology she imagined that her brother was still harboring anger toward Andrew, was convinced that he had an agenda, was after something he wanted from their uncle Robert.

Richard was no doubt warning her to stay alert in

regard to falling prey to Andrew's good looks and any smooth charm he might possess.

Oh, little did Richard know. She was way past all that. Yes, she would most definitely stay alert, but it would be centered on her inner being, her very heart, soul and mind, to make certain that Andrew Malone didn't steal her heart before he returned to Santa Maria.

She would *not* fall in love with Andrew, then be shattered into a million pieces when he walked out of her life forever.

"Stay alert, Dr. MacAllister," she said aloud, then lifted her chin and entered the hospital.

When Kara reached the floor where Robert MacAllister was assigned a private room, she was told that the doctors were in with the patient. Mrs. MacAllister had gone to the cafeteria with one of the nurses to have some dinner.

"All right," Kara said to the nurse at the station. "I'll be back shortly."

"Okay," the nurse said. "Your uncle is a sweetheart, Dr. MacAllister. He didn't even complain that his dinner consisted of green Jell-o."

Kara laughed. "That will change. I doubt that he's been informed yet of the strict diet he's going to be on. My Aunt Margaret is in for hearing a lot of grumbling, which she'll put a halt to when she's had enough."

"She's a lovely lady," the nurse said. "Well, your whole family is super, such nice people."

"I know," Kara said, smiling. "I'm very lucky to have them all." She paused. "I won't be gone too long. Please tell my aunt Margaret that I'm in the hospital and will be back soon if she gets here before I do.''

''Sure thing.''

Kara hurried to the elevator and a short time later entered the nursery on the maternity floor.

''Hi, Diane,'' Kara said to the nurse who greeted her. ''How's my boy this evening?''

''He's doing great,'' Diane said, smiling. ''He ate about an hour ago and is sleeping more peacefully than usual. I'm delighted to see that. It's an excellent sign that the drugs in his system are diminishing. Oh, he looks so cute. I wish you had a camera with you.''

''He's cuter than usual?'' Kara said, laughing. ''I would have thought that was impossible.''

Diane frowned. ''I guess I'm confused. I got the distinct impression that you knew about the present that...oh, what was his name? Malone. Andrew Malone.

''Of course, that couldn't be the same Andrew Malone they're writing about in the newspapers. I bet the Andrew Malone who stopped by here wished he had a different name at the moment.''

''Wait a minute,'' Kara said, raising one hand. ''You've totally lost me. Andrew Malone was here? In the nursery? With a gift for the baby?''

''Yes, about fifteen minutes ago. He said it would be fine with you because you'd already let him hold and feed the baby. I jumped to conclusions, I guess, and thought you knew about the present. Oh, heavens, I didn't do anything wrong, did I?''

''No, no, not at all,'' Kara said. ''What was the present?''

''I put it right on your kiddo. Go look for yourself.

It's too cute for words. It's a little big for him, but the way he's growing it won't take him long to fill it out and be ready to play ball.''

"Play ball?" Kara repeated. "Never mind. I'll go see what you're talking about."

Kara crossed the room to the rear of the nursery and peered into the bassinet where the baby was sleeping with his tiny fists curled next to his cheeks.

"Oh, my," Kara whispered, staring at the infant. "Oh, Andrew, you got him a baseball suit?"

With her gaze riveted on the baby and her mind racing, Kara blinked away unexpected and unwelcome tears.

Why? she asked herself. Why had Andrew done this? He had to have gone to a mall, found a store that sold baby clothes, picked out the darling outfit, then brought it here to the nursery for the baby. All that had required a great deal of effort and thoughtfulness. But why?

Kara reached into the bassinet and lifted the baby carefully into her arms. She settled onto the rocking chair and watched the precious bundle sleep, all decked out like Babe Ruth.

Why? her mind echoed. Yes, all right, it must be apparent to Andrew that the baby was special to her because she continually made time to see him, feed him, hold him. But he had no idea just how important this child was. He didn't know that she hoped, dreamed, prayed that this infant would be her son.

So, the only explanation that made any sense was that the baby had staked a claim on Andrew's heart when he had been hastily recruited to feed him his bottle during the crisis in the nursery.

This was, she knew, the first tiny baby that Andrew had ever held, ever been in close proximity to. She'd heard him talking to the infant, sharing the meaningful story of the bicycle, a very private and special tale.

Yes, that had to be it. When her son—please, let him be her son—had curled his tiny hand around Andrew's finger, he'd also grabbed hold of Andrew's heart.

The adorable baseball suit was evidence that to Andrew Malone, this baby…mattered.

Kara blinked back fresh tears as a lovely warmth tiptoed around her heart.

Just for a second, she thought, she was going to allow herself a fantasy she had no business indulging in. But, oh, it was glorious.

In this fantasy, her fears of loving, falling in love, had taken wing and fled, never to return. She was deeply and irrevocably in love with Andrew and he loved her in return. Not only that, but he loved her—their—son. They would be a family, the three of them. And later, if they were blessed, they would add more children created while making sweet love.

They'd have a house. A big rambling home that was filled with sunshine, laughter and love. There would be a backyard for the children to play in, a swing set, sandbox, toys galore. There would be big trees for shade on hot days and lush green grass to roll and romp in.

What else? Oh, yes, there was a fireplace in the living room that would warm them through the rainy season of winter. She and Andrew would read bedtime stories to the children in front of the hearth, then carry them upstairs to hear their prayers and tuck them into bed with hugs and kisses.

Then she and Andrew would return to the quiet living room, turn out the lights and sit in front of the glowing fire. They'd reach for each other and—

"Enough," Kara said aloud as heat swept through her in a wild current.

Such foolishness, she admonished herself. She had no intention of falling in love with Andrew, or any other man, for that matter. She would raise her son alone, just as she'd planned from the beginning when she'd made her decision to adopt him. That was fine. Good. Exactly the way she wanted it.

Wasn't it?

Oh, Kara, don't, she begged herself silently. She was set on a course of action to be a single parent, and that was that. She was currently engaged in an out-of-character affair with a magnificent man, but it was temporary, would end when Andrew returned to Santa Maria.

"You're all suited up to be part of a team," Kara whispered to the baby. "That team is you and me, my sweetheart. But I'll save that little outfit, and someday I'll tell you about the very special caring man who gave it to you. I think you've stolen his heart, but I can't allow him to steal mine. I just can't."

Kara continued to rock, holding the precious baby in her arms. She frowned as she looked closer and saw a small round spot on the pocket of the baseball suit. She sighed wearily as she realized that the damp little circle had been caused by one of her tears.

Chapter 11

Kara knocked lightly on the door of her uncle's hospital room, and an instant later heard Aunt Margaret call out a cheerful "Come in." After drawing a steadying breath and producing what she hoped was a passable smile, Kara entered the room. She went to the bed that had been adjusted to allow Robert to sit up and kissed him on the forehead.

"You look wonderful," Kara said. "How are you feeling, Uncle Robert?"

"Hungry," he said, frowning.

"Oops," Kara said. "Sorry I asked." She glanced at the tray on the nightstand. "I'll prop the door open a bit so they'll know they can come in and get that dinner tray out of your way."

"You do that," Robert said gruffly. "When they pick it up, I'll inform them that I'm ready for my steak and potatoes."

"Uh-oh," Kara said, returning to the door to flip the rubber stopper down, propping the door about one-third open. "Grumpy already." She took a seat in a chair next to where Margaret sat by the bed.

"I'm humoring the mood while he's in the hospital," Margaret said. "But once we get home? That will be another story."

Robert smiled. "I'll be a perfect patient, my love. I'm grateful to be alive, believe me. An event like this one certainly makes a man aware of his blessings and all the reasons he has to live each day to the fullest. I intend to be around for a long long time."

"I hope so," Margaret said, smiling at him warmly. "I know so."

Robert sighed before frowning. "Well, the time has come, hasn't it? We need to discuss what happened at the party. More precisely, we need to discuss the subject of Andrew Malone and his claim that he's my son."

Kara got to her feet. "I'll leave you two alone. Please don't get overtired, Uncle Robert."

"No, Kara, don't go," Robert said. "You're part of the MacAllister family, and everyone has a right to know the truth. You might as well hear this now. Is that all right with you, Margaret?"

"Yes. Yes, of course," Margaret said, her gaze riveted on her husband. "But you don't have to do this tonight, Robert."

"Yes, I do," he said. "I truly do. This is a great burden on your mind, my Margaret, I know it is. You've been through enough, worrying about whether I was going to live or die, without this situation with Andrew Malone hanging over your head, too.''

Kara sat back down and clutched her hands tightly in her lap. Robert lifted his right hand and stared at a thin white scar that ran across his knuckles.

''That scar,'' he said, allowing his hand to fall heavily onto the blanket, ''is from punching a tree out of hurt and frustration when Sally Malone broke my immature teenage heart.''

''When?'' Margaret said, hardly above a whisper. ''When were you involved with Sally Malone, Robert?''

''A year before I met you, my darling,'' Robert said. ''Margaret, I have never been unfaithful to you. Never. I swear it.''

Margaret closed her eyes for a moment, and when she opened them again, tears were shimmering in her eyes. She smiled at her husband.

''Thank you for that,'' she said. ''I needed to hear you say it. I'm sorry, but I did. I should have had more faith in you.''

''No, there's no reason to apologize. I mean, my God, a young man shows up out of the blue claiming to be my son and...you had every right to wonder when I was intimate with his mother, how old Andrew Malone is. If the situation was reversed, I would need the same assurances I'm giving you, Margaret.''

Margaret dashed an errant tear from her cheek and nodded.

''I've spoken with Andrew Malone,'' she said, her voice not quite steady, ''seen him up close. He *is* your son. He has your eyes, the MacAllister eyes, and his features are yours.''

Robert nodded slowly. "So be it.'' He took a deep breath and let it out slowly. "The year before I met you, Margaret, the summer after I graduated from high school, I worked as a counselor at a youth camp up in the mountains. My father demanded that I do something entirely different before beginning the apprenticeship program at MacAllister Architects.

"He had insisted that Ralph do the same thing two years previously, and so off I went to ride herd on a bunch of rowdy kids, who were feeling their oats because they were away from home and their parents' eagle eyes.

"Sally Malone was working at the camp as one of the kitchen staff. She was there with her older sister...oh, what was her name? Cleo? No, no, her sister's name was Clara.''

"Are you sure you wouldn't prefer that I leave?'' Kara said.

"No, dear, stay,'' Margaret said. "Please.''

Kara nodded.

"Well, it was a case of summer love or whatever,'' Robert went on. "I fell head over heels for Sally. She was sweet, innocent, very wholesome, and...I was convinced I was in love for the first time in my life.'' He shook his head. "Oh, I was such a foolish, lovestruck boy. I believed every word that Sally told me, was convinced that she loved me in return. And how very wrong I was.''

"What happened?'' Margaret said, frowning.

"Sally Malone was not even close to being what she presented herself to be. She was using me for her own purposes. She was involved with an older man back home and decided that a relationship with me would provide her with the sexual experience she needed to please that man.

"There was nothing sweet, innocent and wholesome about Sally. She had an agenda, and I was the unsuspecting pawn in her diabolical game plan."

"That's a lie," Andrew said, bursting into the room and striding to the edge of the bed. "That is a damn lie, MacAllister."

Kara jumped to her feet. "Andrew! Don't. You mustn't upset Uncle Robert because... Don't do this."

Andrew's head snapped around and he glared at Kara. "Don't defend my mother's memory, who she was as a person, a woman? If your uncle feels physically strong enough to fabricate these lies, then, by God, he's strong enough to take them back and tell the truth about what really happened that summer.

"I didn't intend to do this," Andrew said, "but I was in the hallway by the door, hoping to see you when you came out, Kara. I can't, I won't, stand silently by and listen to my mother's name, her memory, being dragged through the mud, made filthy by lies."

Andrew returned his furious gaze to Robert. "Damn you, MacAllister, how can you do this? You actually intend to pass off this story as the truth to your entire family, don't you? What kind of man are you?"

Robert met Andrew's angry gaze directly. "I'm telling the truth as I know it, Andrew."

"Bull," he said, raking a hand through his hair.

"All right," Robert said. "Sally isn't here to defend herself. According to what you said that night in the restaurant, she passed away when you were fifteen years old. You have every right to speak in her place."

"Damn straight I do," Andrew said, a muscle ticking in his jaw. "My mother loved you with all her heart. She gave you her most precious gift—her innocence. And then? When she told you she was pregnant with your baby, you abandoned her, walked away without a backward glance."

Margaret gasped, then pressed her fingertips to her lips.

"Sally Malone wasn't good enough for you, right, Robert?" Andrew went on, a steely bitter edge to his voice. "Oh, sure, she was fine for a romp in the hay during the boring summer. But did you actually intend to have a future with someone far below the MacAllister social status? Not a chance. You used her, played on her innocence, then walked away from her when she needed you the most, laughing at how gullible and easily duped she had been. Oh, yeah, I heard about how you laughed, you bastard."

A rough bark of sound erupted from Andrew's lips. "No, excuse me," he said, narrowing his eyes. "You're not the bastard, are you, Robert? That title belongs to me. I'm the bastard.

"I'm the one who was raised by an unmarried woman, who struggled for every penny she had, who was the most wonderful mother any child could ask for. But I didn't have a father, because you didn't give a damn that Sally was pregnant with your baby when you left her.

"*That* is the truth. *That* is what the MacAllister family is going to be told."

"Dear heaven," Kara whispered.

Margaret drew a shuddering breath as she struggled against fresh tears.

An oppressive silence fell over the room as Andrew and Robert stared directly into each other's eyes. MacAllister eyes meeting MacAllister eyes.

"Andrew," Robert said quietly, breaking the silence, "how old are you? When is your birthday?"

"What?" Andrew said, obviously confused by the questions.

"When were you born?" Robert said.

"Why?" Andrew said.

"Andrew, please," Kara said. "Please answer the questions. They're obviously important somehow. I don't understand why, either, but...please? How old are you? When is your birthday?"

Andrew stared down at the floor for a long moment, then looked at Robert again.

"I can't see the point in this but...all right. I'll be forty years old on April twenty-ninth."

Robert sighed deeply and nodded. "And there lies the truth."

"What do you mean?" Andrew said.

"Oh, don't you see?" Robert said. "We left that camp in early August. Sally, herself, couldn't have known that she was pregnant then, let alone having told me. Andrew, I didn't know that your mother was carrying my child. I didn't know that you even existed until you came to that hotel on New Year's Eve."

Andrew reached out blindly behind him until his

hand connected with a chair. He pulled it forward and sank onto it heavily, his mind racing.

"I didn't laugh at the end of that summer, Andrew," Robert said. "I wept. I cried tears of heartbreak and disillusionment and felt a deep sense of betrayal. I ran into the woods, smashed my fist into a tree and cried until there were no more tears within me to shed.

"For months after I got home I brooded, refused to date, wanted no part of any social life. Time began to heal my wounds, and then I met Margaret. I pushed the memory of Sally Malone into a dusty corner of my mind, was finally able to view what had happened as a bitter lesson learned and moved forward with my life. I came to understand, because of Margaret, what love really was."

Andrew rested his elbows on his knees and dragged both hands down his face. He straightened again and looked at Robert.

"This doesn't make sense," he said, his voice echoing with total fatigue. "You're right, you couldn't have known that my mother was pregnant when you left that camp. But I've always believed that you abandoned her when she told you she was carrying your child and..." He shook his head. "I just don't understand this."

"Andrew," Margaret said gently, "did your mother tell you that Robert walked away from her when she discovered she was pregnant? Did Sally Malone tell you that?"

Andrew turned his head to look at Margaret, then narrowed his eyes.

"No," he said slowly. "No, Clara, my aunt, was

the one who gave me the facts of that summer. It was Clara. All my mother ever said was that she had loved deeply but hadn't been loved in return.

"She said there was no purpose in my knowing who my father was, and I never asked. Clara finally revealed my father's identity after seeing the photograph in the newspaper and the story about the MacAllister reunion."

"Andrew," Robert said, "it was Clara, not Sally, who told me that your mother had been using me to gain sexual experience to please her older lover at home. I didn't hear it from Sally, nor did I ever see her again after Clara delivered her news. She said that Sally didn't care to go through a messy emotional scene with me."

"Oh, my God," Kara said. "Clara lied to you, Uncle Robert, and no doubt lied to Sally, as well, about your having used her. Why would she do such a horrible thing to her own sister? What kind of person would do that?"

Andrew looked up at the ceiling and took a deep breath, letting it out slowly.

"A jealous person," he said, his voice raspy with emotion. "A person who couldn't stand to see her younger sister so happy, so complete, while she herself had no one who loved her.

"A person who has since become an alcoholic who marries men, then divorces them when they can't fill the void within her, the need to have someone make her happy because she doesn't know how to do it for herself.

"A person who realized that long-ago summer that her sister had found someone who loved her, someone who made it very clear that Sally Malone mattered.

"Oh, yeah, I intended to force you to admit to your family that you had gotten a young innocent girl pregnant, then abandoned her, Robert. But what was of the utmost importance to me, what I wanted for my mother, was to hear you say that Sally Malone mattered."

"Sally mattered," Robert said quietly. "I now realize that she was everything I believed her to be. Margaret, my dear, this doesn't diminish my love for you in the slightest, I hope you know that."

"I do," Margaret said. "No one should forget the first time they fell in love. It's special, opens the door of your heart to new feelings and depths of emotion. It may not be forever love, but that person is important and does, indeed, matter."

Kara's heart seemed to skip a beat as Margaret's words echoed in her mind.

No one should forget the first time they fell in love.

She stared at Andrew, her heart settling into a rapid tempo.

No, she thought frantically. She was *not* falling in love with Andrew Malone. She knew she would never forget him after he was gone, but that didn't mean... No!

"Andrew," Robert said, bringing Kara from her upsetting thoughts, "I'm sorry, so very sorry, that Sally was alone during her pregnancy and all the years that she raised you. I don't know what to say to you except that I am so very very sorry."

"It wasn't your fault," Andrew said, shaking his head. "It was Clara's. I know that now. I'm the one who is apologizing. I never should have come to Ventura, gone to that party and... I'm asking you to forgive me for what I did to you and your family." He got to his feet. "I'll understand if you can't forgive me, though."

Andrew cleared his throat as his emotions began to overcome him.

"I'll...I'll be leaving Ventura tonight," he went on, his voice husky. "I won't cause you, or the other MacAllisters, any more trouble. Maybe in time you'll be able to forget that I ever intruded in your lives."

No! Kara's mind screamed. Andrew couldn't leave. Not yet. Oh, please, not yet. Yes, she knew he would go, knew he would leave her, but not yet...please.

Andrew extended his right hand toward Robert.

"Goodbye, sir," Andrew said.

Robert clasped Andrew's hand with both of his. "Andrew, please, wait a minute. Let's talk about this."

"There's nothing more to say," he said, easing his hand free of Robert's.

Margaret got to her feet. "I beg your pardon, young man, but there is a great deal more to be said. Now, you sit back down in that chair and listen."

Andrew opened his mouth to retort, blinked, then sat back in the chair with a thud.

"That's better," Margaret said, lifting her chin. "I don't want to hear any more of this nonsense about us forgetting that you were here, that you exist. You are my husband's son. Whether you like it or not, you are a MacAllister.

"That doesn't take one thing away from Sally Malone or the wonderful mother you say that she was, but the fact remains that Robert is your father, and MacAllister blood runs in your veins every bit as much as Malone blood does.''

"But—"

"I have the floor, young man," Margaret said.

"Yes, ma'am," Andrew said, then shook his head slightly as he realized he felt about ten years old.

Robert chuckled. "Thank you, Margaret. I'll speak for myself now."

"You're welcome, dear," Margaret said, then settled back in her chair.

Kara snapped her mouth closed as she realized it had dropped open at Margaret's outburst and Andrew's compliance with her aunt's orders.

"I'm going to ask something of you, Andrew," Robert said. "I don't have the right to do this, I haven't earned a place in your life, but I'm going to make this request, anyway.

"Please stay on in Ventura for a while. Give me a chance to get to know you, talk with you, share with you. I missed out on nearly forty years of your life, Andrew. Please give me an opportunity to share at least some of your future."

Andrew stared at Robert for a long moment before he spoke.

"You'd be running the risk of doing irreparable harm to the MacAllister family," Andrew said. "You can't expect all of them to accept me with no resentment, no question. Your family might be split into camps, and I won't be the cause of that. I've done enough damage already."

"Let me worry about the remainder of the MacAllisters," Robert said.

"I don't know," Andrew said, shaking his head. "I'm already dealing with enough guilt as it is. I'll have to think about this. I have a business to run in Santa Maria, and I need to get up there. I can't promise you that I'll be back."

"But you aren't saying that you definitely won't return, are you?" Robert said.

"No, I'm not saying that," Andrew said. "I need some time to think this through. There are, in fact, a great many things I have to get settled in my mind, beginning with what Clara did all those years ago."

Robert nodded. "I understand." He paused. "You have nothing to feel guilty about, Andrew. You didn't cause me to be in this bed—I did. I had been ignoring the signals from my heart, pretending nothing was wrong with me.

"Granted, your appearance at the party triggered my heart attack, but if I had gone on as I was, I might not have survived the attack that was inevitable later. Don't beat yourself up with guilt, because it's very misplaced."

"Thank you for that," Andrew said, getting to his feet. "I've got to go."

"I'll be hoping, praying, that you'll return," Robert said, his voice choked with emotion, "son."

"No one…no one has ever called me that," Andrew said, then shook his head as an achy sensation closed his throat, making further speech impossible.

"It's long overdue," Margaret said, smiling at Andrew through her tears. "You have many titles that belong to you, Andrew. You're a son, a brother, an uncle, a cousin, on the list goes. You are a Mac-Allister.''

Andrew nodded jerkily, then turned and strode from the room.

Kara got to her feet. "I have to go to him," she said, her voice thick with tears. "You understand, don't you? I have to. Andrew must be so confused, so... And he's all alone and—''

"Go," Robert said. "Quickly."

"Yes, dear," Margaret said. "Hurry."

Kara rushed from the room.

Margaret stood and leaned over the bed to kiss Robert on the forehead.

"I love you, Robert MacAllister," she said, "and I will until the day I no longer breathe. You are my life, my darling. Just think—after all these years you've just given me another handsome son."

"Andrew may not choose to own that title," Robert said, reaching for Margaret's hand.

"Give him some time," she said. "Andrew has a great deal to make sense of right now, including, I'm beginning to believe, his feelings for our Kara."

"What if he never comes back, Margaret?"

"Don't be silly, dear. Andrew is a MacAllister. He'll do the right thing in the end, because Mac-Allisters always do."

When Kara emerged from her uncle's room, she saw Andrew standing by the elevators farther down the hallway. She resisted the urge to call out to him, years of training keeping her from yelling in the hospital. She hurried toward him.

The doors swished open and Andrew started to

enter the elevator, only to hesitate and look back in the direction he had come from. When he saw Kara, he started toward her. When they met, he gripped her shoulders and looked directly into her eyes.

"I couldn't get into that elevator, Kara," he said, his voice husky, "because I realized I couldn't go without seeing you, saying goodbye."

"Thank you for that," she said, tears misting her eyes. "Oh, Andrew, please don't leave for Santa Maria tonight. You're exhausted and upset and…you shouldn't be driving when you're like this. Can't you wait until morning to make the trip?"

"You're right," Andrew said with a weary sigh. "I'm in no shape to be on the road. I…I just had to get out of your uncle's room. The walls were closing in on me, seeming to crush me, smother me. There's so much I have to come to grips with." He shook his head. "Hell, I'm a wreck, I really am."

"With just cause," Kara said, smiling as she blinked back her tears. "I think we're all on mental overload at the moment. Would you…would you like to come to my apartment and relax? I could make us dinner."

"I wouldn't be very good company, Kara."

"You don't have to carry on a chipper conversation," she said. "But if you'd rather be alone, I understand."

"There's no one I'd rather be with tonight than you, Kara," Andrew said. "If you can put up with my gloomy mood, I'd like very much to go to your apartment with you."

"It's settled, then," she said. "You can follow me over in your vehicle. Okay?"

"Sure. And thank you. You seem to know what I need before I do at times. Is that the doctor in you?"

"No, it's..." Kara hesitated, then lifted her chin. "It's the woman."

Andrew nodded slowly, then they returned to the elevator, where he pressed the button once again. They didn't speak as they rode down to the lobby, but Andrew slipped an arm around Kara's shoulders and tucked her close to his side. He kept her there as they stepped out into the busy main floor of the hospital.

"Get a picture of this," a voice said.

A flash went off and both Kara and Andrew jerked and stopped walking. Andrew dropped his arm to his side.

"Nice photograph," a man said. "Hey, folks, Barry Folger, *Ventura Now.* This is very interesting. Dr. Kara MacAllister and Andrew Malone were seen together—very together—leaving the hospital where Robert MacAllister lies near death after a heart attack after being confronted by Malone, who claims to be Robert's son. Do you two have any comment for the citizens of Ventura and beyond?"

Andrew stepped forward, grabbed the front of the reporter's shirt and nearly lifted the man off his feet.

"Get a shot of this, too," the reporter called over his shoulder. "If he decks me, don't miss it. So much the better."

"Ah, hell." Andrew released the man, managing to shove him backward at the same time.

The reporter staggered, steadied himself, then grinned. "Temper, temper, Malone. You wouldn't want your long-lost daddy to hear that you're in jail on charges of assault, would you?''

Andrew took a step in the direction of the man, but Kara grabbed Andrew's arm.

"Andrew, don't," she said. "He's not worth it. Come on, let's get out of here."

"You print that picture and I'll..." Andrew started, a muscle ticking in his jaw.

"You'll what?" Folger said. "Sue me? Pictures don't lie and I have freedom of the press on my side. I've got a hot scoop here about you two, and I intend to use it. I knew that hanging around this place long enough would pay off. And it did—big time."

"You sorry son of a—"

"Andrew, no," Kara said, tightening her hold on his arm. "Please."

Andrew struggled to rein in his raging temper, then finally looked at Kara and nodded. He pushed past the still-grinning reporter, and he and Kara left the hospital through the front doors.

Outside Andrew stopped, planted his hands on his hips and stared up at the sky, still scrambling for emotional control.

"I've got to get out of this town," he said, his voice low and flat and echoing with fatigue. "All I do is cause problems, one after the next. Now I've made you tabloid news, Kara. Damn it, I've hurt you, too, just by being here."

"No, don't say that," she said. "I could have put distance between us before we got out of the elevator, but I didn't. Whatever ramifications there are from that picture and the story that will accompany it will be as much my fault as yours. We're in this together. We'll weather whatever storm that comes from that ugly man's actions."

"I won't even be here when that story hits the newsstands," Andrew said, meeting her gaze. "I will have left you to face that mess alone. I can't do that. It isn't fair to you. I'll stay on in Ventura and… No, I can't. I've got a business in Santa Maria that I've neglected, that needs my attention. I…"

Andrew shook his head. "This is the last straw. Look what I've done to you. *You.* You mean so damn much to me, are so important and special… Ah, hell, forget it. I'm not making any sense. I don't understand what I'm feeling, what's happening between us, let alone how to explain it to you."

"You're not alone in that confusion, Andrew," Kara said quietly. "You're very important to me, too, but it's still overwhelming and frightening at times. Please, let's just forget all this for now. We'll have some dinner, relax, talk about the weather or whatever."

Andrew managed to produce a small smile. "There you go. We'll have an in-depth discussion on global warming or some such thing. Let's get out of here before that jerk of a reporter decides to follow us. The next few hours are ours. No one else's—just ours."

"Yes."

"I'll meet you at your place," he said, then started off across the parking lot.

The next few hours are ours, Kara's mind echoed

as she watched Andrew stride away. And then? Andrew would be leaving, going back to Santa Maria.

And the haunting unanswered question that was causing fresh tears to sting her eyes was whether or not she would ever see Andrew Malone again.

Chapter 12

"So, there I was," Andrew said, "balancing on the framework of the roof of the house, the kitten clinging for dear life to my shirt—and the skin on my chest, I might add—and hollering its head off, and the ladder flat on the ground."

Kara laughed in delight. "How did you finally get down?"

"Two little boys came along who were searching for their lost kitten. I called to them, telling them I had the kitten, but I couldn't get off the roof. Could they lift the ladder and lean it against the house? No, it was too heavy for them."

"You're kidding," Kara said.

"Nope." Andrew chuckled. "One of the kids said he'd go for help and took off at a dead run. This all took place close to ten years ago, and to this day someone will remember it and razz me about the time the fire department came to rescue me and my cute kitty from the roof of a house I was helping to build. I've never lived it down.''

"What a wonderful story.'' Kara covered one of Andrew's hands with one of her own on the kitchen table. "Thank you for telling me that tale. I could visualize it all so clearly in my mind. I imagine those two children thought you were a real hero.''

"No, actually, they were more impressed with the firefighters when they arrived. It's hard to compete with a uniform, you know.''

Kara's smile faded and she looked at Andrew intently. "Like a baseball uniform? They put the outfit on the baby, Andrew. He was wearing it when I saw him last. It was adorable. *He* was adorable. That was such a sweet and thoughtful thing to do.'' She paused and looked at their layered hands for a second, then met his gaze again. "Why did you buy him that little suit?''

Andrew shrugged. "I don't know. It was another one of those 'it seemed like a good idea at the time' moments. I was wandering around a mall, attempting to fill the hours until I hoped I could see you, and I saw the outfit in a store window.

"The baseball suit was a symbol, of sorts. You know, step up, give it your all, always do the best you're capable of—that kind of thing.'' He chuckled. "I'm sure the baby picked right up on that message of life when they put the thing on him.''

"He did,'' Kara said, nodding. "He told me.''

"Oh, okay.'' Andrew smiled, then grew serious in the next moment. "I guess I've been assuming that the baby will be put up for adoption, have a chance of a normal happy upbringing with a mother and father who love him. I suppose, though, that his birth mother might be able to keep him if she gets her act together. Right?"

"Yes, there have been cases where the baby was placed in foster care while the birth mother underwent rehabilitation for drug use, and they were eventually united. In this case, however, the baby's mother signed release papers before she left the hospital so he could be adopted. She really wasn't interested in giving up drugs."

Andrew nodded. "Then the little guy will be adopted, be part of a real family—mom, dad, dog, cat. Maybe even brothers and sisters down the road. That's good, really good."

Tell him, Kara's mind yelled. The conversation had taken a direction that gave her the perfect opening to share with Andrew the fact that *she* had applied to adopt the baby, that *she* hoped to be his mother. *Tell him, Kara.*

No, no, this wasn't the time. Andrew had so much on his mind, such a great deal to come to grips with already. She couldn't expect him to comprehend something that was so vitally important to *her* when he was already on mental overload.

She'd have to wait. She'd explain it all to him later when he—if he—returned to Ventura. Oh, dear heaven, what if he never came back? What if this night was the last she was to share with Andrew Malone?

"Well, it's nice to know that the baby is going to have a happy ending," Andrew said, bringing Kara from her troubling thoughts. "I'm surprising myself with the fact that the little guy is on my mind a lot. I guess it's because he's the first baby I've ever interacted with. You know, held, fed, bored him into a deep sleep with my pearly words of wisdom.''

"He's a heart-stealer, all right," Kara said quietly. "He's...well, very special, a little miracle."

"Yep. A big miracle is how much better I feel at the moment," Andrew said. "That's due to the delicious dinner you made and the relaxing conversation. Thank you very much, Dr. MacAllister.''

"You're welcome, Mr. Malone."

Andrew pushed back his chair and got to his feet. "The least I can do is help you clean the kitchen.''

"My goodness," Kara said, rising. "Your mother certainly trained you well." She paused and sighed. "Oh, Andrew, I'm sorry. I didn't mean to bring up the subject of your mother. I was just blithering and... Now you'll think about Sally Malone and that will lead you to dwell on Uncle Robert and... I'm so sorry. This was supposed to be an evening off from heavy thoughts.''

Andrew closed the distance between them and pulled Kara into his embrace.

"Shame on you," he said. "You blew it. I would say that it's now your responsibility to occupy my entire thought processes with something pleasant to make up for your mistake.''

Kara encircled Andrew's neck with her arms. "Seems only fair.''

"Indeed."

Kara inched her fingertips into Andrew's thick hair and stood on tiptoe to claim his mouth with hers. He answered the demands of her lips eagerly, hungrily, and passions soared.

Andrew raised his head to take a sharp breath, then slanted his mouth in the opposite direction as he captured her lips once again. His tongue slipped into her mouth, found her tongue, stroked, dueled, danced.

Kara pressed her body more tightly against Andrew's and felt his arousal, glorying in the fact that he wanted her as much as she did him. She drank in the taste of him, inhaled his aroma, savored the strength in his magnificent body and the wondrous sensation of feeling so safe and protected within his powerful arms.

"The dishes," Andrew murmured close to her lips.

"Can wait," she said.

"Good."

Andrew broke the kiss and swung Kara into his arms, causing her to laugh in delight. He strode from the kitchen and carried her into the bedroom, setting her on her feet next to the bed.

They shed their clothes quickly and flung them away, no thought given to where they landed or the wrinkles being created in the fabrics.

Andrew swept back the blankets on the bed, lifted Kara into his arms again, then placed her in the middle of the cool sheets. He followed her down to claim her lips in a searing kiss.

They kissed and caressed, hands never still, touching, exploring, rediscovering wondrous mysteries that were known only to them. Where hands had been, lips followed, tasting, savoring, cherishing.

The flames of want and need grew hotter, consuming them, causing breathing to become labored and hearts to race in wild tempos.

But they waited...waited...anticipating what was yet to come, going to the very brink of what they could bear. A whimper of need escaped Kara's throat. A groan rumbled deep in Andrew's chest.

He left her only long enough to take steps to protect her, then returned to her embrace. He entered her, sheathing himself in her feminine heat, then began a thundering rhythm that took them far far away. Up. Higher. Over the top and into ecstasy.

"Andrew!"

"Kara. My Kara. My Kara."

They hovered, drifted, floated back to the room, the bed, the sated contentment of reality.

Andrew shifted off Kara and settled close to her side, one arm curled across her waist as she nestled her head on his shoulder. Minutes passed in blissful silence as they gathered themselves.

"Just gets better and better," Andrew finally said.

"Mmm."

"I can't...can't deal with the idea of never seeing you again," Andrew said, "but neither can I promise that I'll come back to Ventura, Kara. I would never make a promise I wasn't certain I could keep. There is so much I have to sort through and... Hell."

"I understand, Andrew," she said softly, struggling against threatening tears.

"I don't expect you to sit around waiting for me to get a handle on this muddled mess called my mind. God, I'm so confused about so many things right now."

"I know."

"So, I mean, I have no claim on you or… But the thought of your being with another man is…whew. See? I'm a basket case. Maybe, hopefully, once I get back to Santa Maria, pick up my life, get to work, I'll have a clearer picture of everything, know what I should do.

"Ah, hell, I don't know. All I'm doing now is chasing my own thoughts in an endless circle."

"I…I hope you'll come back to Ventura, Andrew," Kara said, splaying one hand on his chest. "But I'm sure you know that."

"It's nice to hear," he said, sifting his fingers through her hair. "But there's no erasing the fact that you're a MacAllister. If I return to see you, be with you, it would mean taking my place in the MacAllister family unit, being acknowledged as Robert's son and becoming comfortable with that truth myself. That is one heavy trip, let me tell you."

"Yes, I imagine it is."

"I'm a very solitary man, Kara. The number of people in your family is daunting, let alone the emotional involvement being a part of that group would require.

"I grew up with a single mother and a nutty aunt who dropped in between husbands. My grandparents were killed in a drunk-driving accident when I was three years old. I have no memory of them whatsoever.

"I live alone, answering to no one and…and I like my existence just the way it is."

A chill swept through Kara and she pulled her hand back from the warmth of Andrew's chest.

"Yes, well, that's certainly a very safe way to live,

isn't it, Andrew?'' she said, unable to keep the sharp edge from her voice that was caused by the cutting pain of his words.

Andrew shifted enough so he could meet Kara's gaze, frowning as he looked at her.

"What do you mean?'' he said.

"If you keep yourself isolated, exist behind a protective wall where no one can ask anything of you, then you can't be hurt, can you? There's no risk involved in the way you live. But the thing is, Andrew, if you never allow yourself to love, you just might never be loved in return. And I think that sounds very empty, very stark and bleak, and very lonely.''

Andrew's jaw tightened slightly. "I don't see a wedding ring on your finger. Why haven't you run the risk of loving one special man, making a commitment to forever?''

"There are many kinds of love,'' she said, her voice rising. "The love between a man and a woman is far different than the love you feel for your family.''

"I'm not a stupid man, Kara, so I realize that. I loved my mother with my whole heart, but our time together was cut short. When she died, all I had left were memories, with no actual person to center my love on.

"My aunt Clara? Forget it. You have a very clear picture of the kind of woman she is. She's not what you would call lovable. Not by a long shot.''

"No, she's not but—''

"Don't you get it?'' Andrew said none too quietly. "I don't know how to love the way you MacAllisters do. The image of all of you in my mind is…is smothering, draining and…"

Kara wiggled out of Andrew's embrace and sat up, drawing the sheet toward her to cover her breasts.

"I'm a woman, not just a MacAllister," she said, turning to look down at Andrew. "Don't lump me into the MacAllister pile as if I was your sister or cousin or whatever.

"I'm your lover, Andrew, and the emotions that go with that are not the same as what you might come to feel for my family. Separate me from them in your mind, realize that you can be a part of the MacAllister family even if you don't want…even if you choose to end what we…"

Kara shook her head and stopped speaking as tears closed her throat. She raised her knees and rested her forehead on top of them.

"Believe me, I know you're a woman, my lover, not just a MacAllister," Andrew said, flinging back the blankets and leaving the bed. He turned to look at Kara. "I also know that what I feel for you is like nothing I've known before. That does not, however, mean that I understand what it is. You scare the hell out of me, lady."

"Well, you scare the hell out of me, too, mister," Kara said, raising her head and the volume of her voice.

"Fine," he said gruffly. "At least we agree on something here. It's obvious that you don't want to get caught up in a serious relationship any more than I do."

Yes, she did, Kara thought frantically. No, no, she

didn't. But then again, this was Andrew and... Oh, mercy, she was losing her mind.

"I know why I never intend to fall in love, marry, the whole nine yards," Andrew said, splaying one hand on his chest. "I saw what love did to my mother. Oh, sure, she claimed she was happy, that I was enough to fulfill her, that we were a team and all that.

"But as I got older and really looked at the situation, I knew how badly she had been hurt, how devastated she was by Robert's betrayal. I made up my mind when I was still a teenager that that would never happen to me. Never. And it won't.

"But you, Kara? Are you running from love, hiding behind your wall because of your involvement with that loser, Rick, when you were just a kid? That's wrong, really out in left field."

"Don't you dare pass judgment on me, Andrew Malone!" Kara shouted. "You have no idea what's going on in my mind, my heart. And another thing. Your mother was *not* betrayed by my Uncle Robert, remember? She chose well when she loved, she really did. Her heartache was caused by your aunt, not by my uncle."

"Yeah, well, I still don't want any part of..." Andrew swore under his breath and dragged both hands through his hair. "This is great, just terrific. What happened to the relaxing night with no heavy stuff on the agenda? Now we're having an argument about this mess, for Pete's sake."

"Oh. Yes, I guess we are, aren't we?" Kara said, a rather bemused expression on her face. "Hollering at each other isn't going to solve anything."

"No, it isn't. This screamer wasn't a total waste, though. We both know we can be together without any demands for a long-term commitment. Right?"

Yes? No? Kara thought. She was so confused, so muddled, she just didn't know.

"Right, Kara?"

"Oh, well, yes, of course," she said, nodding. "That's right."

"Although I still believe that at some point in your future you ought to take a close look at why you feel the way you do."

Kara narrowed her eyes. "Don't start that with me again. Besides, you would do well to reexamine your views on the subject now that you know your mother was not hurt by loving the man in her heart."

"Truce," Andrew said, raising both hands. "All we have to know is that we are on the same wavelength now. What I can't tell you at this point is whether or not I'll be coming back to Ventura. I…just…don't…know."

Kara nodded, then flopped back onto the pillow, covering her face with the sheet.

"Hello?" Andrew bent over and pressed a fingertip to her sheet-covered forehead.

"I'm exhausted," Kara said, her voice muffled. "Brain dead. I can't think any more tonight. I refuse to say another word."

Andrew slid back onto the bed and tugged the sheet from Kara's face.

"Good idea," he said. "We won't talk. Won't think. We'll just—" he outlined Kara's lips with the tip of his tongue and she shivered from the sensuous foray "—feel." He brushed his lips over hers once, then again. "Yes?"

"Oh, yes," Kara whispered.

Then no more words were spoken.

When Kara awoke the next morning, Andrew was gone.

She sighed, a wobbly, close-to-tears sigh, then reached for the pillow where he'd laid his head and pressed it to her face, inhaling his lingering aroma. In the next moment she flung the pillow to the floor.

"Cute, Kara," she said. "How adolescent can you get? What's next? I'll never wash the fork he ate dinner with last night?"

How was it possible, she thought miserably, that her life had become so topsy-turvy, so complicated, so confusing in a short amount of days...and nights?

Oh, those nights. Those incredibly beautiful, beyond-description nights with Andrew. My, my, my, she thought, her mind shifting into a dreamy state.

The telephone on the nightstand rang, and Kara yelped at the sudden noise. She placed one hand on her racing heart and grabbed the receiver.

"Hello?" she said.

"It's Jack."

Kara shot upright on the bed, her eyes widening. "Jack? Why are you calling so early? Has something happened to Uncle Robert?"

"No, no, nothing like that," Jack said. "I went for an early run while Jennifer and Joey were still sleeping. During my jog, I passed a newsstand where the guy was putting out the morning papers."

"Uh-oh," Kara said.

"Yep, little sister, uh-oh. A photograph of you and Andrew Malone is on the front page of a sleazy tabloid. The story is trashy, indicating you two are getting it on while Robert MacAllister lies near death. I just wanted to warn you so you'll be prepared if anyone says something about it to you."

"I imagine you're furious with me," Kara said wearily. "Pictures don't lie, I suppose."

"No, I'm not angry. What you do with Malone is your business, Kara. My only concern is that you don't get hurt, but you're all grown-up now and I can't protect you from that sort of thing. I just feel...well, that you've cried enough tears in your life. I'd hate to see you torn up because of your involvement with Andrew."

"That's very sweet, Jack. Thank you. You and Richard are the best big brothers anyone could ever hope to have." Kara paused. "Andrew has gone back to Santa Maria."

"Oh, yeah? Is he planning to return to Ventura at some point?"

"He doesn't know. *I* don't know. Uncle Robert asked him to stay so they could get better acquainted, but... I think Uncle Robert will be calling a family meeting when he's stronger, and he'll explain the whole situation regarding Sally Malone, Andrew and what happened all those years ago. He feels the family has a right to know the facts of the situation."

"Uncle Robert doesn't have to do that," Jack said. "It's really none of our business."

"Yes, well, Uncle Robert wants to do it, so... Anyway, it's very complicated and confusing, and...Andrew is a tad overwhelmed by everything right now. I am, too, as a matter of fact.''

"You don't have to answer this, Kara, but I'll ask the question. Are you in love with Andrew Malone?''

Sudden tears filled Kara's eyes and she pressed her free hand to her forehead.

"I don't know!" she said, nearly wailing. "How is a person supposed to figure out such a momentous thing? Huh? Answer me that. I don't have a button to push somewhere on my person that will say yes or no. Forget it. I don't even want to know how I feel about Andrew. I don't. It's hopeless and... Oh-h-h, I'm going nuts.''

"We're back to uh-oh," Jack said, chuckling. "You've got heart trouble, little sister, in spades.''

"I most certainly do not." Kara paused and frowned. "Do I?''

"You'll figure it out in time. Gotta go hit the shower. I'll talk to you later. Remember to be on guard about the junk in the newspaper.''

"Yes, I will and I appreciate your calling to warn me that the jerk actually printed that stuff.''

"One other thing, Kara.''

"Yes?''

"While you're here in Ventura attempting to untangle the mess in your mind, remember that Andrew is up in Santa Maria doing the same thing. Interesting thought, don't you think? As I said, time will tell. Bye.''

"Goodbye, Jack," Kara said quietly.

She replaced the receiver, glanced at the clock, then threw back the blankets on the bed as she realized she was going to be late arriving at the office if she didn't hurry.

As she crossed the room, she hesitated, then stopped to pick up the pillow she'd thrown to the floor. She hugged it to her breasts and drew a wobbly breath.

"Time will tell?" she said aloud. "Yes, I suppose that's true. But at this moment, this tick in time, all I know is, I miss Andrew Malone so very very much."

Chapter 13

He missed Kara MacAllister, Andrew thought, very much.

He tossed the pen he was holding onto the papers on the desk and sank back in the leather chair, squeezing the bridge of his nose to try to relieve some of the pain of the headache that had plagued him the majority of the day.

He leaned his head back, stared at the ceiling and sighed.

It seemed like an eternity, he thought wearily, since he'd stood next to the bed in Kara's apartment and watched her sleep, when in actuality it had been just before dawn that morning.

He'd checked out of his hotel, driven to Santa Maria and stopped off at his apartment long enough to collect his mail and the newspapers from the manager, change his clothes and get something to eat.

A quick flip through the newspapers had made him cringe. He saw that the story of his appearance at the MacAllister reunion party and the subsequent events had been published in Santa Maria.

And, he supposed, the tacky tabloid with the picture of him and Kara leaving the hospital was probably out there on the stands in this city, too. Damn.

Andrew rotated his head back and forth, then stopped as the motion increased the throbbing in his temples.

He'd kept on the move all day, meeting with his top foreman, Harry, and visiting each of the sites of the Malone Construction Company projects to be brought up-to-date on their progress.

He'd finally come back to the office to start plowing through the mountain of paperwork his secretary had left on his desk.

Oh, yeah, he thought dryly, he'd kept as busy as he possibly could, but that hadn't been enough to prevent the image of Kara from continually flashing before his mental vision.

He could see her so clearly at times that he felt he could reach out and pull her into his arms, kiss her, taste her, savor her flowery aroma.

"You're losing it, Malone," he said aloud.

He moved forward again, planting his hands on the desk and gazing off into space.

Malone, he thought. He was Andrew Malone. Andrew MacAllister Malone. Andrew Malone MacAllister. Andrew MacAllister. Hell.

Where did he start? he wondered. Where in the maze in his mind did he find a single thread to unravel the mess he had to deal with?

Should he zero in on his feelings for Kara? What they really meant?

Or maybe he needed to concentrate on whether he wished to pursue a relationship with Robert Mac-Allister—his father. Father. The man who had called him "son" in that hospital room.

But if he did go back to Ventura to get to know Robert, that meant he would inherit *all* the Mac-Allisters, the whole seemingly endless bunch of them. He'd be a son, a brother, an uncle, a cousin. What would they expect of him, ask of him? He wouldn't have a clue how to perform in all those roles, what to do, say, how to act. He'd be smothered by their emotional demands, crushed, unable to breathe.

Andrew took a deep breath and let it out slowly, shaking his aching head.

No, the place to begin, he thought, narrowing his eyes, was with dear Aunt Clara. He now knew the truth of what had happened between his mother and Robert MacAllister that long-ago summer. Clara had destroyed lives and loves, and it was time for her to admit to what she had done, to pay the piper, to stop the endless flow of lies. Even as a teenager Clara had been evil, self-centered and vindictive, and she hadn't changed one iota since.

Andrew's head snapped up as he heard the outer door of the office open. A moment later Harry appeared in his doorway.

"What are you doing here?" Andrew said, leaning back in the chair again. He glanced at his watch. "It's nearly nine o'clock, Harry."

"I was driving past on my way to the store to buy

some ice cream for my wife, and I saw that the lights were on," Harry said. "I spotted your vehicle and decided to see if you'd come across a problem that I might have caused while you were away." He smiled. "Hey, I was making decisions like I knew what I was doing. No telling where all the chips might fall."

"You did a helluva fine job," Andrew said, "and I appreciate it very much. There will definitely be a bonus in your next paycheck."

"I won't argue with that," Harry said. "Thank you. It's unbelievable how much stuff you have to buy to get ready for a baby."

Andrew frowned. "Your wife is going to have a baby? I didn't know that."

Harry shrugged, then leaned his shoulder against the doorjamb. "I didn't mention it, Andrew. You've never seemed to be…well, interested in any of your crew's personal lives. Know what I mean? Hey, I'm not complaining. You're the only man I'd want to work for in this town, that's for sure, but…" He shrugged again.

"I guess…I guess I don't ask about anyone's life beyond the construction site, do I?" Andrew said, frowning deeply. "That's really cold, uncaring. I'm sorry, Harry. Will this be your first child?"

"Yep. We know it's a boy and he's due in two months. My wife is hungry all the time. Man, does she eat. She got a craving for ice cream tonight, so here I am running out to get it. She's convinced that she's fat and ugly, but…well, I gotta tell you, Andrew, I think she's so beautiful. I just wish that… No, forget it."

"Come sit down," Andrew said, motioning toward a chair. "You wish what?"

"I can only stay a minute." Harry walked forward, then slouched into one of the chairs opposite Andrew's desk. "My wife will start to worry if I'm gone too long. I've read the newspapers, Andrew. You've got enough on your mind without hearing my woes."

"No, go ahead. I'm listening."

"Well, it's just that I wake up at night sometimes in a cold sweat, scared out of my mind. I mean, hell, I don't know squat about being a father. What if I do a crummy job of it, mess up my kid's psyche or whatever? How am I going to know what to do, what my son needs from me?"

"I think...yes, I think you just love him," Andrew said. "Be there for him, no matter what. Always take the time to hear what he has to say, understand how he feels about things. You're a fine man, Harry. If you teach your son the values you have, he'll turn out A-OK. But the bottom line is, just love him unconditionally, no measuring stick, no score card."

"I already do," Harry said, smiling. "When I put my hand on my wife's stomach and feel him moving in there, my heart nearly bursts. It's awesome, Andrew. Totally unbelievable."

"A miracle," Andrew said, nodding.

"Yeah."

"I held a baby while I was in Ventura," Andrew said quietly. "Man, he was small. I'd never even been close to a tiny baby before, let alone hold one, feed one. He was so helpless, so vulnerable, and there I was tending to his needs. Me. I felt about ten feet tall.

"I also knew that I was ready to go to the mat for him, would never stand by and allow anything to happen to him or let anyone harm him. Hell, he wasn't even my kid, so I can imagine how you must be feeling. I'm really happy for you, Harry."

"I'm happy for me, too." Harry laughed. "When I'm not scared spitless. You ought to get married and have a couple of kids, Andrew. Hell, you're a natural. I read the newspapers and I now know that you grew up without a dad, but you've got a better handle on what it takes to be a father than I do." He got to his feet. "I'm outta here, but think about what I said. You're overdue to take the big step, get married, be a daddy. Then *you* can go out at nine o'clock at night and buy ice cream. See you tomorrow, boss."

"Yeah. See you, Harry."

Silence settled over the room and with it came vivid images in Andrew's mind.

There she was. Kara, laughing in delight as he handed her a bowl of ice cream, which she rested on her huge protruding stomach.

There she was. Kara, pregnant with his child, the miracle they had created together while making exquisitely beautiful love in the darkness of night.

There she was. Kara, now holding that baby to suckle at her breast as he sat next to them, savoring the sight of his wife and child. The baby—he could see the baby, and he looked just like the little guy he'd held in the nursery at the hospital, and yes, he was wearing the minuscule baseball uniform.

There she was. Kara. The woman he loved with every breath in his body.

"Oh, hell." Andrew lunged to his feet with such force that he tipped over the leather chair, causing it to crash against the wall. "What?"

He stood still, hardly breathing, his heart thundering, the rapid beat echoing in his ears.

And then it came—the all-consuming warmth. It moved through him, touching his heart, mind, his very soul, filling him to overflowing with the wonder of it.

He was in love for the first time in his life. He was in love with Kara MacAllister. And—

"Yes!" Andrew shouted, punching one fist high in the air.

This was what had been happening between him and Kara. *This* was the reason for the foreign emotions he'd felt toward Kara. *This* was love and, by damn, it was wonderful.

He needed to talk to Kara, to see her, hold her, kiss her. He would go back to Ventura just as soon as he could make arrangements for Harry to take over the ongoing projects again.

He'd sit Kara down, declare his love for her, then ask her if she would do him the honor of becoming his wife, his partner for life. She cared deeply for him, he knew she did, and he could only hope and pray that she would realize she loved him just as he did her.

They would have it all—the house, the yard with trees, the kids, the dog.

They'd be a family. A real family. A mother and, oh, yes, a father, who would love their children with their whole hearts. Hot damn, this was so fantastic. It was—

A chill coursed through Andrew with such intensity it caused him to take a sharp painful breath.

It was hopeless, he thought. A pipe dream. A fantasy that would never come true.

Feeling as though the last ounce of his energy had been suddenly drained from his body, he barely managed to set the fallen chair back into place, then sink onto it. He leaned back his head and closed his eyes, weary to the bone.

No matter how Kara might feel about him, she would never agree to marry him. She would not make a commitment to forever. She had made that perfectly clear during their heated exchange on the subject. No, she'd never be his wife, the mother of his children.

And himself? Why was he now able to embrace the idea of loving forever, of taking vows to stay by Kara's side until death parted them?

Somewhere in the maze of his mind, things had shifted, become clear, and now he could see it. Love had not broken his mother's heart. Love had not shattered her dreams. Love had not crushed her hopes and plans. It had been an outside force. It had been Clara.

His mother had chosen well when she gave of her heart and her innocence, for Robert MacAllister was a fine man, who had loved Sally Malone in return.

Sally and Robert would have had it all, if Clara hadn't intervened with her diabolical lies. And he, Andrew Malone, would have been Andrew Mac-

Allister. He would have had a father, a man who called him "son" from the day he was born.

He no longer had just cause to fear love, to be afraid to run the risk of loving, to hide behind his protective wall so that no woman could claim his heart.

He was free. Free of the past. Free of the haunting ghosts. Free to love Kara just as deeply as his mother had loved his father.

But Kara MacAllister would never allow herself to return his love in kind.

Andrew leaned forward, propped his elbows on the desk and dropped his face into his hands.

The silence in the room seemed to press on him with a crushing weight, taunting him with its hollow emptiness and bleak message of his future. It was a nearly palpable force, taking on an identity.

And its name was loneliness.

Time lost meaning. Finally Andrew raised his head and got to his feet. As he came around the desk, he stopped and looked at the chair where Harry had sat.

He had never before in his life had a conversation with another man like the one he'd had tonight with Harry. They'd talked, really shared, bared their souls, confessed their fears. During that brief interlude he had felt connected to Harry as though he was...yes, his brother.

It had been a brief glimpse of what it would be like to be part of a family comprised of people who cared about one another, who stopped what they were doing to hear what was troubling one of their own. An enticing sample of what it might be like to belong to the clan of MacAllisters.

And it had warmed him, filled him, to the very depths of his being.

Oh, yes, Kara had been very right when she'd said that family love was far different from that of the love between a man and a woman.

The MacAllisters, at least those who might accept him as one of them, beckoned like a welcoming beacon on a dreary foggy night, calling to him, showing him the path so that he could come home.

But the part of him that loved Kara was raw and painful, cutting him to the quick with the truth of its hopelessness.

"Oh, God," Andrew said, fatigue ringing in his voice as he dragged both hands down his face.

He turned and walked slowly from the office, switching off the light at the doorway, his steps heavy with the weight of his despair.

The next morning Andrew telephoned Clara, breathing a sigh of relief when he got her answering machine. He left a message that he had returned from Ventura and wished to see her at his apartment that night at eight o'clock.

"It's important, Clara," he said. "Be there."

Andrew slammed the receiver back into place, then stared at it with narrowed eyes, a muscle jumping in his tightly clenched jaw.

"It's truth time, Auntie dearest," he said. "There's nowhere for you to hide from what you did. *You* were the one who made the mistake of not remembering that Sally Malone mattered."

That evening Kara sat in a rocking chair in the family room in Margaret and Robert MacAllister's home. Robert had been released from the hospital that morning and, despite Margaret's arguments against it, had insisted that a family meeting be held that night.

He had rested the entire day as a compromise to his wife, and the MacAllisters were now gathered to hear what Robert had to say regarding Sally and Andrew Malone.

Kara had volunteered to watch the children, since she already knew the story of what had taken place between Sally and her uncle Robert so many years before.

She reached down and stroked the dark silky hair of six-month-old Ryan Sharpe, who was sitting near her feet, happily chewing on a rattle.

The newly adopted Korean baby was seemingly adjusting to his new home and family with ease, and Kara was pleased for Hannah and Ted. Ryan's big sister, Patty, was, at four years old, in her mothering mode and was very protective of her new little brother.

"Aunt Kara?"

Kara looked up to see Matt and Noel, Andrea and John's oldest set of twins, standing before her.

"Yes?" she said, smiling at the inseparable pair.

"We were thinking," Matt said, "that since you don't have a baby, you could borrow our twins. Jeff and Kate are only two, and they still have to wear diapers at bedtime, but they're not so bad."

"They scream a lot, though," Noel said, frowning. "My daddy said they're having a case of the terrible twos, but I think that goes away when they have their birthday and they're three." She paused. "Maybe you'd better wait until they have their birthday. They really holler loud when they pitch a fit about stuff."

Kara laughed in delight. "What a generous offer you two are making. You certainly are grown up at seven years old. But I think you're right. Why don't we wait until Jeff and Kate are three, then I'll decide if I'd like to borrow them for a while."

"'Kay," Noel said. "But baby Ryan is the only other one that's little. I don't think Aunt Hannah and Uncle Ted will let you borrow him yet, 'cause they just got him. This is terrible, just terrible. Where are we going to get a baby for you?"

"Don't worry about it, sweetheart," Kara said, still smiling. "Getting a baby is something I need to do for myself. But I certainly thank you for being concerned about it."

"Maybe Teddy will let you borrow his dog, Scooter," Matt said. "Scooter is pretty cool."

"Don't be silly," Noel said to her brother. "Scooter isn't a baby. He's a dumb dog that ate Sarah's shoe just last week. Teddy said it was Sarah's fault 'cause she left her shoes on the floor, but Sarah said that she was three years old and she could leave her shoes wherever she wanted to, and then Scooter ate it and… No, Aunt Kara doesn't want to borrow Scooter."

"No, I don't," Kara said in mock seriousness, "because I sometimes forget and leave my shoes on the floor."

"Well," Noel said with a dramatic sigh, "I just don't know where we're going to get you a baby. My mommy said that she wished that you had a husband and a baby, and that Uncle Richard had a wife and a baby, so that everyone would have someone to love that was their very own. She said that was 'portant."

"Yes, it is," Kara said quietly. "It's very important, but it takes some people longer than others to find that special person to love. And sometimes, well, sometimes, a woman like me might get a baby to love, but not have a husband, too."

"No kidding?" Matt said, frowning. "No, that wouldn't work. Then the baby would only have a mom, but there wouldn't be a dad for it. That's not a good idea, Aunt Kara. There has to be a dad to do men stuff with. Jocy told me that's what it's called, what he and Uncle Jack do together—men stuff. I do men stuff with my dad. Even Noel does men stuff with our dad sometimes. That's 'portant, too."

Out of the mouths of babes, Kara thought wearily. It was as though Matt was echoing what she'd heard from Andrew on the subject. Whenever he'd spoken of the baby in the nursery being adopted, Andrew had placed great emphasis on that special little guy having a mother *and* a father, a complete family.

No, no, no, she wasn't going to start reexamining her decision to adopt the baby. She'd thought it all through and she knew it was the right thing to do. She wouldn't allow Andrew's opinions or those of a seven-year-old boy to jangle her, cause her to question her intentions.

"Well, if I had a baby, but no daddy for him," she said, "I could borrow daddies from the family, Matt. You'd loan my baby your daddy once in a while, wouldn't you?"

"I guess," Matt said, not sounding entirely certain. "Maybe. Sometimes."

"Wait! Wait!" Noel said, jumping up and down.

"What! What!" Kara said, laughing.

"Well, you see," Noel said, stopping her imitation of a pogo stick, "we all came over here tonight 'cause Grandpa is going to 'plain about our new uncle Andrew. We have a new uncle, Aunt Kara. I don't think you know that, but we really do.

"Anyway, he got lost or somethin' when he was little, but now he got found and he's our uncle. He doesn't have a wife and a baby, either. I asked my mom if he did and she said he didn't. So! Our new uncle Andrew can be your husband and the daddy for the baby you're going to go find someplace. There. It's all fixed."

"I..." Kara started, then inwardly fumed when sudden tears filled her eyes.

"Come on, Matt," Noel said, "I want to watch the video. It's getting to the good part where Ariel gets her voice back and can marry the prince guy."

"Dumb, dumb, dumb," Matt grumbled, but followed his sister across the room.

Kara leaned her head against the wooden slats of the rocker, moving the chair slowly with one foot.

It's all fixed, she thought dryly. Right. She'd just up and marry Andrew Malone, and there they'd be— Andrew, Kara and the precious miracle over in the hospital nursery, who was waiting for a nurturing home and parents to love him forever. There they'd be—a complete family.

Kara sighed.

Oh, the sweet innocence of being seven. Noel had

it all figured out now, and to her, that was that. A done deal. Aunt Kara would marry this new uncle Andrew, and all would be right with the world.

Well, at least she knew that Andrea and John planned to welcome Andrew into the MacAllister family, given that they had already told their children about their new uncle. She could only hope, for Andrew's sake, that the remainder of the family embraced him that quickly and warmly.

Providing, of course, that Andrew returned to Ventura to take his rightful place within the family.

And if Andrew did come back? What would that mean for her? She would have a lover, a no-demands, no-commitments affair with Andrew Malone?

Why did the image of that suddenly seem so empty, so hollow, so incredibly sad? She should be experiencing a rush of joy and anticipation at the mere idea of Andrew returning to her, but...

Kara lifted her head and swept her gaze over the room, drinking in the sight of the beautiful children gathered there.

They were all so loved, she thought. And they each had a mother *and* a father, were part of a unit, a family. They'd welcome her baby, her son, she knew they would, as would their parents, but her baby would have no father to call his own, could only borrow one on occasion from the MacAllister clan.

The memory of Andrew holding the baby in the nursery flitted through Kara's mind, and she smiled.

How marvelous they had looked together, she thought. The big strong man and the tiny child, who was held so safely in those powerful arms. Andrew would make a wonderful husband and father, be there for a wife, a son, a daughter, through the good times and bad.

They could weather whatever storms came their way, because they would stand together, an unbeatable force. Their home would overflow with love and laughter.

Fresh tears filled Kara's eyes and she sighed again, this time in sorrowful defeat.

There was nowhere to hide now, she thought miserably. Andrew had managed to chip away at her protective wall, brick by emotional brick.

She had shielded herself from love, from the frightening risk of losing her heart to a man, because she had been held fast in the iron grip of the past, in the clutches of a boy, Rick, who should have been dismissed from her mind years before.

She had brought that nightmare to the surface and was free of it for all time. It was over at long last.

But now she stood alone, vulnerable, exposed to heartache and loneliness. The truth was before her in crystal clarity, refusing to be ignored.

She was in love with Andrew Malone.

Two tears spilled onto Kara's cheeks and she dashed them away before any of the children saw that she was upset.

She was so foolish, she thought. She'd fallen in love with a man who never intended to love anyone, who wanted no part of a serious relationship, who didn't need a wife and family to be complete, fulfilled.

She was in love, truly in love, for the first time in

her life, and she was consumed by the ache of a heart that was shattering into a million pieces.

She had planned to tell the family tonight about her hopes to adopt the baby, since everyone was gathered together. But she didn't have the emotional fortitude to do it this evening. Her news would have to wait until another time, because she was a breath away from bursting into tears over her own stupidity, and lack of sophistication, and starry-eyed dreams about a future with Andrew.

A future that would never become a reality.

Because Andrew Malone did not and never would love her as she loved him.

Chapter 14

Just before eight o'clock that night, Andrew opened his apartment door to admit a beaming Clara, who had been announced by the doorman on duty downstairs. Clara breezed past Andrew, and he caught the heavy mingled odor of liquor and expensive perfume.

Clara dropped the armload of newspapers she had been carrying onto the coffee table and clasped her hands beneath her chin, smiling at Andrew as he walked forward slowly to stand by the end of the table.

"You beautiful clever boy," Clara said. "You outsmarted those high-and-mighty MacAllisters, didn't you? Oh, I am so proud of you, Andrew."

"I have no idea what you're talking about, Clara," Andrew said wearily.

"Don't be modest, dear," she said, settling into a chair. "It doesn't take a genius to figure out that

Robert MacAllister faked a heart attack when you confronted him at that ritzy party in order to create a smokescreen, a means to keep you away from him, unable to make your demands.''

Andrew shook his head and sat on one end of the sofa, frowning at his aunt.

''Please continue,'' he said dryly, waving one hand in the air. ''This is fascinating.''

''Well, it's easy to see what Robert did,'' Clara said, ''and, of course, with his money and power he was able to get the doctors to release phony medical updates on his condition and all that nonsense. But you put that marvelous mind of yours into action, didn't you, darling? Yes, you certainly did.''

Clara jumped to her feet and riffled through the newspapers, finally grabbing up the tabloid and holding it in both hands to show Andrew the picture of him and Kara in the lobby of the hospital.

''You seduced Kara MacAllister,'' Clara said, her eyes dancing with excitement, ''to get inside the MacAllister family that had circled the wagons around their mighty leader.''

Andrew struggled to keep his rising temper in check as Clara dropped the paper and returned to her chair. She crossed her legs and folded her hands in her lap.

''Tell me everything,'' she said. ''What did you settle for? Money? Oh, how delicious. I know you're quite wealthy, but a person can never have too much money. Or did you decide to go for a permanent place within the MacAllister family? That's what I'm hoping you did. That's where we belong.

''We'll move to Ventura and be part of high society, where the MacAllisters belong. Oh, I can hardly wait. Tell me, Andrew. What did you get?''

Andrew narrowed his eyes. ''The truth. That's what I *got*, Clara. The truth about what really happened between my mother and Robert MacAllister that long-ago summer.''

''That doesn't make sense,'' Clara said, frowning. ''You knew the truth before you left here. Robert took advantage of your sweet innocent mother, then abandoned her when she discovered that she was carrying his baby. What more could you possibly need to know?''

''Knock it off, Clara,'' Andrew said, lunging to his feet. ''I realize why what I said is going right over your head. You don't know what the word *truth* means. You've told so many lies over the years that you probably can't separate fact from fiction any longer.''

''What are you raving about, dear?'' Clara said, raising her eyebrows. ''Facts are facts. Sally raised you entirely alone with no emotional or financial support from Robert.''

''Because he didn't know I existed!'' Andrew yelled. ''Robert MacAllister had no idea that my mother was pregnant when that summer camp ended. She didn't know at that point, either, as far as that goes.

''You fed so many lies to me, Clara, kept them coming, festering inside of me. I never questioned what you were saying, never figured out the time-table of the ending of camp and when I was born. My birth date makes it impossible for anyone to have known that my mother was pregnant when the camp was over.''

''Don't be ridiculous.'' Clara smoothed the material of her skirt over her knee and averted her eyes from Andrew's angry stare. ''Sally most certainly did know she was pregnant. Some women can tell very early on, and Sally was one of them. She was even having morning sickness while we were still in those mountains.''

''You just don't quit, do you?'' Andrew said quietly, shaking his head. ''Clara, I know the truth. I know about the devious stories you concocted, then told to my mother and to Robert. Lies. All of them were lies. Both Robert and my mother believed you and felt betrayed and used by the other.''

''That's not true!'' Clara shouted. ''The Mac-Allisters got to you, didn't they? They brainwashed you with a farfetched fairy tale, then sent you packing empty-handed. My God, you're as gullible as your mother was.''

Clara took a deep breath, then pressed her hands to her flushed cheeks.

''I've got to calm down,'' she said. ''Yes, all right, I'm fine now. It's not too late to salvage this situation, Andrew. You simply drive back down to Ventura and inform Robert MacAllister that you've thought it all through and you're no longer buying his phony explanation that he didn't know that Sally was pregnant. Yes, that's the ticket. Thank goodness one of us is thinking clearly.

''You can threaten to give the press all the juicy intimate details of what took place between you and that—whatever her name is—Kara, the MacAllister woman you seduced. Oh, it's perfect and it will do the trick. I know it will.''

"You couldn't stand it, could you?" Andrew said, his voice low and steely edged. "When you realized that a fine young man had fallen in love with your sister, with sweet innocent Sally, you became incensed, made up your evil mind to destroy what those two had together, because you couldn't bear the thought that someone loved Sally and no one loved you."

"That's absolutely crazy," Clara said, meeting Andrew's gaze again. "I was attempting to protect my poor little sister from—"

"I know what you did," Andrew hollered. "You shattered loves and lives that summer, sentenced my mother to a lifetime of loneliness and me to growing up without a father. Admit it, Clara. Damn it, for once in your liquor-drenched life, would you tell the truth?"

"I won't listen to any more of this malarkey," Clara said, getting to her feet. "When you come to your senses and realize that the MacAllisters have twisted your mind with *their* lies, I'll accept your apology for these terrible accusations. Then I'll help you make plans to rectify the situation in Ventura, get what is coming to us...to you."

"Sit down," Andrew said. "You're not leaving here yet."

Clara did as he asked, the color draining from her face.

"I don't like the tone of voice you're using with me, Andrew. I deserve some respect here," Clara said, her voice not quite steady. "I am your aunt, the one who raised you after our beloved Sally died. I'm willing to forgive you for falsely accusing me of things I certainly didn't do, but I demand that you speak to me in a pleasant manner."

"How do you live with yourself?" Andrew said, dragging a hand through his hair. "Actually you can't, can you? You drink to drown the guilty memories of what you did so many years ago.

"I want you out of my home and out of my life, Clara. You've done enough damage to last three lifetimes, and I never want to see you again. As gentle and loving as my mother was, she might have forgiven you, but I'm not Sally and I will never forgive you.

"Actually I feel sorry for you, Clara. You're pitiful. You don't have a clue how to be happy, and you can't bear it when people around you are. That's sick. It's sad and it's sick."

"Don't you dare feel sorry for me!" Clara shrieked, getting to her feet. "I was the beautiful Malone sister. I was so pretty and outgoing, had men flocking around me from the time I was a young teenager. I was the one who turned heads, who deserved to be loved, not your mousy little insipid mother. She didn't even wear makeup or know how to dress properly.

"Robert MacAllister should have fallen in love with *me* that summer. I spotted him the first day of camp and made up my mind that he would fall in love with me, that I would become a MacAllister, have everything their world offered. *Me*. It was supposed to be mine, all of it. Sally stole what was rightfully mine!"

Andrew nodded slowly. "And so, eaten alive by jealousy and rage, you set out to destroy what Sally and Robert had together."

"Yes!" Clara curled her hands into tight fists at her sides. "Oh, they were so gullible, the two of them. They believed every word I said, even allowed me to comfort each of them in turn. I also managed to keep them apart so they couldn't possibly talk it through, realize that what I had told them was all lies. I had brains along with my beauty, you see, Andrew. I accomplished exactly what I set out to do."

"But you couldn't stop there, could you?" Andrew said. "When I was growing up, you'd get me alone, poison my mind against my father, cause me to vow never to love because look what love had done to my mother."

"I was afraid you might convince your mother to tell you who your father was," Clara said, a frantic edge to her voice. "Afraid you'd seek him out and discover the truth. Afraid Robert might make a place for you in his life before you were old enough to understand that I deserved to be right beside you when he did. I do deserve that, Andrew. I do. I do.

"When you became a man, you were so independent, moved through life as though you didn't need anyone special, anyone close to you. I was terrified that if I told you your father's identity, you'd shrug and dismiss it as unimportant, do nothing to get what was rightfully ours—yours.

"Then the story came out in the newspapers regarding the MacAllister reunion, and I was so furious about how much Robert had that I threw caution to the wind and decided the time had come for you to know who your father was. I was right to do that, Andrew, I was. You went there, to Ventura, confronted Robert and... But now they've turned you against me. It's not fair. It's not."

"Ah, Clara, you're so pathetic," Andrew said, fatigue in his voice. "I don't have the energy to be angry at you anymore, I guess. It's pointless. You need help, professional help. I'm just grateful that my mother never learned what an evil sick person you are. She loved you, Clara."

"And I hated her!" Clara yelled. "She always landed on her feet, Miss Syrupy-Sweet Sally. She always found the nauseating bright side to every situation like a damned Pollyanna.

"My God, our parents disowned her when they discovered that Sally was pregnant, threw her out of the house to fend for herself. Did Sally crumble and cry? Oh, no, not her. She lived in a horrible little room in a boardinghouse and worked as a clerk in a drugstore for pennies.

"Then you were born. 'Oh, look at my beautiful son,' Sally said to me. 'This is the happiest day of my life, Clara. I am so blessed, Clara.' She nearly starved to death raising you, but she thought life was wonderful."

Tears filled Clara's eyes and spilled onto her pale cheeks.

"And somehow...it was wonderful," she said, sobbing. "You and Sally were so happy together, acted as though you lived in a mansion, instead of a shabby apartment where one of you had to sleep on the sofa. You had nothing, *nothing*, yet it was as though...as though you two had everything.''

"We had what counted, Clara," Andrew said quietly. "We had unconditional love and endless trust in each other. We were a team, stood united, together.''

"And I had no one to love me," Clara said, nearly choking on her tears. "I tried to be happy. I married men who were supposed to make me happy but... Damn it, it wasn't fair. Even after Sally died and I moved you into my home, gave you decent clothes for the first time in your life, the finest food, expensive gifts, you didn't love me. Not even then.''

"You can't buy love, Clara," Andrew said. "You have to earn it, give as much as you receive. You've never done that.''

Clara closed the distance between them and gripped his shirt with both hands. Tears tracked paths through the heavy makeup on her cheeks, and dark smudges of mascara were beneath her eyes.

"Don't leave me alone, all alone," she said, crying openly. "I can't bear to be alone anymore. Please, Andrew, tell me you didn't mean it when you said you never wanted to see me again. I'll kill myself. Yes, that's what I'll do. I'll commit suicide and it will be on your conscience for the rest of your life.''

Andrew grasped his aunt's wrists and pulled her hands away from his shirt.

"I won't turn my back on you if you do what I ask, Clara," he said. "You have one chance. One.''

"Anything. I'll do anything you want.''

"Check into a rehabilitation clinic. Get help for

your drinking problem. Tell them the truth about everything you've done and allow them to show you the way to be happy, how to like yourself.''

Clara's eyes widened in horror. "You can't be serious. Bare my soul to total strangers? They'd take Sally's side, I know they would. They wouldn't understand how everything I should have had was taken away from me by other people, and I simply took steps to attempt to set things to rights.

"As for my drinking? I enjoy a drink, several drinks. That doesn't mean I'm an alcoholic who needs to go to some drab place and get dried out. I could quit drinking this very moment if I chose to. You're asking too much, Andrew. It's ridiculous.''

"Fine. Then don't ever expect to see or speak to me again. It's up to you.''

"Well, I...'' Clara wrung her hands. "I really could use a vacation. This whole situation has been very stressful for me. Some of those clinics are very posh, like resorts. I suppose I could go to one of those and... I'll play your silly game, Andrew, if that's what it takes to get you to come to your senses and realize that I deserve a place in your life.''

"You'll have to make it clear wherever you go that I'm to be kept fully apprised of your progress there,'' he said, narrowing his eyes. "Understand?''

"Yes, whatever,'' she said, waving one hand in the air. "I'm leaving now. You've upset me terribly and I'm exhausted. I may have made some mistakes in the past, Andrew, but you've treated me horribly here tonight. I'll be waiting for your apology for that.''

Clara rushed from the apartment and Andrew sank

onto the sofa, leaning back his head and closing his eyes.

He was totally drained, he realized. He wouldn't be able to move a muscle even if the building was on fire. But, well, he'd done it. He'd tackled the first step. Whether or not he ever saw Clara again was up to her.

Next step? Hell, he couldn't even think about that now. Not tonight. Maybe in the light of the new day he'd be able to think clearly.

Yes…maybe…tomorrow…he'd know what…to do.

"Oh, Kara," Mary MacAllister said, her eyes misting with tears. "He's such a beautiful baby."

Kara smiled and nodded as she stood next to the rocking chair in the hospital nursery, watching as her mother held the infant.

"I know," Kara said. "I love him so much, Mom. This waiting to hear the judge's decision about whether or not I can adopt him is so difficult. I don't know what I'll do if my petition is denied."

"They wouldn't dare deny it," Ralph MacAllister said. "I'll go to that judge myself if I have to, tell him that my daughter will make a fantastic mother, and unless he has sawdust for brains, he'll realize that. That's a MacAllister you're holding there, Mary. Guaranteed."

"Oh, I love you," Kara said, rising on tiptoe to kiss her father on the cheek. "Both of you. You're the best parents in the world."

"That's true," Ralph said. "We're dandy grandparents, too."

Kara sighed. "I was planning on telling the whole family at once about my plans to adopt this little miracle, but the opportunity just hasn't presented itself because of what happened to Uncle Robert. But since you decided it was best to fly back to Florida tonight, I couldn't let you leave without meeting my son. Oh, please, God, let him be my son."

"He will be," Mary said. "I feel it in my heart. He's yours, Kara, is meant to be yours. I truly believe that. He...he...he... When are you going to give this darling a name?"

"Not until I know he's truly mine," Kara said. "I just can't bring myself to do that until I'm certain I'm going to be his mother." She paused. "You do realize that there may be some problems down the road due to his being addicted to drugs when he was born."

"So?" Ralph said. "Deal with them when and if they happen. That's simple enough. Just take it one day at a time, enjoy your baby and don't worry about what might or might not come to be."

"I'll remember that, I promise," Kara said. "Oh, I'm going to miss you two so much. It's been wonderful to have you here during these weeks."

"We've enjoyed it, too, dear," Mary said, "but we feel we should get out of the way. Margaret and Robert don't need extra people sleeping under their roof while Robert is recuperating. We've extended our visit as it is because of what happened, but it's time to go home. You will call us the moment you receive word on the judge's decision, won't you?"

"Of course I will," Kara said. "Listen, you can tell Aunt Margaret and Uncle Robert about the baby, as well as any other MacAllisters you might see before you leave. I think we've had enough family meetings to last us a while. I'll let word of this event of mine pass from one person to the next. That's fine.''

"Well, you know there will be a big MacAllister-clan baby shower for you once you receive the official word that he's yours," Mary said. "Oh, how I hate to miss that party. I adore baby showers. And that one will be for my own daughter and grandson. Mmm. Florida is seeming very far away all of a sudden. Jack gave us our grandson Joey and there's another baby coming along there and—''

"Hot damn, we're moving back to Ventura," Ralph said, rubbing his hands together. "I knew you'd see the light eventually, Mary. It took babies to do it, but I'm ready to pack up and leave Florida, haul ourselves back here where we belong.''

"Which would not mean you'd start going to the office of MacAllister Architects every day, Ralph MacAllister," Mary said sternly. "You and I will discuss this once we are in Florida, Ralph. There will be rules laid out and promises made.''

"I'm in trouble," Ralph said, smiling at Kara.

"You're definitely in trouble," Kara said, matching his smile.

"Kara, dear," Mary said, continuing to rock the sleeping baby, "there's something else on my mind that I must address before we board that plane.''

Kara sighed. "Andrew Malone.''

"Well, yes, my darling, Andrew Malone," Mary said.

"You saw the story and the photograph in that awful newspaper, didn't you?" Kara said.

"Yes," Mary said. "Jack brought us that tabloid so we wouldn't be caught off guard if someone made reference to it or... But even before that, it was apparent that you and Andrew were spending time together.

"Richard was having a fit, then finally calmed down and...well, the whole family is aware that something is...how shall I put this?—going on between you and Andrew."

"Now, Mary," Ralph said, "don't get nosy." He looked at Kara. "All right, young lady, what's going on between you and Andrew Malone?"

I'm in love with Andrew, Mom and Dad, Kara thought. *How's that for a bulletin? I'm in love for the first time in my life, and I'm so miserable I could cry for a week because the man of my heart will never come to love me in return. Never.*

"Oh, heavens," Kara said, striving for a breezy tone of voice, which didn't quite materialize. "It's a big hoopla over nothing. I just felt that Andrew was isolated, all alone, during the crisis with Uncle Robert, so I befriended him, and everyone jumped to ridiculous conclusions, including that tacky reporter, and anyway, Andrew returned to Santa Maria and no one knows if he's even coming back...if any of us...will ever see...him again. So, that's that and..."

"You're in love with Andrew," Mary said. "That's as clear as the nose on your pretty face, Kara darling."

"Yep," Ralph said, nodding and stroking his chin with one hand.

"Yes," Kara said, her eyes filling with instant tears. "But it's hopeless and I really don't wish to discuss it. Please. I just can't talk about it right now."

"Honey," Mary said, "it may seem hopeless at the moment for reasons you certainly don't have to explain to us. But don't underestimate the power of love, of its ability to solve what seem to be insurmountable difficulties."

Kara sniffled and shook her head. "No, it's definitely hopeless. Trust me on this. I do not have a future with Andrew Malone. I'm going to raise my son alone and be a happy fulfilled woman and mother. I'll be fine, you'll see, just fine."

"Mmm," Mary said, then exchanged frowns with her husband.

"We're here if you need us, pumpkin," Ralph said. "Don't forget that."

"I know," Kara said, "and I love you both more than I can ever begin to tell you."

"Want me to get your brothers to go deck Malone?" Ralph said, raising his eyebrows.

"No, thank you, Dad," Kara said, smiling through her tears.

"Well, the offer stands. Okay, Mary, my turn to hold that bundle for a while. For mercy's sake, Kara, give that kid a name."

"I will," she said softly, "when the time is right, when I know he's really my son. Legally, not just in my heart like he is now. When...when he's truly a MacAllister."

Chapter 15

During the following week, Andrew kept himself as busy as he possibly could. On the days when paperwork didn't need his attention at the office, he donned old clothes and his hard hat and worked side by side with the men on his various construction sites.

He made it a point during breaks and lunch to chat with the guys, ask them about their families, girlfriends, whatever might be on their minds.

While the men where surprised and, therefore, hesitant at first to open up to the boss, Andrew's undivided attention soon had them competing for his time and attention.

When one of the construction crew tentatively broached the subject of the past articles in the newspapers, Andrew found that he was comfortable saying that Robert MacAllister was, indeed, his father,

a fact he had just recently discovered. Since he and
the Ventura MacAllisters had given the press nothing
more than "no comment" replies to their questions,
the reporters had moved on to fresher stories, leaving
Andrew in peace, to think. The men accepted his
short explanation with nods and shrugs, and that had
been that.

Andrew thoroughly enjoyed the camaraderie and
found himself looking forward to updates on what
was happening in the men's lives.

When a nervous young crew member left work
one day with the intention of proposing to his girlfriend that night, Andrew was among those waiting
to hear the results the next morning, and he cheered
with the others when the grinning man approached
them with a thumbs-up.

He was practicing the role he might have as part
of a large family, Andrew knew, pretending he had
taken his place within the MacAllister clan. And he
liked it very very much.

He was also acutely aware that he had no idea if
the MacAllisters would choose to accept him in their
midst, didn't know if Robert had explained what had
happened between him and Sally Malone, or what
the reaction of the other MacAllisters had been.

Kara would know how things stood. But as much
as Andrew wished to hear her voice, he exerted a
great deal of self-control and didn't allow himself to
pick up the telephone to call her, not while he was
still mired in confusion.

His days were busy and fulfilling, but the nights
were long and empty, his sleep coming in snatches,
as he tossed and turned and thought about Kara.

When he did manage to sleep, he dreamed of her, sensual dreams that often caused him to jerk awake drenched in sweat.

He loved her. Ah, man, how he loved Kara MacAllister. But the hopelessness of ever having a future with her, the chilling knowledge that it would never come to be, caused a knot to tighten in his gut and an icy wave of loneliness to consume him again and again.

Sitting in his office late at night, one week to the day since the confrontation with Clara, whom he had not heard from since, Andrew decided it was time to return to Ventura. To stay away longer would be not to deal with the very real possibility that the MacAllister family members beyond Robert, Margaret...and Kara wanted nothing whatsoever to do with him.

He now knew he wanted to be a part of that clan, albeit in a limited manner due to the miles between them but counted as one of them just the same.

At nearly forty years old he was going to have, for the first time, brothers, sisters, cousins, nieces, nephews...and a father. A father who was wealthy, powerful, highly respected as a person and a businessman, and who had a moral code that would make any son proud.

Father, Andrew mused, sinking back in the leather chair behind his desk. He moved the word and its meaning through his mind, then allowed it to travel to touch his heart, his very soul, warming him as it journeyed.

He, himself, wished to be a father. He truly did. He wanted to be Kara's husband and the father of the children they would create together. He wanted a child to call son or daughter, a real house, instead of an apartment.

And a dog. He mustn't forget the dog. They'd name it Duke or Butch or...

Ah, hell, he thought, dragging both hands down his face, why was he torturing himself like this? He would never be part of the picture he was painting in his mind.

Kara would never agree to marry him, would not allow herself to acknowledge whatever feelings she might have for him, because she was adamant never to become involved in a serious relationship, a forever love.

"Damn it," he said aloud, shaking his head.

So, okay, he would get Harry to take over the reins again, then drive down to Ventura to spend some time with Robert.

And Kara?

What should he do about Kara MacAllister?

Stay as far away from her as possible? Not seek her out, escape from having to deal with knowing how much he loved her and how out of his reach she really was? Take what he could get in the form of a no-strings, no-commitment affair with her? Make love with her while being certain he didn't *declare* his love for her?

He didn't know. He couldn't sit here, a hundred miles away from Kara, and form a plan regarding her. He would just have to do what felt right when he was back in Ventura, close to her. He'd—

The sound of the outer door to the office opening, then being shut, brought Andrew from his complicated thoughts. He stared at the doorway to his office, wondering if Harry had gone out for ice cream again for his pregnant wife and had stopped by to shoot the breeze for a bit.

Andrew's eyes widened and he got to his feet quickly as three tall and well-built men entered his office. Three very familiar men.

"Good evening, Andrew," one of the men said, no readable expression on his face. The trio halted halfway across the large expanse, spreading out in a line. "I'm Michael MacAllister, and these—" he swept one arm toward the other two "—are my brothers, Ryan and Forrest."

Andrew came around to the front of his desk, folded his arms over his chest and nodded. The men advanced to stand about three feet in front of him. Andrew tensed his muscles and shifted his weight slightly to rest more on the balls of his feet.

"You didn't return to Ventura," Michael said, "so we came to you."

"And?" Andrew said.

"Our father explained what took place between him and your mother," Michael went on, "and made it clear that you're our brother or half brother."

"So it would seem," Andrew said, his gaze riveted on Michael.

"Since I'm the oldest," Michael said, "or I was until you showed up, I get to do this."

With that, Michael drew back his fist and delivered a stunning blow to Andrew's jaw. Andrew staggered backward from the painful impact, nearly sprawling onto his desk. He straightened, steadied himself, shook his head slightly to clear it, then curled his hands into tight fists at his sides.

"Okay," he said, his eyes narrowed. "If that's the way you want it to be, it's fine with me. Come on, all three of you, but you better have packed a lunch because I'm not going down easily."

One silent second ticked by, then two, then three. The brothers exchanged glances, then nodded at each other.

"You'll do," Michael said, a grin breaking out across his face, "as a MacAllister." He stepped forward and extended his right hand. "Welcome to the family...brother."

Andrew eyed Michael warily, looked at his hand, his face, his hand again, then finally grasped Michael's hand with his own.

"You've got a strange way of accepting someone into the fold," Andrew said, unable to curb his own smile.

"That was partly a payback for the manner that you chose to make your existence known," Ryan said. "You could have picked a better way than crashing a family gathering. But we're also just checking you out. Hey, do you want me to arrest this jerk for popping you?"

Andrew shook hands with Ryan, then Forrest.

"No," Andrew said, still smiling. "Don't haul him in, Ryan. We'll just leave it that I owe him one and let him worry about it."

The three hooted with laughter, then sobered in the next moment.

"Our father, *your* father," Forrest said, "wants to see you. He's starting to get stressed out, wondering if you're going to come back to Ventura, and he's supposed to stay level, not get uptight about anything. We want to know—now—what you intend to do.''

''I've had a great deal to think about,'' Andrew said. ''I'm sorry if I caused your—our father to become upset. I haven't had much experience in being part of a family and... Anyway, I'd made up my mind to go back to Ventura, get to know Robert better, even though I had no idea how the rest of the family felt about me, the fact that I exist.''

He rubbed his still-aching jaw.

''Now I know,'' he said, smiling. ''Anyone else waiting to take a shot at me?''

''Nope,'' Michael said, then flexed his right hand. ''You've got a MacAllister jaw, that's for damn sure. I nearly busted my hand.''

''It would appear,'' Ryan said, ''that you've left some unfinished business with our cousin, Kara. We haven't seen much of her sunny smile since you left town. We really miss Kara's smile. Just thought I'd mention it.''

''Yeah, well,'' Michael said, ''*you're* going to deck him if he doesn't set things to rights with Kara, Ryan.'' He peered at his hand. ''I'm now officially among the walking wounded here.''

''You're such a wimp, Michael,'' Ryan said, shaking his head. ''So? Ready to go, Andrew?''

''I have to make arrangements here. I've got a lot of projects in the works. I should be able to be in Ventura tomorrow evening.''

''Fair enough,'' Forrest said. ''We'll tell our father to expect to see you the following day. That way, he won't insist on staying up longer than he should to-morrow night. Okay?''

"Sounds good," Andrew said, nodding.

"And Kara?" Ryan said. "What do we tell her?"

"You're a real nag, do you know that?" Michael said. "I don't know how Deedee puts up with you. Jeez."

"She loves me, idiot," Ryan said, glaring at Michael. "And besides that, I happen to be a wonderful guy, so put a cork in it." He looked at Andrew again. "Well?"

"Don't say anything to Kara about my returning to Ventura," Andrew said quietly. "I'll handle that situation myself."

"Got it. Let's hit the long road," Michael said. "There's a hundred miles between my lovely wife, my soft bed and an ice pack for my hand. We're outta here, gentlemen and Forrest. Say, you up for a game of touch football sometime, Andrew?"

"Sure," Andrew said, nodding.

"Good," Michael said. "You're on my team."

"Hey, wait just a minute here," Forrest said. "You can't just snag him for your team."

"I certainly can," Michael said. "It's based on seniority privilege. Andrew and I are the oldest MacAllisters. Eat your heart out, Forrest. See you soon, Andrew."

"Yes," Andrew said. "Soon."

As the three men left the office, Andrew sat on the edge of the desk and replayed the entire scene in his mind. A slow grin crept across his face, and he once again massaged his jaw.

"I'll do," he said, nodding in approval, "as a

MacAllister. And I'm even on a team to play touch football.''

In the next moment he frowned.

Kara had been unhappy since he'd left Ventura? Wasn't smiling her sunny smile? What did that mean? She missed him? Wished he was there, close to her, holding her, kissing her, making love with her? Talking, sharing, caring?

Realizing she was in love with him and rejoicing in that momentous fact?

"Don't go crazy, Malone," he said with a snort of self-disgust. "It isn't going to happen. Not now, not later, not ever."

The next evening, after indulging in a long leisurely bubble bath, Kara dried herself with a fluffy pink towel, then hummed as she smoothed rich, lilac-scented lotion over her entire body.

She wrapped the towel around herself like a sarong that fell to midthigh, then tucked the end between her breasts to keep it in place. She smiled as she realized she was humming a lullaby, then turned to look at her reflection in the mirror above the sink.

"Hello, Mommy," she said, still smiling. "How are things up on cloud nine, Dr. MacAllister, mother of a beautiful baby boy?"

She hugged herself in pure joy as she relived the telephone conversation of a few hours ago that was going to change her life forever.

She'd been alone in her office, catching up on patients' charts after Lucy had gone home for the night. Her pager had buzzed, and as she saw the number on the tiny screen, her heart immediately began to beat in a wild tempo. With a visibly shaking hand she'd lifted the receiver and pressed the numbers.

"Answer, answer," she'd whispered, as she heard the ringing on the other end.

"Hello?"

"Mindy? It's Kara."

"Oh, Kara, I'm glad you got back to me so quickly," Mindy said. "I'm still down at the courthouse. The judge's secretary pulled me aside and said that the judge was planning on working late and getting some cases taken care of. She knew your file was in the stack on his desk. I've been pacing around here like I was in a maternity waiting room." She laughed. "Which, in actuality, I was."

"What do you mean?"

"Kara, Kara, Kara, you've been approved to adopt your baby! I have the documents in my briefcase even as we speak. Congratulations, Mother. You have a son."

"I...oh...I..." Kara said, then burst into tears.

"I love it," Mindy said. "You're so typical it's wonderful. Have a good happy cry, then start making a list of what you need to buy for your kid. I know you've been too superstitious to set up a nursery. I've got to dash. My family is waiting dinner for me. I'm sincerely happy for you, Kara. You're going to be a fantastic mother. He's a lucky little boy. Bye."

"Thank you, thank you, thank you," Kara had said, sniffling. "Oh, and goodbye."

Kara walked slowly out of the bathroom, then stopped and looked heavenward.

"Thank you," she whispered. "I'll be the very best mother I can possibly be."

A knock on her apartment door caused her to gasp in surprise.

She wasn't expecting anyone, she thought. She'd spent ages on the telephone sharing her happy news with her parents and as many of the MacAllisters she could reach. They'd all been thrilled for her. Andrea had said that the first order of business was to plan a baby shower for Kara-the-New-Mama, but none of them had said anything about coming over to celebrate with her tonight.

The knock was repeated and Kara hurried across the living room, acutely aware of her skimpy attire. She looked through the peephole on the door and her eyes widened.

"Andrew?" she said, her breath catching. "Oh, dear heaven, it's Andrew."

She slipped off the chain, unlocked the door and opened it enough to peer around the edge.

"Andrew?" she said, feeling like a parrot echoing herself.

"Hi," he said, shoving his hands into his trouser pockets. "I know I should have called first, but...I wanted, needed, to see you."

"Oh." Kara glanced down at her towel-clad body and mentally shrugged. Andrew had seen her in less than this, had visually and physically traced every inch of her body. It was a tad late for modesty around this man. This man, who she loved so much and who would never return that love in kind. "Come in."

Kara stepped back and opened the door wider so that Andrew could enter the apartment. He walked past her and she closed and locked the door.

"I..." Andrew started, turning to look at her. He

stopped speaking as he slid his gaze over her from head to toe. "Ho-boy, I definitely should have telephoned before barging in here. You...you are so beautiful, Kara, and I know what's beneath that towel and..." He shook his head. "Whew."

"Well, so be it," Kara said, smiling. "It's... wonderful to see you, Andrew." *I love you, Andrew.* "I missed you."

"I missed you, too," he said. "I really did."

"Does your being back here in Ventura mean that you've decided to become a part of the MacAllister family?" Kara said.

Andrew nodded. "Yes. I made that decision even though I didn't know how anyone beyond you, Margaret and Robert felt about it. I didn't intend to push myself on the others if they chose not to accept me. Then Michael, Ryan and Forrest paid me a little visit last night." He rubbed his jaw with one hand. "They welcomed me into the family."

"Did one of them punch you?" Kara said, none too quietly.

"Hey, don't get excited," he said, raising both hands in a gesture of peace. "It's okay, it really is. It was a...a guy thing, you know what I mean?"

"Men are so weird," Kara said, rolling her eyes heavenward.

"Mmm." Andrew dragged one hand over the back of his neck. "You're killing me here, Kara. Either go put some clothes on or..."

"Or what?" Kara said, smiling sweetly.

Oh, what was she doing? she thought frantically. She should march into the bedroom and get dressed.

Her affair with Andrew had to end, because it was going nowhere but down a direct path to heartbreak.

But she wanted Andrew, wanted to make exquisite love with him. This was such a special night in her life. She had just become an honest-to-goodness mother.

It was foolish, she knew that, but she wanted to share this momentous event with the man she loved, the man she wished would have the role of father to her new baby son.

"Are you saying that this towel I'm wearing is...disturbing you, Andrew?" she said.

"That's putting it a tad mildly," he said, chuckling and shaking his head.

"Well, then, it just has to go," Kara said.

She flipped the end of the towel from between her breasts, and the fluffy material fell to the floor, leaving her standing naked before Andrew.

He opened his mouth to speak, realized there was no air in his lungs and drew a deep breath, letting it out slowly.

"Well..." He cleared his throat. "Hell."

Andrew closed the distance between him and Kara, wrapped one arm around her waist and pulled her against his aroused body, his mouth melting over hers.

Kara raised her arms to encircle his neck, and her lashes drifted down as she savored his kiss.

The kiss was hungry, urgent, speaking of too many long lonely nights of aching for each other, missing each other, wanting each other.

Without breaking the kiss, Andrew lowered Kara to the plush carpeting on the floor, lying half on and half off her as his tongue delved into the sweet darkness of her mouth to find her tongue.

Kara shifted her hands to push gently against his shoulders, and he raised his head to meet her gaze, his breathing labored.

"You have too many clothes on, Mr. Malone," she said close to his lips.

"You've got that straight," he said. "Don't move. I'll be right back."

"I can't move," she said, smiling. "You dissolved my bones. Hurry, Andrew. I want you so much."

Andrew shed his clothes, took steps to protect Kara, then returned to capture her mouth once more. They were on fire. Within moments they were unable to wait any longer.

Andrew moved over Kara, entered her and began a thundering rhythm that she matched, raising her hips to draw him closer.

They were flung up and away, seconds apart, each calling for the other in reverent whispers. Each declaring their love for the other in silent messages from passion-laden hearts and minds.

Andrew collapsed against Kara, his energy spent. He rolled onto his back, taking her with him as he wrapped his arms around her. She stretched out on top of him and raised her head to meet his gaze.

"Was that tacky?" he said, smiling at her. "I mean, I could have carried you to the bed, you know. But when you dropped that towel…"

"I'm wicked," she said, matching his smile. "Naughty me."

"Fantastic you," he said. "Damn, you feel good on top of me. We fit together so perfectly."

"I noticed that. Am I smushing you?"

"Never, Dr. MacAllister."

Mommy MacAllister, Kara thought. The time had come to share her glorious news with Andrew.

"Let's go into the bedroom," she said. "I have something I want to tell you."

"Okay," Andrew said. "If I can find the strength to move, that is."

When they entered Kara's bedroom, she swept back the blankets on the bed.

"How's that little guy in the nursery doing?" Andrew said, settling onto the bed and patting the space next to him.

Kara's head snapped up and she stared at Andrew for a long moment, having the irrational thought that he was reading her mind. She shook her head slightly, then joined him on the bed, snuggling close to him, their heads resting on the same pillow. They shifted so they could see each other.

"The baby?" she said. "He's fine, doing really well. He's gained some more weight and it appears that he's fully withdrawn from the drugs that were in his system."

"Good. That's good." Andrew paused. "I remember standing outside the nursery window on New Year's Eve, which seems like an eternity ago, watching what I thought was a mother who had come from a party to feed her baby. I didn't know it was you, because your face was in shadow. I was deeply moved by that scene, more than I can say. It filled me with a foreign warmth, because it was such a lovely picture and...I'm rambling."

"Andrew, I—"

"Then you came out of the nursery," he went on, "and I realized that I had it all wrong. You weren't a mother who had wanted to spend the beginning of the New Year with her child. You were just helping out by feeding the baby while you waited for word of your uncle's condition. But I still can't forget how I felt from what I first saw. It was a very beautiful picture."

Tears misted Kara's eyes, and her heart nearly burst with love as she listened to Andrew's words.

"That picture," she said softly, blinking away her tears, "was real. It was exactly what you perceived it to be, Andrew."

He frowned in confusion. "What do you mean?"

"I received word earlier this evening," she said, her eyes beginning to sparkle with joy. "The judge approved my petition to adopt the... Oh, Andrew, that darling baby, that special little miracle you gave the baseball outfit to is...is my son."

"What?"

"I'm going to adopt him," Kara rushed on. "I'm his mother now. I'm so happy, so grateful, so... I can't even describe how I'm feeling."

"Wait a minute here." Andrew slid his arm from beneath Kara and sat up, turning his head to look back down at her. "You're adopting the baby in the nursery? The one I held, fed, gave the baseball uniform to?"

"Yes," she said, sitting up next to him. "The judge approved my petition to adopt him just hours ago. Isn't that wonderful? I'm a mother, Andrew. Can you believe this?"

"No," he said, moving off the bed. "No, I can't

believe it." He spun around to look at Kara. "You're intentionally creating a situation where that boy will grow up without a father because you want to be a mother?"

"What are you saying?" Kara said, the color draining from her face. "What are you so angry about?"

"Hey, I understand that there are women out there raising kids on their own due to divorce or death or whatever," Andrew said, his voice rising. "But to purposely deprive that child of a father because you know full well you never intend to marry?

"That's selfish, Kara. It's selfish and wrong, and no, I can't believe you'd do such a thing to that boy." He dragged one hand through his hair. "I grew up without a father. I know what it's like. What you're doing isn't fair to that baby, Kara."

"Not fair?" Kara said, the volume of her voice matching Andrew's as she grabbed the sheet to cover her breasts. "I'm going to love him with all my heart, be the best mother I can possibly be and—"

"When you have time." Andrew planted his hands flat on the bed and leaned forward to speak close to Kara's face. "You have a very demanding career, in case you've forgotten due to the glowing maternal mode you're in. What do you plan to do— fit the kid in around the edges of your schedule, hand him over to an expensive nanny to raise?"

"How dare you—"

"No," Andrew interrupted. "How dare *you* do this to that baby? He deserves a mother *and* a father. Even the most dedicated single mother in the world—and I know this is true, because Sally Malone was one...can't be both. It just doesn't work. The kid comes up short time after time. I lived it, Kara. I know what I'm talking about.''

"Your mother was all alone when she raised you," Kara yelled. "I'm part of a huge supportive family, remember? My son will have plenty of father figures in his life, who will be there for him when he needs a man's touch and wisdom and advice.

"And as far as my being too busy to devote enough time to my baby, I plan to... No, damn you, Andrew Malone, I have no intention of justifying to you my decision to adopt that baby. He's *mine*. *My* son. This has absolutely nothing to do with you."

Andrew straightened from his bent-over position on the bed, feeling as though he'd been kicked in the gut. A chill coursed through him, and his voice was raspy when he spoke again.

"No, it doesn't, does it?" he said. "This has nothing at all to do with me. I'm just the guy you sleep with when I happen to be in town. I'm not really involved with you, let alone with your...your son. You're right. I'm out of line.

"But this ends it between us, Kara. I can't see you anymore as your lover. As one of the MacAllisters? Yeah, I suppose we'll bump into each other, play a little touch football—what the heck, huh? I...I've got to go. I hope you and your...son will be very happy together. He's a neat little guy."

"Andrew?" Kara said, a frantic edge to her voice. "Wait. Can't we discuss this calmly, rationally? Andrew, please, I—"

"There's nothing more to say."

Andrew strode from the room, and Kara covered

her mouth with trembling hands to stifle the sob that threatened to escape from her throat. A few minutes later she cringed as she heard the apartment door slam behind an exiting Andrew.

She sank back against the pillow and gave way to her tears, feeling as though her heart was splintering into a million pieces that could never be put back together again.

Chapter 16

Andrew rolled onto his back on the bed in his hotel
room, swearing viciously as the sheets wrapped
around him. He yanked free of the clinging material,
then sighed wearily.

A quick glance at the clock told him it was nearly
3 a.m., and he had not been able to doze, let alone
fall into a deep restorative sleep, since he'd gone to
bed hours before.

The raging voices in his mind were tormenting
him, forcing him to relive the scene with Kara earlier
that night over and over.

*You're intentionally creating a situation where
that boy will grow up without a father, because you
want to be a mother?*

*That's selfish, Kara. It's selfish and wrong. Selfish
and wrong. Selfish...selfish...selfish...*

I'm going to love him with all my heart, be the best mother I can possibly be.

Selfish...selfish...

He deserves a mother and a father.

My son will have plenty of father figures in his life, who will be there for him when he needs a man's touch and wisdom and advice.

He's mine. My son. This has absolutely nothing to do with you.

Nothing to do with you. Nothing...nothing... nothing...

Andrew groaned, closed his eyes for a long moment, then opened them again to stare into the darkness.

A nightmare, he thought. The horrendous argument with Kara over her adoption of that baby had been a living nightmare. He'd been cruel, had flung harsh words at Kara like punishing blows.

He'd made her cry,

The tears had been shimmering in her beautiful eyes as he'd left the bedroom. He'd made the only woman he'd ever loved cry.

Then he'd walked out of her apartment and her life forever, having told her that he couldn't, wouldn't, remain her lover, that it was over between them.

"Because she's going to adopt that baby?" Andrew said aloud. "Because she intends to provide a home for a child who had no one to love him, no chance of a decent future, of being a happy little boy?"

Selfish...selfish...

Ah, damn it, he was so confused. As that scene in

Kara's bedroom replayed relentlessly in his mind, it
was as though he was watching a stranger who had
taken possession of his body. Someone he didn't
know, who had stood in judgment of Kara and found
her guilty of a terrible wrong. A man who had cut
Kara to the quick with his biting and cruel accusations.

Selfish…selfish…

Something wasn't right here, Andrew thought,
franticness edging its dark cold tentacles around him.
He'd made it sound as though being raised by a single mother, by Sally Malone, had resulted in him
having a miserable childhood.

And that just wasn't true.

Yeah, sure, there had been times when he was very
young that he'd envied his friends who had fathers.
But in the big picture he had been happy as a child
because he'd had a mother who loved him unconditionally.

Where in hell had his sudden and angry reaction
to Kara's news come from?

He didn't know. He just didn't know.

Somewhere within his subconscious, he supposed,
had been buried pain that he hadn't been aware of,
a deep-seated festering resentment that he had not
had a father.

How could that be possible? Sally had been a wonderful mother. No, they hadn't had a lot materially,
but he'd sure as hell had what counted. Love. The
kind of love Kara would give that baby in the nursery.

God, none of this made sense. What had transpired
in Kara's bedroom was confusing and terribly unset-

tling because he couldn't get a handle on why it had happened.

All that he was certain of was that what he had shared with Kara, every memory-making moment, was over, done, finished.

He'd destroyed what they'd had together, and heaven help him, he didn't even know why he'd done it. That baby was going to have a fantastic mother in Kara MacAllister and be welcomed with warm embraces into the huge MacAllister family.

That little guy was truly blessed.

Selfish...selfish...

There they were again, Andrew thought, closing his eyes. The anger. The accusations. The judgment passed, the verdict guilty.

And it all stood between him and Kara like a solid impenetrable wall. He'd lost Kara due to beliefs he hadn't even known he possessed on an issue of vital importance in their relationship.

Oh, yeah, he was most definitely in a stranger's body, thinking a stranger's thoughts, had uttered the words of a bitter and vindictive man he didn't even know existed within him.

Selfish...selfish...

Andrew pressed the heels of his hands against his throbbing temples, attempting to quiet the haunting voice in his mind. But it refused to be exorcised.

As the dim light of dawn began to creep beneath the draperies, Andrew flung back the rumpled sheets on the bed, having not slept at all. He strode toward the bathroom, the harsh taunting voice following him into the shower.

* * *

Late that afternoon Andrew sat in a recliner next to the one where Robert MacAllister was sitting in the living room of Margaret and Robert's large home.

Andrew had telephoned them after having breakfast in the hotel coffee shop, and it was agreed that he would visit at ten o'clock.

He had been nervous when he'd pressed the doorbell, then was greeted by Margaret. Within minutes of settling in he'd begun to relax.

The conversation with Robert, his father, had flowed easily, going from one topic to the next. They'd touched briefly on the subject of Clara, what she had done that long-ago summer and what had resulted because of it. But they hadn't lingered there because there was no point in rehashing the past, what could never be changed.

Andrew and Robert had discussed MacAllister Architects and Malone Construction, marveling at the fact that Andrew had built more than one structure following plans drawn up by MacAllisters.

In the early afternoon Margaret had appeared in the room carrying a tray holding lunch. Robert wrinkled his nose at his offering, then smiled at his wife as she narrowed her eyes, daring him to complain.

"It looks delicious, dear," Robert said.

"No, it doesn't," Margaret said. "But those are the breaks, *dear*. Eat it and like it."

Robert had shot Andrew a dark glare when he'd chuckled, causing Andrew to lose control and laugh uncontrollably. Robert and Margaret were caught up in the infectious sound, and soon they were all laughing, at ease with each other, glad that they were together.

Now in the late afternoon Andrew could feel his previous night's loss of sleep catching up with him. The chair he was sitting in was too comfortable, made to entice a person to sink deep within it and take a nap.

"I really should be going," he said. "I don't want to tire you out, Robert. I'm sure they have rules about your recuperation."

"They have rules about everything," Robert said dryly. "I have to raise my hand and humbly request that I be allowed to visit the rest room."

Andrew smiled. "That's stretching it a bit."

"True," Robert said, smiling. "But as long as I'm griping, I might as well throw everything in the stew that I can think of, farfetched and all."

"Go for it," Andrew said. "Although I wouldn't recommend laying it on Margaret."

"Are you kidding?" Robert said, raising his eyebrows. "My ticker might be under par, but there's nothing wrong with my brain. I like living." He paused and became serious. "This whole situation has shown me just how very blessed I am to be surrounded by the family I have, and also how grateful I am to be alive. Oh, yes, Andrew, I do, indeed, like living."

Margaret came into the room carrying a pad of paper and a pen.

"And there's the most important reason why," Robert said quietly, gazing warmly at his wife.

"Why what?" Margaret said, sitting down in an easy chair.

"Man talk, my sweet," Robert said. "What are you up to over there? You're obviously making one of your ever-famous lists."

"My lists, which I endure such kidding about," Margaret said, lifting her chin, "have kept order in the midst of what might have been chaos for many years, Mr. MacAllister."

"Indeed they have, Mrs. MacAllister," Robert said, nodding. "So, what's this tome pertaining to?"

"Kara," Margaret said, "and her new baby boy."

Andrew stiffened, feeling every muscle in his tired body tighten nearly to the point of pain.

"And?" Robert said.

"I just spoke with Kara on the telephone," Margaret said, "to be certain this plan was all right with her. There was a chance, you know, that she wished to buy all new baby furniture and who knows what else for her son.

"But she was delighted with what I told her, especially since her plans for her medical practice will result in her having less income."

"So what's the mystery plan that Kara agreed to?" Robert said.

Margaret consulted the list. "Well, let's see. Jillian and Forrest have a crib and changing table that Kara can have. Jennifer and Michael are sure there are a playpen and a high chair somewhere in their garage, and they'll find them and scrub them. Ryan and Dee-dee still have a baby swing that isn't being used...and on it goes."

"Sounds like our new mother is in business." Robert slid a glance at Andrew. "You *do* know about Kara's son, don't you, Andrew?"

Andrew nodded, but didn't comment.

"Margaret, back up here," Robert said. "Why is Kara going to have less income? I think I missed something that's in the works."

"Well," Margaret said, settling more comfortably in her chair, "for the adoption proceedings Kara had a home study done by a social worker and... Anyway, she was giving serious thought to how she could be a doctor and a single mother, without either role compromising the other."

"It can't be done." Andrew frowned, immediately furious at drawing attention to himself on the subject of Kara and her baby.

Margaret looked at him. "You don't believe that a woman can have a child *and* a career, Andrew?"

"There are just so many hours in the day," he said. "You also left out a couple of adjectives. Kara is a *single* woman, who has a very *demanding* career." He paused. "This is none of my business, really."

"Isn't it?" Margaret said, looking at him intently. "I got the impression that Kara's adopting this baby would be very much your...business, as you say."

"No," he said quietly. *This has absolutely nothing to do with you.* "It has...it has nothing to do with me."

"I see," Margaret said slowly.

"So?" Robert said. "Finish your story, Margaret. Kara will have less income in the future because...?"

"Oh. She has a doctor friend who is divorced and raising two children alone. Kara knew that the woman was becoming very frustrated by her lack of time to accomplish everything that needed doing, both professionally and personally.

"Kara approached her with the idea of joining her medical practice. They would both have more free time, albeit less money, but it would make it possible to fulfill both their roles.

"It was understood that if Kara's petition to adopt was denied, then that was that. But if she was approved to adopt the baby, the other woman assured her that she would jump at a chance to do what Kara proposed. Isn't that splendid? Our Kara is so brilliant."

Yes, she is, Andrew thought. It was a dynamite idea. The baby was going to get equal billing with Kara's medical practice. Granted, Kara's income would diminish, but the way the MacAllisters were rallying around, she would reap the benefits of good old-fashioned hand-me-downs, including everything from equipment for the nursery and probably to clothes and toys.

"Don't you agree, Andrew?" Margaret said. "This is a solid, well-thought-out plan that Kara has, and it should proceed very well."

"What?" Andrew said, as he was pulled from his thoughts. "Oh, yes, it sounds great. Very good. Fine. I guess the only thing that baby will be lacking is a father."

"Whoa there on that one," Robert said, smiling. "That munchkin is now a MacAllister, remember? Our boys are probably already squabbling about who gets to teach Kara's son how to throw a baseball.

"I might put my money on Forrest for that. He'll claim he's the most eligible because he has three daughters, none of whom are the least bit interested at this point in their lives in learning the finer points of tossing a ball into a mitt.''

"No, I'd have to put my money on Richard," Margaret said. "He doesn't have any children at all. He'd plead his case based on that.''

"You've got a point there," Robert said, nodding.

"This is silly," Margaret said, laughing. "We've got Kara's son playing baseball, and the sweetie pie is only a few weeks old. Kara said the baby has to get up to five pounds before they'll release him from the hospital. He's almost there.

"The boys will help Kara set up the nursery within the next few days so that she's all set when the baby can come home. I'll be talking to our girls about a baby-sitting schedule until the woman joining Kara's practice can give her notice where she's on staff at a San Francisco hospital and move down here.

"After that, Kara can decide whether she wants to trade with the others for baby-sitting time when she is working or bring in someone from the outside. All in all, things are very organized and should go very smoothly.''

"Yep," Robert said. "Does this newest Mac-Allister have a name yet?"

"Well, Kara said that his middle name will be Ralph, after her father," Margaret said. "But she hasn't settled on a first name yet." She laughed. "It's certainly a good thing that too much love isn't hazardous to health. That baby is going to be so loved by so many people.''

"Of course," Robert said. "He's a MacAllister."

Selfish…selfish…wrong…wrong…selfish…selfish…

The haunting words echoed once again in Andrew's mind, and he shifted uncomfortably in the chair, realizing that he had nowhere to put them, nowhere to make them stick. Kara's son would, just as she had said, have more than enough male influence in his life.

But yet…

There was a dark shadow hovering over him, Andrew thought. A sense of confusion and doubt, of not having a firm grip on what was still disturbing him regarding Kara's plans to adopt the baby. The stranger who had emerged from within him remained powerful and forbidding.

Ah, damn, he was driving himself nuts again, plagued by a whole new set of questions with no answers.

He was tired. Just too tired to tackle this maze. Something definitely wasn't right, wasn't clicking, but he was far too weary to figure out what it was.

Andrew pushed himself to his feet.

"This has been a terrific day," he said, "and I thank you for the warm reception and the delicious lunch, but I'd better shove off."

"You're more than welcome to stay for dinner, Andrew," Margaret said.

"No. No, thank you," he said. "I brought a briefcase full of paperwork with me that I have to tend to tonight." *Liar.* "I'll speak with you tomorrow, regarding my coming by again, if that's all right."

"It's more than all right," Margaret said, getting

to her feet. "We'll be counting on it. I'll see you to the door, Andrew."

"No," Robert said. "You don't always escort any of our other sons to the door when they leave, Margaret. It depends on what you're doing at the time. Andrew isn't a guest here. He's a member of the family, who knows where the front door is." He shifted his attention to Andrew. "Thank you for today...son."

Andrew met his father's gaze for a long warming moment, then finally nodded. He turned and left the room, closing the front door behind him with a quiet click.

Late that night Kara sat in the rocking chair in the hospital nursery holding her baby, who was sleeping peacefully in her arms.

"Dream of rainbows, my precious," she said softly, "and ice-cream cones, fluffy kittens and bright red bouncing balls. Oh, I love you so much. You're mine now. My son. And I'm your mommy. We're going to have a wonderful life together."

Selfish...selfish...wrong...wrong...wrong...

Kara leaned her head against the high back of the chair, closing her eyes with a weary sigh as she continued to rock back and forth.

How strange, she thought. It was actually possible for a person to be filled with immeasurable joy in one arena of her life, while being shattered, empty and incredibly sad in another.

A chill swept through her as she once again replayed in her mind the final scene in her bedroom with Andrew.

He had been so angry, had lashed out at her with harsh and hurting words. He viewed her as a selfish woman who intended to satisfy her maternal needs at the expense of an innocent baby who had no voice in the matter.

Darn it—no, *damn* it, it wasn't fair. Andrew had, apparently, been comparing her baby's upbringing with his own and found it terribly lacking due to Kara not having a husband, a father for her son.

Kara raised her head and gazed at the sleeping baby again.

Andrew had the right, she supposed, to his opinion regarding her, a single woman, adopting a baby boy. But Andrew was the one who was wrong. Her son would be surrounded by father figures, would never lack for role models or—

Oh, what sense was there in rehashing it all? Constantly reliving that ugly scene wouldn't change the ultimate outcome.

Everything she had shared with Andrew was over. She would never again be the recipient of his touch, his kiss, never again make sweet love with him.

They would cross paths at MacAllister-family functions, and they'd nod politely, inquire after the other's health or some mundane thing, but that would be it.

From across a room or a backyard, when the MacAllisters gathered, she'd watch Andrew and view the distance as being a world apart, never to be united again.

"Oh, my baby," she whispered, tears brimming in her eyes. "I love Andrew Malone so very much. I want to marry him, spend the rest of my life with him. I want him to be your father.''

Tears spilled over onto her cheeks.

''Andrew gave you your spiffy baseball uniform, do you know that, sweetheart? I'm going to keep it for you, and when you're old enough, I'll tell you about the magnificent man who sat in this very chair and held and fed you. The man who went shopping and bought you that baseball outfit because it represented a message about life that he wanted you to know.''

Kara sighed.

No, she guessed she couldn't tell her son about Andrew Malone, because he would be at MacAllister gatherings and her son would question why the man who had given him a present as a baby paid little attention to him now that he was a big boy.

Her baby would never know who gave him the cute little uniform.

And Andrew Malone would never know that she loved him more than she would ever be able to describe, because of the limitation of words.

Andrew, who would continue through life as the solitary man he proclaimed himself to be, allowing family love into his existence, but never the committed forever love of a woman. Oh, no, never that. He was alone and liked it that way just fine.

As fresh tears stung Kara's eyes, she shook her head in self-disgust and got to her feet.

It was time to go home and attempt to get some sleep, she thought, crossing the nursery to the baby's bassinet. In her bed. Alone. With no Andrew beside her to reach for her and draw her into his strong but gentle embrace.

No, Andrew wouldn't be there.

Not tonight.

Not ever again.

Chapter 17

Andrew's days fell into a pleasant routine. He slept late in the morning, then spoke with Harry on the telephone to get an update on the Malone Construction projects in Santa Maria.

After a leisurely breakfast in the hotel coffee shop, but before he went for his daily visit with Robert, he drove to MacAllister Architects, where he spent time talking to Michael, Forrest and Jack, who were more than willing to show Andrew the plans they were contracted to draw up.

On more than one occasion Andrew was able to make suggestions from the builder's point of view that would save the client money, a fact that would be very much in the architect's favor.

"You know," Michael said, on the fifth day since Andrew had returned to Ventura, "I was thinking. Suppose we had a construction expert as a consultant, as in you, Andrew, to see ways to get the results the client wants but shave off some bucks while doing it. Talk about a full-service outfit.''

Forrest nodded. ''I like it. Andrea has a degree in landscape architecture, Andrew. I don't know if you knew that. If the client wants us to, we can include Andrea's presentation for the landscaping.''

''Smart,'' Andrew said, nodding in approval. ''That would make a very neat package.''

''Yep,'' Jack said, ''and I like Michael's idea that we could also say we have a construction consultant on standby to confer with to enable the customer to cut costs. Dynamite.''

''Interested, Andrew?'' Michael said.

''I definitely would be, but…'' Andrew shook his head. ''No, it's not very practical. I live a hundred miles away, remember?''

Michael leaned back in the high stool that was in front of a drafting table covered in paper and laced his fingers behind his head.

''What's keeping you in Santa Maria?'' he said.

Andrew laughed. ''My company. The office is there and…'' He paused. ''Then again, we do build all over the state.''

''I rest my case,'' Michael said. ''You could set up a main office anywhere you want to. You must have a topnotch guy in charge up there now to enable you to be down here. Right?''

''Yeah,'' Andrew said, nodding. ''Harry is the best. Just steps in and takes over, and the men like and respect him. He's in for the long haul, too, because he owns a house and his wife is expecting a baby. He's a good man.''

"So there you go," Michael said. "You bump up the guy's paycheck, leave him in charge of the Santa Maria branch of Malone Construction and open an office down here. You'd get a consulting fee from MacAllister Architects for your input on money-saving options to our plans, and we're off and running."

"I'm really liking this," Forrest said.

"Ditto," Jack said.

Michael laughed. "I mean, hell, Andrew, how are we going to whip these guys' butts in touch football if you're not here to play on my team?"

"That cooks it," Andrew said, smiling. "You've convinced me. I'll move down here tomorrow." His smile faded. "Seriously, I will definitely give this some thought."

"Fair enough," Michael said.

"There's something else we need to do," Forrest said. "Kara's going to need a house in the not-so-distant future. She can't raise her son in an apartment. The kid needs a yard to play in, make mud, climb trees."

"Have a dog," Andrew said, then frowned as he realized he'd spoken before he'd realized he was going to do it. He cleared his throat. "Never mind. Forget it."

"A dog," Michael said, nodding slowly as he looked at Andrew intently. "You think Kara's son should have his own dog?"

"What kind of dog?" Forrest said, his gaze also riveted on Andrew.

"Big or small?" Jack said. "Mutt or pedigree? Male or female?"

"Hell, I don't know," Andrew said, very sorry he'd opened his mouth on the subject. "A dog is a dog, for Pete's sake. I just figured it would be fun for the kid to have a..." He glanced at his watch. "I've got to shove off. Your—our father will be wondering what happened to me if I don't get over to the house."

"Okay," Michael said, "but think about moving down here." He redirected his attention to the plans in front of him on the drafting table. "And zero in on what kind of dog Kara's son should have after we build her a house with a yard."

"Cripes," Andrew said, then strode out of the office, muttering under his breath as he went.

"Andrew is in love with Kara," Michael said.

"Yep," Forrest said.

"Yep," Jack said. "And Kara is in love with Andrew."

"Yep," Forrest said again.

"Yep," Michael echoed. "But Jenny said they haven't been together since Andrew came back."

"Jillian says there's something off-kilter between Andrew and Kara," Forrest said. "A glitch, a problem, a war zone, a trouble-in-romance-land thing, a—"

"We get the point, Forrest," Jack said. "Don't beat it to death."

"Yes, well, they'd better get their acts together," Forrest said. "I'm officially entering Andrew in that bachelor bet business of yours, Jack. I'm putting my money on him going down for the count with our Kara and marrying her."

"I wonder what's wrong between them?" Michael said thoughtfully.

"I don't have a clue," Jack said. "The thing is, having been down that road myself, it could be that they don't know, either. Or maybe one of them doesn't get it. Or... Love is very powerful complicated stuff."

"No joke," Michael said.

"Damn," Forrest said. "What if Andrew and Kara never get it straight?"

"They will," Michael said decisively. "They're not dopes. After all, they're both MacAllisters."

The three men nodded, then got back to work.

Late in the afternoon of the sixth day since his return to Ventura, Andrew told Robert and Margaret that he was going back to Santa Maria the next day.

"So soon?" Robert said, frowning.

"I don't even want to think about the paperwork that must be a mile high on my desk," Andrew said. "I really have to go tend to things."

Robert nodded. "I can understand that. Michael told me about the proposed plan of your moving down here permanently, Andrew. Have you given it further thought?"

"Some," Andrew said. "I'll really tackle the idea when I get back to Santa Maria. I'll have to talk to my main man, Harry, and... There's a lot of things to consider."

"Oh?" Margaret said. "Such as?"

"Just...things," Andrew said, not looking at her directly.

"She misses you, Andrew," Margaret said.

Andrew's head snapped up and he stared at Margaret. "What?"

"Kara misses you, dear, as much as you miss her," Margaret said.

"I never said that I..." Andrew shot a pleading look at his father.

Robert laced his fingers over his chest as he smiled and shook his head. "Sorry, son, you're on your own. The bee is in Margaret's bonnet and I've learned—the hard way—to keep my mouth shut."

"Robert, hush," Margaret said. "I'm simply chatting, that's all. Have I made a major production out of the fact that Kara is bringing the baby home tomorrow? That the big event is at eleven o'clock in the morning, and Kara declined the offer to have someone from the family with her, wishing to take her son home herself, just the two of them? No, I certainly have not. Have I—"

"Wait a minute," Andrew said, leaning forward in his chair. "She's bringing the baby home? The little guy is up to five pounds? Are you sure? Is the hospital scale right? I mean, hell, what if he comes home too early, is too small and... No, I guess a scale in that place would be on the money, wouldn't it?" He smiled. "I'll be damned. The champ made it in record time, didn't he?"

"Indeed." Margaret picked an imaginary thread from her skirt. "I believe Kara said something about the baby wearing a...oh, what was it? Yes, a tiny baseball uniform as his going-home outfit. She said it was very special to her, that tiny suit."

Andrew sank back in his chair. "She did? Kara said that? Are you sure?"

"Yes," Margaret said, an expression of pure innocence on her face as she looked at Andrew again. "Is that information important for some reason, dear?"

"What?" Andrew said. "Sorry. I was off somewhere for a moment there."

"Have you decided yet what kind of dog you're going to get the boy once Kara has her own house with a yard?" Robert said.

"You know about the dog?" Andrew said, his voice rising along with his eyebrows.

"Of course," Robert said. "The dog would be a MacAllister dog. Therefore, I know about it."

"Oh, man," Andrew said, chuckling. "This family is something else."

"This family," Margaret said, "cares deeply about its members. This family, Andrew, is also yours. It's heartbreaking to know that there is something keeping you and Kara from having the happiness together that you both want and deserve."

Andrew frowned. "You sure don't pull any punches, do you?"

"Not where my loved ones are concerned," she said, lifting her chin.

"Are you aware," Andrew said, his jaw tightening slightly, "that Kara wants no part of a serious relationship? Isn't interested in marriage, forever and ever, the whole nine yards?"

"Nor are you, Andrew," Margaret said. "I had this very same conversation with Kara, and she informed me of that fact. Loudly and clearly, I might add."

"I *used* to feel that way. People change, you

know," Andrew said none too quietly, then cringed as he saw both Robert and Margaret lean forward to stare at him. "Oh, hell."

"Do tell," Margaret said.

Andrew dragged a hand through his hair and shook his head. "You're implying that Kara may have changed her views on the subject of a lifelong commitment. I believe that you're wrong."

"*You* no longer feel as you did on the subject," Margaret said. "Why isn't it possible for Kara to have given it second thoughts, too?"

"Have you heard from Clara?" Robert said.

"What?" Andrew said. "Where did that come from?"

"Have you?" Robert said.

"Sort of," Andrew said. "There was a message from the head honcho of a clinic is Northern California on my answering machine at my apartment. Clara has checked in there for an extensive rehabilitation program and has listed me as the person to be kept informed of her progress. Why are you asking about Clara?"

"Because," Robert said, "nearly forty years ago the direction that lives would take was determined by Clara's intervention. She's no longer in the picture, can't be blamed anymore. The responsibility for the future rests entirely in your and Kara's hands. Think about that, Andrew. Think about it long and hard."

Andrew got to his feet, and his voice was low and weary-sounding when he spoke. "There's something…hanging over me, tearing me up, and I can't get a handle on it. I'm aware of what it's centered on, but I don't have a clue why it's there. Until I do know, there's no point in my talking to Kara about...about anything."

He drew a shuddering breath.

"I've got to go. I'll speak with you before I leave for Santa Maria tomorrow. Thank you for...everything."

Andrew covered the distance to the front door of the house in long strides and closed the door behind him with a trembling hand.

When Andrew started off on a nocturnal trek that night, he was immediately aware of how many people were out walking their dogs. He slid glances at the canines, attempting not to appear like a potential dog-snatcher.

Choosing a dog for Kara's son, he thought, required a great deal of research. You had to be assured it was the proper breed to play in a yard, then later sleep next to the bed of a special little boy.

You know about the dog? he'd asked Robert incredulously.

The dog would be a MacAllister dog, Robert had answered. *Therefore, I know about it.*

Andrew chuckled and shook his head, earning him a wary look from a woman who was walking in the opposite direction on the sidewalk. Andrew turned the corner and slowed his pace.

Robert's having been informed of the conversation about the dog was the type of thing that he'd convinced himself would make him feel smothered, cornered by the large MacAllister family, unable to breathe.

The same held true of Margaret and Robert's unsolicited remarks about Kara and his relationship with her.

Those two incidents, as well as others, should be prompting him to hightail it back to Santa Maria, then find excuses for why it wasn't convenient to make a return visit.

Andrew shoved his hands into his pockets and trudged on, his way lit by a multitude of stars twinkling in the black-velvet sky.

The truth of the matter was, he was soaking up the caring and sharing exhibited by the MacAllisters like a thirsty sponge.

Those people really understood, truly knew how to make someone know that he *mattered*.

Andrew nodded and continued walking along the quiet street.

Although the MacAllisters were obviously quick on the draw to pass along newly acquired information, he also knew, somehow, that if he ever told one of them something in confidence, it would go no further than the person he was speaking to.

The clan, when gathered, was a formidable force, prepared to lay it all on the line for one of their own if need be. It would be done without question, because that was just the way it went if you were a MacAllister.

And he was.

He was now as proud of that half of himself as he was of the Malone part.

He could easily understand why Kara had felt honored when asked if she would legally become a

MacAllister, and why she changed the name on the headstone at her baby daughter's grave.

Kara, Andrew thought. This was the first time when envisioning her in his mind that he wasn't consumed by loneliness and despair.

Tonight there was a small glowing ember within him that he realized was the wondrous emotion of *hope*. It was due to what Margaret and Robert had said about Kara missing him as much as he missed her, and the theory that Kara could very well have changed her negative views on commitment, on forever love, just as he had.

It's heartbreaking to know that there is something keeping you two from having the happiness together that you both want and deserve.

Margaret's heartfelt words echoed in Andrew's mind and he sighed.

That *something* was encased in the dark shadow that hovered over him, refusing to allow him to see it clearly, understand what it was, deal with it. It was focused on that baby, who had staked a claim on Kara's heart and wrapped tight little fingers around Andrew's heart, as well.

Even if Kara *did* love him and had, indeed, freed herself of the ghosts of the past as he had done, was ready to embrace a future with him, that unknown *something* definitely stood between them.

He could apologize to Kara for his harsh words regarding her adopting the baby, for calling her selfish for intentionally creating a childhood without a father for that little boy. He could ask her to forgive him for what he had said, assure her that he no longer felt that way, realized that her son would have a rich and full life with her, even if she was a single mother.

He could then go on to say that he was in love with her, wanted to marry her and be that baby's father. Wanted to be part of a family that would have a home filled to overflowing with love. A house with a yard big enough for a dog.

"Yeah, right," Andrew said, shaking his head. "Like Kara would buy all that, no questions asked. Not a chance, Malone."

No, not Kara MacAllister. She'd make him back up, readdress what he'd said regarding her being a single woman raising a son. She'd no doubt accuse him of glossing over his feelings on the subject, might very well believe that he still felt as he had when he said those horrendous things to her, but was dismissing them now because he was asking her to marry him.

The ugly scene in her bedroom would remain as the barrier between them, no matter what their feelings for each other might be.

Andrew stopped walking, narrowed his eyes and stared into space.

Yes, that was the wall that created the dark and haunting shadow that stood between him and Kara. It was the *why* of his initial reaction to Kara's excited announcement that she was adopting the baby in the hospital nursery.

He had lashed out at her so cruelly.

Why?

He had labeled her a selfish woman who wished to fulfill her maternal needs with no regard for the child she was using to satisfy those needs.

Why?

He had made it sound as though he'd had an empty hollow childhood because of a lack of a father, which simply wasn't true.

Why?

Kara would demand answers to those questions. He needed to know what they were before he could obtain any inner peace, be in an emotional place where he was fit to ask Kara to be his wife, declare his love for her, ask her if she returned his love.

Somehow he had to transport himself back to the exact moment when Kara told him about her plans to adopt that baby, then halt the scene rolling in his mind, examine it, reach deep within himself for the answers to the damning question of *why*.

Andrew spun around and began to retrace his steps.

He would return to the hotel and not allow himself to sleep until the mystery was solved, the wall crushed into dust and the dark shadow flung into oblivion for all time.

And while he struggled to find within himself what he was seeking, he would hold fast to the glowing ember of hope that Kara MacAllister loved him.

Chapter 18

The next morning Andrew stood among a group of trees bordering the parking lot to the hospital. He glanced yet again at his watch, relieved to see that it was, at long last, nearly eleven o'clock.

He'd been standing there for three hours, wanting to be certain that he didn't miss witnessing Kara leave the hospital with the baby. He was totally exhausted, had hardly slept the previous night, yet he was exhilarated at the same time.

He had the answers he had been seeking.

Slowly but surely through the long dark hours of the night, as he concentrated on that final scene with Kara, relived over and over the emotions he'd been experiencing then, it began to come together like an intricate puzzle, the pieces linking into a picture that he could comprehend.

There was just one final step he felt he had to take.

He had to see Kara with the baby as she left the hospital to take her son home for the first time.

That would be the final test. The last piece of the puzzle that was still missing. The assurance he needed that he truly did understand where his reactions to Kara's news about adopting the baby had stemmed from during that horrendous scene in Kara's bedroom.

Andrew's muscles ached from standing so long and from tensing every time a car drove into the parking lot. He was afraid that someone would call security regarding the man skulking around the edge of the lot for hours, but so far he had apparently gone unnoticed.

Andrew stiffened and his heart began to beat in a wild tempo as the front doors of the hospital swished open and Kara emerged carrying a car seat in her arms.

She stopped, looked up at the brilliant blue sky, then smiled as she gazed into the car seat. Andrew could see her lips moving as she said something to the baby, then she started off again, crossing the lot to where her car was parked.

Andrew stepped quickly out of sight behind a large tree, his mind racing. He closed his eyes and mentally saw the last piece to the puzzle click firmly into place, then dropped his chin to his chest in heartfelt relief.

Yes, he now knew *why*.

"Ah, Kara," he whispered. "Now it's up to you. Will you forgive me for hurting you? Do you love me as I love you? Do you, Kara?"

Andrew peered around the tree and saw Kara drive

out of the parking lot. He walked slowly to his own vehicle, deciding he had to endure another hour before he would go to Kara's apartment, give her time to get the baby settled in and enjoy, privately, the first moments of having her son home where he belonged.

One more hour.

Then he'd go to Kara MacAllister.

And before this day was over, his entire future would be determined.

Kara hummed softly as she placed the last bottle of the batch of formula she'd prepared into the refrigerator. She left the kitchen, crossed the living room, which was a bit crowded with the furniture from her office, and went into the second bedroom that was now officially a nursery.

She stood by the crib and watched the baby sleeping peacefully, his tiny hands splayed next to his face.

"You're really here, sweetheart," she said, tears of joy misting her eyes. "I can hardly believe it. You're home, my precious, and I love you so much. I'm going to stand here like a silly first-time mommy and watch you sleep. You're so beautiful."

Kara frowned when she heard a knock on the apartment door.

Who could that be? she wondered. The family knew she wanted to be alone with the baby today. She'd had Lucy juggle her patient appointments so that these hours to savor this momentous event were hers.

The knock was repeated.

"Well, darn it." She left the room and hurried to answer the summons, still frowning at the unexpected intrusion.

Kara opened the door without checking through the peephole to see who was there, and her eyes widened as she found herself staring at Andrew Malone.

"Hello, Kara," he said quietly, no readable expression on his face.

"Andrew, what—"

"May I come in?" he interrupted. "I need to talk to you. It's important."

"How did you know I was here, instead of at the office?" she said.

"You're a MacAllister, who brought her son home today," Andrew said, a slight smile forming on his lips. "I'm a MacAllister, so I know about it. It falls into the same category as the dog for the yard."

"Pardon me?" Kara said, obviously confused.

"Never mind. May I come in?"

"Well, I..." Kara sighed. "Yes, all right."

Andrew entered the apartment and Kara closed the door behind him, leaning back against it as she felt her knees begin to tremble from the close proximity to Andrew. She drank in the sight of him as he crossed the room, then turned to face her.

Focus, Kara ordered herself. *Don't dwell on how much you love this man, how much you've missed him, ached for him, longed to see him, touch him, feel his kiss and... No.*

She lifted her chin. "This is a very special day in my life, Andrew. I have no intention of allowing you to mar it in any way. I'm aware that you believe me to be a selfish self-serving woman who adopted a baby boy to satisfy my maternal needs, with no regard for the fact that the child wouldn't have a father. I don't wish to rehash all that. I refuse to do so. So it's probably best if you just leave and—"

"I love you, Kara," Andrew said, cutting off her rush of words.

Kara stopped speaking and frowned. "You what?"

Andrew shoved his hands into his trouser pockets and drew a deep breath.

"Could we sit down?" he said.

"Good idea," Kara said.

Kara sank gratefully onto a chair as Andrew sank onto the sofa. He leaned forward, rested his elbows on his knees and linked his fingers, his gaze riveted on Kara.

"Kara," he said, his voice gritty, "I am deeply in love with you. I've stepped out of the past, I'm free of the hold it had on me, and I'm looking to the future, a future I want to spend with you—you, as my wife, my soul mate, my partner."

"But—"

"Please, hear me out," Andrew said.

Kara nodded, her heart beating so rapidly she could hear the echo of it in her ears. She clutched her shaking hands tightly in her lap and stared at Andrew.

"You've stolen my heart, Kara MacAllister, and so has that baby, your son. The thing is, I don't want my heart back. I want you to keep it and to hear you say that your heart belongs to me."

"You're in love with *selfish* me?" Kara said, narrowing her eyes. "Oh, really? You'll pardon me, I trust, if I find that hard to believe, Andrew."

Kara paused and the color drained from her face.

"Oh, wait just a minute here," she said. "You said that my baby, my son, has also stolen your heart. Is that what this is all about, Andrew Malone? Your paternal instincts have kicked in, gone into overdrive, and you want to be a father? So, you'll put up with me in order to be a daddy to that baby who is sleeping down the hall?"

"Ah, hell," Andrew said, staring up at the ceiling for a long moment. "I was afraid that was what you would think." He looked at Kara again. "Please, listen to me, Kara. Let me explain what happened, what I've finally figured out after many sleepless nights."

"Go for it," Kara said, folding her arms over her breasts.

"Will you hear me with an open mind?"

"Don't get picky," she said. "Count your blessings that I haven't already thrown you out of here."

"Right." Andrew cleared his throat. "Kara, when you told me you were planning to adopt the baby, I reacted badly, said such hateful things to you, hurt you so damn much."

"No joke," Kara muttered.

"The thing is," Andrew continued, "I didn't know *why* I lashed out at you the way I did. That *why* has caused me to just about lose the last thread of my sanity. The things I accused you of simply weren't true, weren't how I really felt at all, yet I'd hurled that garbage at you and... It didn't make sense to me, not even close. But I finally have the answers to what happened when you said you were going to adopt the baby.''

"Oh?" Kara said, her heart increasing in tempo even more.

"Kara, at that moment, which I've relived a hundred times or more, I felt as though my world was crumbling into dust, leaving me nothing, sentencing me to a lifetime of loneliness, emptiness and... You were so excited about the baby, about being his mother, becoming a family...just the two of you.

"You didn't need me, or want me, or love me. You never intended to marry, nor become involved in a serious relationship. You and that boy would have a wonderful life together, I knew that.

"I lashed out at you from a place I'd been flung to that was raw with pain and loss, and the image of a future that was cold and dark. I loved you so much and you were out of my reach forever. It hurt. God, it hurt, and I raged in fury because of that blinding pain.

"I've untangled the maze in my mind—finally. I even watched you this morning as you left the hospital with the baby to be absolutely certain that I wasn't mistaken about what I'd discovered about myself.

"And now? Now, Kara, I don't know how to make you believe me, how to keep you from thinking that I'm saying all this because I've grown to love that baby boy and you are an obstacle to my being his father.''

Sudden unexpected and unwelcome tears filled Andrew's eyes, and his voice was choked with emotion when he spoke again.

"I love you, Kara, with all that I am. That is the honest truth. I want to marry you and spend the rest of my life with you. I don't...don't know what else to say, how to put it to make you believe me. You are my life, my future happiness, my reason for being.

"And, yes," he continued, hardly able to speak as tears clogged his throat, "I love that baby boy. *I* want to be the one to teach him to play ball—not Forrest, or Richard, or... Me. His father. I want to buy him a dog to play with him in the yard of the home we'll have. I want to rake leaves into piles for our son to romp in with his puppy, and...I love you, Kara, I swear to God I do."

Andrew stopped speaking, shook his head and dragged trembling hands down his face.

Kara stared at Andrew, then drew a wobbly breath. A warmth began to fill her, slowly at first, then rushing like a wild current, consuming her, wrapping itself around her heart, her mind, her very soul.

"You do," she said, her voice ringing with awe and wonder. "You really do love me. I know it's true. I can feel it—" she spread her hands over her heart "—in here, where it's meant to be. Oh, dear heaven, Andrew, I love you, too.

"I never dreamed that you... You said you wanted no part of... I was so happy about the baby, but so very sad and lonely at the same time because you were never going to be a part of my life, a part of his life and... Oh, God, Andrew, I love you so much."

They moved at the same time, rushing to embrace each other, holding fast, allowing tears to flow unchecked. They rocked back and forth, clinging to each other as though never again to let go.

Andrew finally gripped Kara's shoulders and eased her away from him enough so that he could look directly into her tear-filled eyes.

"You believe me?" he said. "You honestly believe I love *you* as well as that baby?"

"Yes. Oh, yes, I do. I've freed myself of the past, too, Andrew, just as you have. I didn't even realize until I met you what a tight hold it had on me, but that's all behind me now. I believe that you love me, and heaven knows how much I love you."

"Oh, man," Andrew said, his shoulders slumping with relief. "Thank you." He paused and attempted to get his emotions under control. "Kara Mac-Allister, will you do me the honor of becoming my wife? Will you marry me, stay by my side until death parts us?"

"I can't answer that yet," she said. "There are still things that need to be discussed."

"Are you worried because I live in Santa Maria and your medical practice is here?" Andrew said. "I've covered all that with the MacAllisters. I'm going to open an office in Ventura, live here and have my business in Santa Maria run by my top man, Harry. I haven't talked to him about it yet, but I'm certain that he'll—"

"No, no, that's not it," Kara interrupted, "although it's nice to hear that where we might live is not going to be a problem." She paused. "Andrew, I have to know that you realize there might be long-term problems for the baby because he was born addicted to drugs. There's just no way to know at this point.''

Andrew framed Kara's face in his large hands. "He's our son, Kara. We'll tackle whatever we have to if and when it comes. Nothing could ever diminish my love for that little guy. Nothing.''

Kara nodded, unable to speak for a moment as fresh tears filled her eyes.

"All right," she finally said. "There's just one other thing. Andrew, I have chosen to believe you, believe *in* you, because our love has got to be based on a solid foundation of trust. Without that, we have nothing.''

Andrew nodded.

"But there's something I need to tell you that is separate and apart from that foundation. The proof of what I'm about to say is in that folder over there on the coffee table.''

"I don't understand," Andrew said. "What are you talking about?''

"In that folder," Kara went on, "are the legal papers pertaining to the baby's adoption. Also in there is a copy of the birth certificate that was completed at the hospital this morning and will be properly filed with the State of California.''

"And?" Andrew said, still confused.

"I never thought I would be with you again, Andrew, except at family functions where we could keep our distance from each other. Yet I knew how much I loved you, would always love you. I knew what a wonderful man you were, what a fantastic husband and father you would have been if you'd chosen to be.

"I didn't care what anyone in the family you might think, might surmise by it, because I felt so strongly about it and I knew I was going to do it."

"Do what?"

"Andrew, even though I said we were to be based on a foundation of trust, this is asking too much of you. I don't expect you to believe me as it certainly sounds as though I'm making this up as I go along to reinforce my declaration of love for you. I'll understand, I truly will, that you'll need to see the proof of what I'm saying in that folder.

"You are the man I love. The only man I have ever, will ever, love. And so, I named my son after you, even when I thought I would never have my love for you reciprocated. I...I named the baby Andrew Ralph MacAllister."

Andrew's breath caught. His head snapped around and he stared at the file on the coffee table.

"It's there in that folder," Kara said. "The birth certificate showing the baby's name. Go look at it so you can verify what I'm telling you."

Andrew shifted his gaze slowly from the file folder to look directly into Kara's eyes.

"I don't need to see that birth certificate," he said, his voice raspy. "I believe you, believe *in* you, just as you said you believed in me. Our foundation of trust is solidly in place. I'm honored that you named the baby after me, Kara, more than I can even begin to tell you. Andrew Ralph MacAllister." He smiled. "Damn, that's one fine name for our son. Thank you, my love, thank you so much." His smile broadened. "*Now* will you agree to marry me?"

"Yes!" Kara flung her arms around Andrew's

neck. "Yes! Yes! Yes! Oh, I love you. I adore you. I... Oh, Andrew, I'm so happy I think I'm going to burst. Kiss me, kiss me, kiss me."

And he did.

Andrew captured Kara's mouth in a kiss that tasted of tears. It was a kiss of commitment to forever, of love declared and love returned in kind. It was a kiss that erased the pain, the misunderstandings, the confusion and dark emptiness of loneliness.

It was a kiss that was eternal love—rich and deep and real.

Andrew nestled Kara against his body, savoring the feel of her pressed to him, inhaling her flowery aroma, drinking in the taste of her.

Kara splayed her hands on Andrew's broad strong back, as she allowed her lashes to drift down so she might take deep within her the taste, the feel, the aroma, the very essence of Andrew.

Andrew raised his head just enough to take a sharp breath, then spoke close to Kara's lips.

"I want you, my Kara," he said, his voice raspy with passion.

"And I want you, my Andrew," she whispered. "I truly—"

They both stiffened, then jerked apart as the sensual spell encasing them was broken by the sound of a wailing baby.

"Nice timing, kiddo," Andrew said dryly, then smiled. "Hold that 'I want you' thought, Kara. I believe our son is making his presence known."

Kara laughed. "I'd better go check on him, but I'll definitely hold the thought in question."

"*We'll* check on him," Andrew said, slipping one arm around Kara's shoulders. "Together."

When they entered the nursery and crossed the room to stand next to the crib, they exchanged smiles as they saw that the baby had fallen back to sleep.

"Hey, little guy," Andrew said. "Did you call this meeting to order or not?"

"Not," Kara said. "He changed his mind."

"Margaret told me you were going to bring him home in that baseball uniform he's wearing," Andrew said quietly, his gaze riveted on the sleeping infant. "I nearly lost it right there in front of her and Robert when I heard that."

"I'm going to keep that outfit for him in his treasure box when he outgrows it," Kara said. "Someday we'll explain to him how he came to have it. It will be a very special story."

"Kara," Andrew said, shifting his gaze to her. "How would you feel about changing the baby's name?"

Kara frowned. "But you said you were honored that he was Andrew Ralph——"

"I am," Andrew interrupted. "What I'm fumbling around about here is that I want to adopt him, make him legally my son, just as you're legally his mother. His name could be Andrew Ralph MacAllister Malone."

"Oh, Andrew, yes, that would be wonderful. I'll telephone my social worker tomorrow and ask her how we should proceed." She turned to look at the baby. "Do you hear that, Andy? We're going to be Malones, as well as MacAllisters. It just doesn't get any better than that."

"Speaking of names," Andrew said as they left the nursery. "It's about the dog. This is a boy's buddy, you understand. It can't have a name like Fluffy, or Muffy, or Twinkie."

"Twinkie?" Kara said with a burst of laughter.

"Definitely not Twinkie," Andrew said. They entered Kara's bedroom by unspoken agreement. "It's got to be something like Butch, or Zeke, or Zack, or—"

"Shut up," Kara said, encircling Andrew's neck with her arms.

"You want to name Andy's dog Shut Up?" Andrew said, raising his eyebrows.

"No-o-o," Kara said, then outlined Andrew's lips with the tip of her tongue. "I want *you* to hush, not talk, not think. Just make love to me, before Andrew Ralph MacAllister Malone decides he's hungry."

"I can handle that, Mrs. Malone-to-be," Andrew said.

"I'm sure you can, Mr. Malone," Kara said.

Then no more words were spoken, because none were needed as their hearts sang a litany of everlasting love.

The announcement in the Ventura newspaper regarding the engagement of Kara MacAllister and Andrew Malone was picked up on the wire services and printed in papers all across California.

A spring wedding was planned, the announcement said, and it would be a private affair with only members of the family in attendance. The couple would reside in Ventura, and their house was currently under construction. The couple would be joined in the large home by their son, Andy, their dog, Zork, and their cat, Twinkie. The pets would temporarily live with Mary and Ralph MacAllister, the bride's parents, who moved back to Ventura from Florida.

Andrew received a telegram from Clara that said that someday she might have the courage to ask his and Robert's forgiveness, but she was concentrating now on learning how to be at peace with herself and find happiness on her own. She was extending her best wishes to Andrew and Kara on their pending marriage, and also to their son.

"I hope she makes it," Andrew said to Kara, nodding in approval after reading Clara's telegram aloud. "If Clara finds even half the amount of happiness that I have, she'll be doing just fine."

He shifted his gaze to the baby, who was nestled in the crook of his arm as they all sat on the sofa in Kara's living room.

"Right, Andy?" Andrew said. "Everyone deserves to be happy."

Andy burped.

"He has spoken," Kara said, then laughed.

Her laughter was infectious, and Andrew laughed with her, the joyous sound filling the room to overflowing and dancing through the air on magical golden sunbeams.

* * * * *

THE BABY BET continues in
Silhouette Desire in October 2000, with
BABY: MacALLISTER-MADE,
as confirmed bachelor Richard MacAllister
loses a wager about never falling in love!

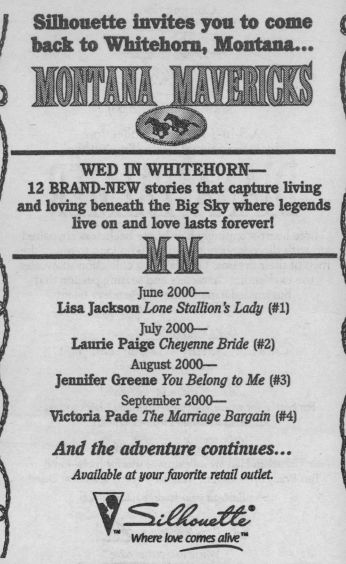

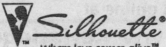

ATTENTION, LINDSAY McKENNA FANS!

Morgan Trayhern has three brand-new missions in Lindsay McKenna's latest series:

**Morgan's men are made for battle—
but are they ready for love?**

The excitement begins in July 2000, with
Lindsay McKenna's 50th book!

MAN OF PASSION
(Silhouette Special Edition® #1334)
Featuring rugged Rafe Antonio, aristocrat by birth,
loner by choice. But not for long….

Coming in November 2000:

A MAN ALONE
(Silhouette Special Edition® #1357)
Featuring Thane Hamilton, a wounded war hero on his way
home to the woman who has always secretly loved him….

*Look for the third book in the series in early 2001! In the
meantime, don't miss Lindsay McKenna's brand-new,
longer-length single title, available in August 2000:*

MORGAN'S MERCENARIES:
HEART OF THE WARRIOR

Only from Lindsay McKenna and
Silhouette Books!